THE LAST DRAGON SKIN CHRONICLES BOOK 1

THE EMPTY CROWN

GEORGINA MAKALANI

Also by Georgina Makalani

The Last Dragon Skin Chronicles:
The Empty Crown
The Lost Endeavour
Shadows Awaken
The Darkened Crown

The Magics of Rei-Een:
The Hidden Princess
Hidden Promises
The Hidden Phoenix

The Raven Crown Series:
Raven's Dawn
The Caged Raven
Raven's Edge

Other Stories:
The Mark of Oldra
The Heart of Oldra

The Legend of Iski Flare (Novella series):
The Legend Begins
Red Wolves
The Riddle of Daralis
The Last Child
The Tree Maiden
Reflections
The Beast
Circus of Wonder

Short Stories:
Stuffed Frogs and Spinning Teacups
Searcher
The Silence (in Glimpses)

1

Ana sucked in a deep breath and closed her eyes, then opened them almost immediately. It didn't matter whether she looked or not; it didn't make it any easier. The weatherworn grey stone bridge stretched out before her, its opposite end lost to the darkness. She took another steadying breath, her heart still beating so fast it was going to leap from her chest this time for sure. Holding up her lamp and pulling her cloak tighter around her, Ana stepped out onto the bridge, too aware that the world dropped away to nothing beneath her.

The cruel chuckle of the guard at the other end of the bridge echoed through the early morning darkness. The sun was still far from lighting the sky, and the light of the lamp in her unsteady hand made the bridge appear to move.

"You know this is my third bridge this morning," she called into the dark.

"And yet you appear just as scared. Or is it easier for you by the time you reach this bridge every morning?"

"No," she called back. "Each one is just as frightening as the one before."

She didn't like being reminded of where she was, or of her fears, and the guard chided her every day. Yet in some way it made this last bridge easier. His unseen conversation confirmed that she wasn't alone. And the distraction assisted her in making the distance, for it was the longest bridge she had to cross each day.

Ana would never tell him how much he helped her. There were some things a maid never did, and one of those was make conversation with a soldier. It didn't matter how lowly a rank he was, for it took very little before it would turn to gossip and suggestions would be made that the friendship was more than it should be for a girl like her. Too many maids had unwittingly lost their freedom or their jobs to such gossip.

Ana blew out a long breath as she neared the end of the bridge. She ducked her head in acknowledgement to the guard and kept walking, thankful to be on solid ground again. Although she could never escape her fear, for her whole world was made up of sheer drops and difficulties.

Sheer Rock was a series of islands off the northern coast of the Kingdom of Ilia, and it was just what the name suggested. The islands had formed from a strange geological event Ana did not understand; sheer drops surrounded each island to the sea hundreds of feet below. The islands were large enough that she could go whole days without seeing the edge of the world. Except when she crossed the bridges. Each island was connected by a bridge to the next. Some islands had several bridges that connected them to their neighbours, and there was a single long, broad bridge that connected them to the mainland. Despite their connection to the kingdom, it was heavily guarded and not somewhere she had been anywhere near since her father had died.

Before that day she hadn't given the distance to the sea below a second thought. She had skipped across bridges, stood on cliff tops, laughed with ease. She shook the image away that was starting to form in her mind of the day her father had gone over the edge of a bridge and her world had changed. Along with the loss, a fear of heights had developed and, despite her best efforts and derision from others, it was something she hadn't been able to shake.

She stopped on the path, trying to calm herself. If she appeared before the cook looking like she felt, she would be paying for it for the rest of the day. She looked up towards the castle. It was the Seat of the Lord of Sheer Rock and took up most of the island it was situated on. Ana tried not to shiver. She had upset the lord the day before when she had slipped on a sheet of paper that had drifted from the desk, and spilt the tea she'd been carrying across the rest of the papers.

The lord had glared at her but said nothing. Ana knew she was in serious trouble despite not being chastised. She had lifted the cloth from her belt, but the lord had only pointed to the doorway. The memory of those piercing blue eyes as she stood from the desk made Ana shiver again. The lord was a beautiful woman, slender with blond wavy hair pulled loosely from her pale face. And yet Ana had never found anything of beauty in her.

Ana had bowed low, murmured a request for forgiveness and backed out of the room. She had been given other duties for the rest of the day, but it had been a position of standing to serve the lord directly. She only hoped the cook would send her back again before she was replaced by another.

Ana moved quickly through the castle to the kitchen, where she blew out her lamp and hung her coat. "Am I still being punished?" she asked over her shoulder.

"My little Ana," the cook said, her dimpled face glowing with her smile. "There is a special guest arriving today, and the lord has asked for you to serve them."

"Really?" she asked, relief washing over her.

The cook nodded. "But in the meantime, you are to help me. They'll be waking soon enough, and the bread needs to go in the oven."

"Thank you," Ana said, kissing the cook's soft cheek.

"Nothing to do with me," she said, pulling Ana into a tight hug.

Ana stood in the doorway and tried not to stare at the strange man who stood before the lord's desk. He was tall and angular. His short grey hair stuck out in strange places, although his trimmed grey beard was neat. There was something unsettling about him and his lavishly embroidered burgundy cloak. Something within screamed at her to run.

Without looking up, the lord waved her forward. Ana tried to focus on where she was going rather the strange man, but it was difficult. She glanced towards the only other man in the room, a tall, broad soldier standing to the side in the black shiny armour of the King's Men. He was older than she'd first imagined from her view in the doorway. He was handsome, or at least he would have been but for the scar that cut across his cheek.

Ana looked forward, refocusing on the man before the desk and realising with a shudder just who he was. The regent's mage, or was he the king's mage? She looked back to the soldier, still and staring off into the distance, and the scar on his face was gone. She was tempted to raise her fingers to her own cheek, but was hampered by the tray in her hands. Her feet stopped as she stared at him.

"Do not hover," the lord snapped, her harsh voice carrying through the large open room.

Ana nodded, but her legs refused to move. Only her head would turn towards the lord's desk. The mage's cold gaze raked over her, and she was sure those grey eyes could see far more of her than she wished. She gulped down her rising fear and stepped forward again. She carefully set the tray on the edge of the table and, as the soldier turned his attention to her for the first time, she pushed it loudly across the surface of the desk to ensure it wouldn't fall.

"She is the gifted one," the mage said, his cold stare still focused on her.

The lord nodded.

Ana glanced back at the rugged soldier; thankful he was in the room although not sure why she felt that way.

"You may step forward and greet me, for I shall make your life worth living." The mage waved her forward with a large sweep of his arm, bowing his head as he spoke, but Ana knew it wasn't out of any respect for her.

She stayed just where she was and although she opened her mouth, she was very quick to close it again. Ana wasn't sure what this man was proposing, but she knew it was not something that would make her life any better. As with anyone of her station, she was only there to make the lives of others easier.

"Her mother," the man said, stretching out a long finger towards her.

Ana was still rooted to the spot, although she was desperate for him to say more. It was as though he had stopped mid-thought.

What of my mother? What does this man know of her?

The lord nodded. Without a glance at Ana, she surprised her by saying, "We don't talk of my sister."

The world appeared suddenly hazy. Ana's mother had died when she was very young. Her father had raised her as best he could, and she still missed him terribly. But she'd had no idea there was any connection between her family and the Lord of Sheer Rock. If she was family, why was she living in the small, dusty cottage and serving the lord as she did?

"What did she do?" Ana asked before she could stop herself, and the soldier turned sad eyes towards her. "What did she do?" she asked more confidently.

"She was of no real consequence," the lord said.

The grey-eyed mage stood over her then. He was taller than she thought, wiry, and he smelt odd. She didn't want to sniff at him, but she couldn't quite place the bitter scent that clung to him. As he reached for her, she stepped back.

"Ana, do as you are told." The lord pushed up from the table. She looked bored by the event, as though Ana was nothing.

The long, cold fingers of the mage wrapped around Ana's jaw, and he pulled her face closer as he leaned down to peer into her eyes. "So green," he murmured. "What do you see?"

She tried to shake her head, but she couldn't move, his grip too tight. She was sure his hold was bruising her face. He moved his face closer to hers, continuing to stare into her eyes, and she felt the world move for a moment. She pulled at his hold to find the soldier standing behind her, a solid mass preventing her escape. Her heart beat so fast she was sure it was going to explode from her chest. This was more frightening than crossing the bridge.

"They will take you with them." The lord looked away and sat back at her desk. "He is looking for girls like you."

"I don't have any skills a mage would need," Ana stammered, "and I haven't got anything with me. I can't travel today."

"There is no need," the mage said, his fingers now wrapped too tight around her arm. She wondered why he needed the soldier. "The capital provides."

"The capital?"

"The king's regent wishes to see you."

"Me?" Ana asked, wondering why in all the world the regent would want to see her. How did he even know who she was? But then, she had thought she knew who she was. And as she glanced back at the lord standing by her desk, Ana realised there was far more to the world than she knew.

"You would do well to know your place," the mage said, his tone deep and unfriendly.

"I don't have any gifts," she said quickly.

The lord came around the desk then, her face dark and dangerous. Ana wanted to step back, but the soldier prevented her movement. "Do not embarrass me," she said, her voice low, and Ana knew she was in more trouble than she had ever been. "You will do as you are told, or it ends here."

The soldier coughed politely, and Ana glanced up at the opening in the wall. For those who displeased the lord, there was one punishment. In the wall of the lord's office was a large round opening into the world beyond, over the cliffs and the Endless Sea. The view was spectacular from a distance, and there had been many days Ana had watched the sun on the waves, or great violet clouds making their way across the dark water towards them.

Now she could only see the walkway that led to nothing when she glanced over her shoulder. Ana shook her head violently. She struggled with the bridges, let alone standing out over nothing. The walkway was wide enough to just hold three men side by side and long enough that two of them could have lain end to end. But there was no railing, and the wind could come up and pull you away before you even realised you were scared.

She had once found the lord standing just outside the round doorway, the wind pulling at her blond hair and her deep green robes. Ana was both amazed and frightened. Now they were threatening her with the walkway, and she wasn't quite sure why.

"I will go to the capital," she whispered.

"You do not have the choice," the lord said, her anger dissipating to be replaced by her usual apathy. She sighed and waved them away.

"Why have you kept her to yourself for so long?" the mage asked.

"I have not used her gifts," she said quickly. "I have no need."

"Are they not worthy, or are you better than the regent?"

"I know my place," she said, anger flaring again behind her blue eyes. Ana wanted to run. "You have come all this way. Test her if you must before you take her."

"That may be an idea," the soldier said, and Ana glanced at him. His voice was rough and quiet, yet it carried a confidence to it. The scar she had been so sure marked his face was still absent, and she sensed that this man would be a dangerous enemy.

She turned back to the mage as he cleared his throat. She wasn't quite sure what they thought she had, and she didn't know whether it was a good thing to let them find it or if she should keep it hidden. If she even knew how to hide it. She tried not to sigh, sucking in a deep breath instead and trying to exude the same confidence the large soldier showed.

But as the old man raised his fingers towards her and placed his cold, clammy hand on her forehead, her urge to run returned.

"Look at me," he said. "Look hard."

She focused on him, standing with his eyes closed and his hand on her head. As she studied his fine, sharp features and his too-thin body, she wondered if he was unwell. His eyes snapped open and he slapped her hard across the face, hard enough to knock her to the ground.

The mage cleared his throat as he glared at her. "You were to look, to see what is already there. Do not try to use your gift on me."

She shook her head. "I don't have any gifts," she said, bringing her hand to her stinging face. There was far more strength behind this man than she thought, and for the first time she wondered what gifts he had.

"You will do as you are told," he said, standing over her. "You will look, and you will tell me what you see."

She nodded, but she stayed where she was as he put his hand back over her head and closed his eyes. She did the same, feeling the strength and power within his hand. In the darkness behind her lids, the mage stood tall. A small boy appeared beside him, tear stained and scared, asking for help, pleading. But he shook his head and pushed the child away, taking something from him. Something the child had held out to him.

A crown. A simple yet heavy golden crown. He held it in his hands and then handed it directly to another man, who placed it on his head as the child disappeared.

"The boy king," Ana murmured, opening her eyes.

"You are not what I wanted." He sounded disappointed and, Ana thought, a little afraid. "What a waste," he said with a sigh.

The soldier pulled her to her feet. Although she felt the same strength in him, it was different and kind. Despite the blood she sensed on his hands, he was gentle as he placed her feet on the ground. When he let her go, the older man pushed hard against her chest, although she wasn't sure his hands had touched her. She slid too quickly towards the window. The soldier reached for her, but was not fast enough, and the lord's impassive face looked away as she sat back at her desk.

The air was cold around her as she blew out the window and onto the walkway. She shivered and squeezed her eyes closed, sensing the emptiness around her. The tears started before she could stop them. Ana wanted to be anywhere but here. Even on a bridge, she thought as the wind pulled at her clothes and hair and threatened to lift her away.

When she was a very small child, she would run along the wide edges of the bridges, looking down into the void between the islands as her father ran along beside her, smiling. Then he had fallen. She allowed herself to relax, trying not to hold her body rigid as she thought of him.

He hadn't fallen from a bridge. She may have been a child, but she remembered him clearly, and she remembered the same feeling of standing out on the walkway with him. The wind had pulled at her hair and her dress, cold and sharp against her face. He had pushed her back inside; the sharp nails of the lord had taken her arm and then he was gone.

Ana opened her eyes and stared at the woman sitting at the desk now. Had she watched her father's death or tried to ignore it as she did Ana's?

The soldier at the edge of her vision tried to subtly wave her forward. The older man reached out a hand towards him, and he dropped his arm. Ana felt the hopelessness of the situation. She wanted someone, anyone, to help but knew it wouldn't come. Fear had disappeared in the certainty of what would happen. She wondered if her father had felt the same in that moment before his death.

The old mage raised his hand.

"Long live the king," she said, and then she was falling.

2

Dray sprang forward as though he had a rope tied around his waist, pulling him to the opening in the wall and across the narrow stone that stretched out across the void. How he managed to grab her, he wasn't sure. But he hung half off the walkway, dangerously close to slipping off entirely, his hand tight around the girl's arm. Her eyes were squeezed shut, her already pale skin even paler.

She opened incredibly green eyes to stare up at him, and he blew out a relieved sigh. He heaved her up. As she landed on the edge of the walkway, she clung to him like a scared child. Although if he had nearly fallen, he might have been keen to do the same to whoever had saved him from such a fall.

The old mage glared at him, and he knew there was no going back. Dray stood carefully, trying not to tip over the edge with the weight of the girl on his arm. She stood with him, and they inched their way along the walkway. The lord looked even more dangerous than the mage in that moment.

"No matter what gifts she has or what offence she has caused, it is not reason enough to throw her to her death," Dray said, unsure where the words came from. He walked back through the round doorway, trying to look like he wasn't about to throw up. The girl, on the other hand, looked like she just might.

"Ana is of no concern to you. She is a maid."

"A maid?" Dray asked, looking down at her. She nodded. "I thought she was your niece."

"You are not in a position to question the decisions of others," the mage said, his sharp face looking even sharper if that was possible.

Dray opened his mouth and then closed it. She had called for help, and they had just watched her fall. He couldn't let that happen. Although he wasn't quite sure why, he was determined to help this girl.

Looking over these people who represented the boy king in the world, Dray wondered what the king thought of his kingdom, if he thought of it at all. His uncle had ruled long enough that many of the people considered him more of a king than the boy himself. But no matter the state of the world, he couldn't just walk out with her on his arm.

He set his jaw and seized the back of her dress with his free hand, pulling her from his arm and held her up before him. "If she is a problem, then she is better locked away," he murmured. "Allow me to do the job I was employed for."

The mage raised a hand. Dray was tempted to put his hand on his sword, but it currently held the maid. He had thought she might struggle or make a scene, but she hung limp in his hold as though she knew she was lost whichever way she went.

"You know how long I have looked for her," the mage growled.

"She is young," Dray murmured. "The young don't think of what might benefit them. Let me lock her away somewhere safe until you are ready for her, rather than kill her now."

"That may have been why I searched," the mage responded, a confidence in his voice Dray doubted. The man might appear to have power others only dreamt of, but Dray had yet to see any evidence of it. He seemed to fear far more than a man with power should. Dray had been around enough of them to know just what men in power could do.

He looked down at the girl again. She might be important, or she might just be a maid. Either way, he couldn't let her die at the whim of a nasty old man. He took a deep breath, feeling the same desperation she had called to him with from out on the Walk.

Her wide green eyes seemed to draw him as he lowered her to the floor, and with his hand still firm on the back of her dress, he directed her towards the door. He half expected some further complaint from the lord or the mage. Yet neither moved nor spoke.

In the hallway beyond the lord's rooms, the intermittently spaced lamps did little to light the dark grey stone other than a small area around each one. No one else appeared, but Dray continued to direct her forward. Although somehow his arm had reached across her shoulders had pulled her in close as his pace had increased.

He expected someone to come after them, but perhaps they had believed his story. He stopped then and looked back.

"Which way?" he asked softly.

"Down…"

"No. Out. How do we get out?"

There was a long pause before she answered. "Go straight and then down the main stairs. From the foyer you can exit the castle. But…"

"Just wait until we are outside," he murmured, racing out onto the landing and checking to ensure there was no one around the large open entrance. Half of his men could have waited at the base of the stairs and the space would still not have been full. He moved carefully, half pulling her. She put her hand to his arm, and he stopped. In the corner of his eye, he saw another maid at the far end of a corridor leading from the landing, and then she was gone again.

Several soldiers stood by the doors of the castle and several of his own men stood nearby. He wondered how the others waiting beyond the doors would great him with the maid. He grabbed her wrist as she stepped forward, and she looked up at him with those bright eyes again. He shook his head once.

She chewed on her lip for a moment and then turned back the way they had come. She waved for him to follow and turned down a narrow hallway. They didn't pass anyone as they headed down narrow steps and, for a moment, he was sure they were moving through the walls.

Dray thought he could smell the kitchen, and Ana paused in a doorway. She sighed and looked up at him before she continued along the hallway. It was only a matter of minutes until they were standing in the sunshine. After so long in the dim light of the castle, Dray was sure it should have been night.

"This way," she said, slipping along the side of the castle, leading the way with her hand in his. They were moving quickly and, whether by luck or something else, they had managed to leave the castle unseen. Ahead of them was a wide bridge, and Ana stopped dead as a guard stepped forward.

"Found yourself a helper, Ana?" the guard at the end of the bridge asked. "You finished early today."

"We have an errand to run for the lord," she said quickly, dropping Dray's hand and taking a single step forward.

"You got your job cut out there. That lass can't cross a bridge without—" He stopped as he took in Dray and the insignia on his chest, then stepped forward.

"Is it your job to question the task set by the lord?" Dray asked.

The man shook his head quickly and pulled himself to attention.

"Come along," he said to Ana. Stepping close, but not so close to arouse the suspicion of the guard, he gave her a gentle nudge. She looked up at him and then started walking.

He could feel her tension. He wondered at first if it was due to the incident that had just occurred, but then he thought there might be more to it. With his hand in the small of her back, Dray glanced over his shoulder to the guard and tried to move her faster across the bridge.

"They will not be far behind," he whispered.

She nodded and yet continued at the same pace, although he was sure she focused on the small space before her feet. Once they were off the bridge, she sighed and then stopped.

"Where are we going?" she asked, shivering a little and wrapping her arms around herself.

Dray glanced around them and then looked into the distance. "The mountains, unless you have somewhere?"

"She would know where to find me on Sheer Rock," she said, another shiver covering her body.

"Mountains it is," he said. "Can we move a bit faster?"

She shook her head and blew out a long breath. "We have three more bridges to cross."

He sighed and then looked at her properly. She was shivering, and not just because of the cool sea breeze pulling at her hair. "You are scared of the bridges."

"I'm not good with heights," she admitted quietly. "Why did you save me?"

He took her hand and pulled her along the road. She allowed him to lead her and moved as fast as she could, almost keeping up with his long stride. He was keen to run, but if they came across anyone else, he didn't think it would be a good idea.

"Why?" she prompted.

He stopped and looked at her slight frame. "I couldn't see another innocent die."

"Are you so sure I am innocent?"

He laughed then and noticed they were closer to houses than he had previously realised.

"Ana?" someone called. She pulled Dray to a stop, then let go of his hand. "Did you spill something on the lord again?" a young man asked, walking towards them.

She shook her head, and Dray was pleased she was smiling at

the boy, not raising suspicions.

"Tim," she said warmly. "You would give the soldier the impression I'm clumsy."

"She is," he said, his friendly tone matching his smile. "And why are you travelling with a soldier?"

"We've been sent on an errand."

"You don't even have your cloak," he said, the friendliness slipping away. As he leaned closer, concern etched his features.

"The sun is warm and we won't be long," she said, although Dray could see the gooseflesh on her skin. "I got distracted," she added with a wave of her hand, and he relaxed.

"Well hurry back, the winds will be up soon."

She nodded and smiled, then indicated that Dray should head in the direction of the bridge. She waved fondly to Tim and they were off again, trying to walk quickly and yet not appear to be rushing.

She paused as they hit the next bridge, but with a deep breath she continued to walk across it. It was narrower than the previous bridge. He looked back, realising they were not headed straight for the main bridge that led to the mainland from this crazy part of the kingdom. The islands were so high from the water, he wondered why anyone would live here. Although he had to admit it would be easy to defend.

"Where are we going?" he asked.

"If we try to cross the mainland bridge, we would be spotted immediately and you will be standing beside me on the Walk."

He nodded and allowed her to lead the way. It took time as they wove through streets and between farms, and eventually there was nothing but green open fields that dropped off at the sides with a rocky outcrop at the far end. Dray wondered at the girl so clearly afraid of heights. He tried not to laugh at the irony of it. Then she was gone, and he was sure she had slipped from the edge. He raced forward.

"Stop," she said behind him, and he did. "You'll go over the edge if you aren't careful."

"I thought you had," he said, turning to her standing amongst the rocks.

She shook her head and grinned. "I have another way."

3

Ed pulled the hood tighter around his ears as he looked up at the squeaking sign swinging in the wind. The cold rain had numbed his fingers and his nose, and despite the sun being high in the sky, he sucked in a frustrated breath and headed into the tavern.

Water ran from his cloak in rivulets as he stomped his numb feet on the entrance mat. Or at least he hoped it was a mat; it was the same colour as the road outside, and just as muddy. He had travelled most of the way so far by keeping from the main roads. But the storm was continuous, the rain sharp and cold, and he needed a warm bed.

He lowered his hood slowly as he stepped into a dimly lit room and the smell of stale ale and farm animals hit his senses. He would have shied away from such a place not so long ago, but in the storm, he had little option. He shook the rain from his cloak. Some of the people at the closely packed tables looked up, but their looks didn't linger. He was sure no one would recognise him. It appeared that no one was looking for him.

If they were, news of his disappearance might have reached these people. Ed doubted his uncle had noticed he was no longer in his room. He wasn't around people often enough to hear news, and he wasn't sure if the word was out. Taverns like this rarely carried the sort of news he sought. There had been many days during his journey when he'd wondered if he would find the man he searched for.

"You after a meal?" a round older woman asked, working her way between the tables to reach him. She didn't look very friendly, nor did she sound it, and he wondered if he should have sheltered out on the road somewhere.

"Need a room for a night," he said, trying to sound gruff and confident.

She nodded once and walked away, working her way back through the tables to the bar at the far side of the room. He tried to keep up, but despite her little legs and his long ones, she was able to move through the tight gaps more easily than he.

"We got one room," she said, turning sharply and pressing a key into his hand. "Up the stairs, second on the right." She took her time to look him up and down. "Two crowns."

"Two," he stammered, and her face hardened. "Two seems fair," he murmured as he felt out two gold coins in his pocket.

Ed closed his hand tightly around the key, thankful he hadn't kept all his coin together as he pressed them into her outstretched hand. He worked his way through the crowded room and up the stairs, barely a glance raised in his direction. He counted along the doors until he reached his allocated one and found it unlocked.

It opened silently into a small room with a narrow bed more like a soldier's cot against one wall and a small table with a single chair. He blew out a sigh and pushed the door closed behind him, locking it quickly and then testing it. It seemed to hold, but he wondered how solid it would be if someone were determined to get to him in the night.

He threw the wet cloak over the back of the chair and sat on the edge of the bed before he lay down. It had been too long since he'd had the opportunity to lie down. He might have been too rash to run from the capital as he had. But he couldn't go on as he was. There was no chance for him to be what his parents had hoped. Although there had been a time he didn't want it, as he'd grown he had begun to understand the importance of what they hoped he would be.

He closed his eyes, taking in the sounds of the storm. The wind and rain battered the building, and he was grateful to be under a roof. He hoped this was the right thing to do.

The dining room filled with patrons produced a continuous muffled sound to compete with the sounds of the storm. Ed should have considered food as well, but he wasn't up to it. His stomach hadn't travelled well, and the idea of food made him nervous. He was sure he could travel further if he avoided illness.

A sharp bang on the door startled him into a seated position, and he waited. Then it came again.

"I have your meal," the older woman called through the door.

He wanted to tell her to take it away, but instead he got up, opened the door and showed her in. She glanced at the muddy mark on the bed where he had lain down with his boots on and scowled at him again. She dropped the tray on the table, slopping the ale in the pewter mug. The watery-looking stew didn't move at all, and a chunk of bread sat solid on the tray.

"Just one night?" she asked.

He nodded once, still looking at the food and wondering if anyone would want to eat it.

"Where ya goin'?"

"North," he murmured. "To find family."

She looked him over and, for the first time in the last few weeks, he was worried she might actually recognise him.

"Nice boy like you should have a horse." She smiled a little, revealing crooked yellowing teeth as she rubbed at her chin with her knuckles.

"Lost it," he said, feeling more unnerved by the smile. "Spooked by the lightning."

"Really?" She raised her eyebrows slowly, and Ed knew she didn't believe anything he said.

He nodded slowly and looked back at the stew.

"You got money to buy a new one?" she asked.

"No," Ed said quickly. "It isn't too far now, I hope. I can walk for a couple of days."

"Nothin' 'round here within two days' walk."

"I'm sure the farm is not far away. Thank you for the food," he said, guiding her towards the door. She backed up as he continued; he had height on her if not weight. The door had remained open, and he wondered if someone else might have heard their conversation. As she backed into the hallway, he glanced quickly each way. The hard look had returned to her face when he bowed his head, thanked her again and then shut and locked the door.

The innkeeper might be more danger than the soldiers he had thought would follow. He wiped the ale from the battered spoon on the edge of his cloak and poked at the stew. It remained unmoving. He dropped the spoon and took a single sip of the ale instead. It was bitter but drinkable, and he carried the cup and the bread back to his cot.

He wanted to prise his boots from his cold damp feet, but he worried what he might find within, and he wasn't sure he would be able to get them back on. If the little round woman turned out to be the trouble he suspected, he might need to leave in a hurry.

Ed sighed and then wondered, not for the first time, if this was a good idea. He gulped at the ale and then sat it down on the floor. His stomach made a strange noise as he bit into the bread. If they wanted to rob him, they might have done something to his food. But he hoped it was clear he didn't have the money they thought he might.

She wasn't the first to have mentioned a horse. Although it would have been both useful and faster, it would have drawn too much attention. He would have had to explain why he wanted a horse from the stable, and if he had managed to take one unseen, anyone he passed would have recognised it.

He was tempted to leave the tavern even though he had spent too much on the small room, but the wind and rain still lashed at the building. There was no use hurrying in this weather to he wasn't sure where. With his shoes still on, he lay back and pulled the thin blanket over him. His clothing still damp, he shivered and closed his eyes as the dim light shone through the narrow window.

You can't hide when you stand out.

Ed could have dressed better, and he could have carried more with him, but it had been far more important that he leave unseen. All he had to do was find the man his mother had told him to find, and the world would be what it should. He hoped. Although he had no real idea of what it should be. And other than a feeling that he lived to the north, possibly in the Edge Mountains, he didn't even know his name. To be so well known to his mother, Ed had assumed he was the Lord of the Mountains or worked with him.

But for a man on foot not used to travel, the mountains were still a long way off.

4

The wind pulled at the soldier's cloak, and Ana tried not to focus on the thick material. She might have been terribly underdressed, but she wasn't lying dead at the base of the cliffs. She sucked in a breath and continued beside the big man. He was older, grey just touching the sides of his thick dark hair. And he was handsome.

The scar she had seen so clearly across his face was undeniably absent, and she wasn't sure if it had been a trick of the light or something she had done or thought. He glanced at her and she looked away, not wanting to stare. Yet as he turned forward, her eyes found his face again.

"Are we going the right way?" he asked, his deep voice echoing down the tunnel.

She nodded. "It is hard to tell down here with this hazy light, but yes."

"You have been this way before?"

"Not all the way across, but I have been in these tunnels a few times. I have heard whispers of others crossing here. Smugglers and the like, probably."

"Smugglers?" he asked, stopping.

"Are you scared?" She was unable to hide the smirk in her voice.

"No, but you should be."

"I just survived the Walk," she said with a laugh that bounced from the tunnel walls. "I don't think a smuggler could be nearly as scary."

"Have you lived in Sheer Rock your whole life?"

She nodded.

"Yet you are scared of heights. The whole world is up high. How many bridges did you have to cross a day?"

"Three and back," she murmured. If she never had to cross another bridge, she would be happy. And she had no idea how this tunnel led them to the mainland from Sheer Rock without crossing a bridge.

His hand was strong and heavy on her shoulder. She looked up into his intense gaze. "Why?" he asked.

She shrugged him off and kept walking. "Why is anyone scared of anything?" she whispered.

"Usually for good reason." His long strides quickly caught her up.

"You talk a lot for a soldier," she grumbled.

"How many soldiers do you know?"

"Only those at the bridge, and maybe some in the castle. I don't really talk to them. Talking to soldiers can get you into trouble."

"You seem to be able to get yourself into trouble well enough."

She stopped then and watched him walk ahead of her. He stopped, looking around and then back.

"I don't know why he wanted to push me off the Walk," she said.

"Don't you?"

She stared at him a bit longer as she wondered why this man had risked so much to save her. He didn't know her, he didn't know her background and she certainly didn't have any gifts someone might want to use. Maybe the old man had only come to find her because he knew she was the only one who knew what he was. But then she supposed everyone knew or knew of the mage. And she was sure the regent knew just what kind of man he was.

"Whatever I might be, it doesn't explain why you would

abandon your position to save me," Ana said.

"Maybe I was looking for an excuse."

"Or you thought I was…" She wasn't quite sure what he might think she was, and she was equally unsure of what she wanted him to think she was. He looked down then, and she noted the brighter light behind him. "Come on," she said, pushing around him and heading for the way out. Although what they did once they found it, she wasn't sure. Would they continue to travel together?

They continued in silence to find the tunnel ended in a rough opening into nothing, and Ana felt even more sick than she had on the Walk. The world dropped away from them, the orange afternoon light showing just how big a gap there was between them and the mainland. They looked across at the opposite cliff. She knew the water was below and, as the soldier leaned out, she grabbed at his cloak. Feeling the familiar panic rising in her throat, she sat down and pressed her back into the wall.

"There is a bridge," he said.

"I think I would rather die," she murmured.

"You might. It is a rope bridge."

Ana tasted bile, and she swallowed. He squatted down before her, his hands on her knees.

"I could carry you over," he said gently.

"I don't know if we can be seen from above," she said.

He moved back to the edge and leaned out again, looking up. "I can't even see the bridge. We are a long way down, but we may be in a different part of the island."

She nodded, willing the tears that threatened to stay away. She wondered how long until Tim realised she wasn't coming back. She rubbed the back of her hand over her cheek.

The soldier was leaning over her again. "We can wait until it is dark."

"They might realise where we have gone."

"How did you know of this place?" he asked, his voice soft and coaxing.

"My father mentioned it at some point. I came looking one day and…"

He waited. When she didn't continue, he squatted down again and nudged her with his elbow.

"It doesn't feel as high," she said.

He nodded in response, and she wondered how her life could have shifted so suddenly that she was here with this man.

"I don't know your name," she said, holding out her hand. "I'm Anaise; everyone calls me Ana."

"Drayton," he said, shaking her hand firmly. "My friends call me Dray."

"It is nice to meet you," she said politely. "Now, what exactly are we doing, where are we going to go and how long can I follow you before you dump me somewhere?"

He sat back and looked her over. "I hadn't planned on dumping you anywhere," he said, "but I haven't really thought about this and where we can go."

"You said into the mountains."

"I know someone in the mountains who may be able to help."

"Someone you can leave me with," she said, climbing her feet and brushing her skirts down. "Maybe I should take my chances with the lord."

"I don't think your aunt is very willing to give you any chances."

"Don't call her that," she said, looking towards the opening. He was right; there was no other option but to follow him across the divide. She sucked in a deep breath and headed for the opening.

Holding tight to the edge of the tunnel, the rough rock pressing into her hand, she leaned out and looked towards the water. Just below the level of the tunnel was a narrow bridge of wood and rope. She pulled herself back, looked at the soldier and then dropped to her knees. "I don't think I can do it."

"You are scared every day, and yet you cross so many bridges."

"They are solid," she murmured. "And the bullying comments

of the watch help distract me."

"Do you want me to bully you?" She looked up at him, but he smiled. "Let's just hope it holds our weight," he murmured, unclasping his dark cloak and stepping forward.

He helped her to her feet, tied the cloak around her and pulled the hood up over her head. When she peered up at him, he grinned; she was almost lost in it. Then he turned his back and dropped to his knee.

"Climb on," he said. When she hesitated, he added, "You can close your eyes. You will be protected from the wind, and I can get us across."

"You won't drop me?" She hated how scared she sounded.

"I promise."

She pulled her skirts up about her knees and leaned against him. He was so solid, and the straps of his armour dug into her, but she wrapped her arms tight around his neck and her legs about his waist. He stood slowly, his rough hands on her legs as he shrugged her higher on his back. He muttered something and then leaned forward, the cloak falling about her and shielding them both.

When he stepped up to the edge of the tunnel, she could see the bridge dip away before them.

"I need to breathe," he whispered hoarsely, but her arms wouldn't loosen around his neck. He waited, and she tried. She didn't want to kill him on the way over. "Close your eyes," he said more clearly when she released the pressure from his throat.

The structure moved beneath them. His hands must have been on the ropes, and she missed them against her skin. Ana tried not to tighten her grip around his throat, squeezing her eyes closed tighter instead. She was sure they rocked from side to side as he moved forward, and she waited for them to tip over the edge. But they didn't, and after what felt like an age, the swaying stopped and they were on solid ground.

"You can let go," he said, and she opened her eyes. There were in a small cavern. As he squatted down, she released her hold on him and straightened out her skirts. She reached for the clasp of the cloak, but he put his hand on hers. "Keep it for now," he said. "It is colder in the mountains."

"I'm used to the sea wind," she said.

He smiled and shook his head.

She looked back out at the opposite cliff. She couldn't make out the bridge or the opening they had come through. "Thank you," she said, not turning back. Then she was sitting on her seat in the dust and her heart felt like it was cracking and no matter what she did to try to calm herself, she shook all over.

"A fire would help, but I fear we won't be able to get one going for some time. It is the shock," he murmured, his hands on her shoulders, lifting her from the ground and directing her to the back of the cavern. It was much darker there, and she shook even more. What had she been thinking to run with this man?

Then he was gone, and she was standing alone in the dark. "Drayton?" she called.

"Looking for a way out," he said, his voice distant.

"You won't leave me here, will you?" she asked.

"I have just risked not only my life but my career for you, little maid. I'm certainly not going to leave you behind now."

"Little maid?" she asked, the strength coming back. "Do you know who I am?"

"No," he whispered, too close. She jumped. "But you are important enough that the regent's own mage would have you killed."

"He knew the boy," she stammered.

"What boy?" Drayton asked. "What did you see?"

"He took the crown from the boy king and gave it to someone else. Maybe the regent," she told him without hesitation.

"I thought the boy didn't want to be King."

"He looked so sad. I think he wanted help."

"He trusted the wrong man," Drayton said, further away again.

"Dray," she called. "Please don't leave me."

"I have promised I won't. Or do you not like the dark either?"

"I'm not a child," she snapped. "I just feel a bit wobbly after the crossing and everything else that has happened today."

A strong arm closed around her shoulders and she leaned into him, thankful he was there. She couldn't help but wonder what might have happened if another soldier had accompanied the mage. A mage was a powerful thing, she thought, seeing him watching her on the Walk as though she were there again. He might be able to find them. "We need to keep moving," she said.

"We will. Catch your breath and we can find a way out. If the tunnel led to here, it must continue."

"I can't."

"You are going to be a difficult travel companion," he muttered, rubbing her arm. Then she was standing alone again in the dark.

"You have no idea," she said, walking back into the cavern, her arms outstretched. It was much darker than the other side, and she wondered if she was going to be able to find her way out of this. Then the rough wall beneath her palms changed to smooth, and she stopped. She was sure she could feel cool air. "Drayton, I think I found it."

"Maybe you are gifted," he said, and then his hand was on her shoulder. "Lead the way, little gifted maid."

"You could call me Ana. Although if we come across anyone, they are going to wonder at a soldier with a maid."

"I will claim you are my sister," he said, his hand closing around her arm as she felt her way along the stone.

"It is so dark," she murmured.

"Then let's hope there is no one hiding along the tunnel."

She stopped, and he bumped into her.

"Do you know if anyone still uses these tunnels?" he asked. "Have you seen anyone in the ones on Sheer Rock?"

"No," she murmured. But then she spent most of her days in the castle. She was rarely down here now, and it was when there were generally more people around. "My father mentioned their use, but he always talked about it as though it was long ago."

"Then let's hope he didn't lie to you," he said, giving her a gentle nudge forward.

Ana stepped forward, but the idea niggled at the back of her mind. There was so much her father hadn't told her, and she didn't know if that was because she had been a child or if he might never have told her the truth of who she was.

5

A distant light flickered in the darkness. Dray stopped and murmured his disappointment that he had given the girl his cloak. The light indicated people, and the reflection on his armour would give them away for sure.

"What do we do?" Ana asked in a hushed voice.

"Keep going," he whispered, determined that they couldn't go back.

She nodded and moved forward, a little slower than before, her hand still on the smooth stone wall. He wondered where they might be. There might have been other tunnels, and perhaps they had taken one that led away from where they needed to go. Or one that led them into more trouble.

At the sound of voices, Ana stopped. "There," she whispered. She stepped out into the middle of the narrow tunnel and then disappeared.

Dray's heart dropped. He took a tentative step forward before a hand closed around his arm, and he jumped.

"In here," she whispered.

There was a small alcove off the tunnel where she had slipped inside. Covered in the cloak, she was invisible in the dark space. He moved in around behind her, hoping she could shield his armour, and waited. The voices grew closer and the light brighter.

Two men continued past them with torches, murmuring amongst themselves, and didn't appear to have seen them. The light flickered and then faded to nearly nothing.

Dray pushed Ana behind him and leaned out. The light and voices had disappeared, but he had no idea where to. He could only hope they made it out before the men returned, as he wouldn't be able to explain their presence in the tunnel.

He led her out the way the men had come from. Although the light was poor, he could feel the incline of the path. They were headed up, and that could only be a good thing. They continued to walk for well over an hour, and Ana had started to lag behind him when he saw light ahead. Thankfully they hadn't come across anyone else.

"We are nearly there," he said.

"And where is there?" she asked, too far away. He stopped. "My feet hurt," she said. Although there was something to her voice. Not a whine at her predicament, but something he couldn't place.

He reluctantly returned to find her hidden in the cloak. "What is it?" he asked.

Ana shook her head, the hood moving about her. He wanted to laugh. She seemed quite determined.

"Ana," he said softly. As he took another step towards her, she stepped back. "They might return. We need to get out of this tunnel."

"Do you know what my mother did?" she asked in a quiet voice.

"What?"

"The lord said that my mother wasn't worth talking about. What did she do? And did they push her off the Walk too?"

"I don't know," he said, wrapping an arm around her shoulders and trying to guide her towards the light.

She pulled against him. "If I leave, I may never find out."

"You have left," he said, his voice firm. "And you may still be able to learn who she was and what happened. There would be records in the capital and…"

"The capital?" she interrupted. "Are we going to the capital?"

He opened his mouth and then closed it. Dray had no idea at all where he was going or what he was going to do with this scrap of a girl before him. All he knew was that he couldn't leave her, and he couldn't allow the mage to find her.

"Can we start here?"

"Start what?" she asked, her bright eyes looking at him from beneath the hood.

"Trying to find out what is going on."

"I thought you knew what they wanted. You were with them. You travelled with that smelly mage."

"Smelly?" he asked, unable to hide the laughter from his voice. "What did he smell of?"

Ana shook her head, and he tried to read her bright eyes in the dim light of the tunnel. "What did he smell of?" he asked more clearly.

"I don't know," she said too loudly, and he pressed his hand to her mouth.

"Someone might hear you," he murmured, looking back down the tunnel for any sign of a light.

She wriggled out of his hold and kicked him sharply in the shin.

"Hey," he cried as she took off ahead of him. *What has gotten into her?*

He raced after her and found her just outside the tunnel standing by a large rock, looking over the looming mountains and the thick tree line. He glanced about. They were too exposed, he thought as he blinked into the light. He had no idea who might be following or where they might appear from. He took her arm and dragged her across the rocky ground and into the trees.

"What are you doing?" he asked, the exasperation thick in his tone.

She straightened up, pulled her shoulders back and then

deflated.

"Well?" he asked again.

"I need to know," she said.

"What do you need to know?"

"She is my aunt," she said, her eyes wide. "My whole life she has treated me as though I am… a maid," she blurted.

He raised his eyebrows at her.

"Well, I'm not," she snapped. Her hands found her hips, and he was tempted to take a step back despite her almost comical look in his oversized cloak. His shin still stung from her sharp boot.

"What are you then?" he asked.

"I'm… I'm not," she said quietly.

"You aren't now, whatever you might have wanted. We are fugitives," he muttered, looking around the trees that appeared to move in closer as though listening to them.

She looked up, taking in their height. "We don't have trees like this," she said. Then she sighed and pulled his cloak tighter about her.

"We'll need a fire," he said, "but not here."

She nodded, and they walked side by side towards the trees. She stopped then and turned back. He turned with her. In the distance, they could make out the Sheer Rock islands. They were green. As he opened his mouth to offer some comfort, she turned and headed deeper into the trees.

"Are you well enough to walk?" he asked, and she turned a harsh look on him. He put his hands up in defence. "I was thinking of your feet," he said. She ignored him and continued on. They made their way through the trees and higher into the mountains. It was starting to get dark when he suggested they stop.

"I can keep going," she murmured.

"I can't."

She stopped and turned back, looked him over and then nodded. He could have walked all night, but he needed time to work out what they were doing and where they were going. He had an idea of someone who might be able to help them, an old soldier who had retired in the mountains. But it was a long shot, and the mage might have considered they would try that way. While they had been scurrying around under the ground like rats, the mage might have been leading the men back across the bridges and into the mountains by road.

He sighed as he looked at the girl sitting on a rock. *What am I doing?*

"Can we light a fire?" she asked.

"A small one."

"Do you need your cloak back?" she asked, holding it close around her. He shook his head.

Ana chewed on her lip as she watched him pull together dry branches from around where they stood. With the ground so hard and rocky, he didn't think they would get much rest. Nor did he think it would be easy to find the old general from here.

The fire crackled into life and Ana moved closer, holding her hands out to the small flames. He leaned against a nearby tree within the warmth of the flames and watched her. *Who is this girl?*

"I'm hungry," she murmured.

"Me too," he agreed, still trying to work out what or who she really was. "There will be little here to eat."

"There might be some plants," she said, looking around doubtfully. "We aren't well prepared for this."

"No," he agreed. "That is the problem with running away."

She gave a sad smile, and he turned back to the flames. After a little while he looked up and noticed her watching him. The sky so far above them had darkened further, and in the shadow of the trees he could only see her by the glow of the flames. "Do you want to sleep?"

She nodded, but continued to watch him.

"Do you want to lean on me? It might be warmer."

Ana climbed to her feet and took the cloak from around her shoulders.

"You will need that," he said as she sat down beside him.

"We can share it. You won't be much use to me frozen to death."

"Have you seen that?" he asked quickly, as she continued to study his face.

She reached out and ran her fingertips across his cheek. "Did you have a scar here?"

"No," he said, lifting her hand from his skin. He took the cloak from her and wrapped it around their shoulders. She pulled her knees in close and then grabbed his hand.

Hers was so small in comparison, so young, yet it was marked and calloused. "What have you done?" he asked, studying it.

"I work, like you do."

His own hands were weathered and worn from carrying and working with a sword.

"You have blood on your hands," she said unemotionally.

He cleared his throat. "I'm a soldier."

"Captain Drayton Sterling," she said. "What did you do?"

"Whatever they told me." He realised then he hadn't told her his full name, and more questions arose than he could string together. "And what is your name, little maid?" he asked instead.

She looked up at him with her green eyes. "Anaise Merrin," she said.

"Merrin?"

She nodded and then sat back from him. "Do you know the name?"

He tried not to sigh. "I might," he murmured.

She looked hopeful, but he shook his head. "It is familiar, but I can't answer your questions."

She sat back against him.

"What if they find us?"

"The mage?"

She nodded against him. He closed his arm around her and held her close. "Well, if we don't freeze to death in the mountains, they will kill us."

"Why was he looking for me?" she asked. He had thought she might react to his words differently, but then they had already tried to kill her.

"They have been searching out gifted ones, to help the kingdom."

"Help them do what?"

"Become stronger? I don't know. I just do as I'm told."

"You have done that your whole life, I would imagine. Although, you aren't doing very well at it at the moment."

"Your point?"

"Why do something different now?"

"I'm not so sure that what they are doing is helping the kingdom."

"Do you think I'm gifted?"

"I thought you were just a maid."

They sat in silence for some time. She huddled closer, and he leaned his head on her hers. She was very much like a little sister, he thought, if he could remember his own. Then he ran a hand over his cheek, where Ana had traced along a line that wasn't there.

"I saw the scar," she said. "The moment I entered the lord's office, I saw it deep and red. And when you took my arm and dragged me from the room, I saw the blood on your hands, smelt the bitter coppery scent of it."

He looked beyond the small fire into the darkening trees. "What did the mage smell like?"

"It was familiar, but I can't quite place it. It will come to me," she said, trying to stifle a yawn.

Her dark hair had slipped from its ribbon and fallen about her face. Despite her determination, her eyes wouldn't remain open. He pulled the cloak around them and then looked at his hands. In the dim light of the fire, he couldn't see anything but their outline. He wondered at the blood Ana was so sure was there.

6

Despite the rain and wind hammering the side of the building and the cot that wouldn't have been fit for a soldier, Ed had slept solidly throughout the previous afternoon and into the early morning. He stretched and sat up slowly, his cloak and shoes still damp. The cold stew still sat on the table. Although his stomach grumbled, he didn't touch it. He pulled his small bag over his shoulder, gave the room a quick glance over and sat the key on the table.

There was no one in the main room of the tavern when he reached the bottom of the stairs, and although he thought she might be watching from some corner, he couldn't see the innkeeper either. The sun hadn't yet started to light the sky as he stepped outside, but he knew it wasn't far away. Although the rain had stopped, the air was damp and the road wet.

He pulled his cloak tighter around him and regretted not taking the opportunity to wash. But the layer of dirt he had acquired helped keep him warm. The mountains were still some distance away, and he headed off quickly, wondering how long it would be until he found another bed.

The road cut through the dark landscape like a pale snake, and his boots crunched too loudly on the gravel in the near silence of the early morning. He walked until the sun slowly began to light the sky. He heard a stream, or at least running water, and before long he was standing on the edge of a narrow stone bridge.

He looked down into the clear water, adjusted the bag over his shoulder, then crossed the bridge and followed the small path down to the water. The stream was icy cold as he submerged his water skin into it, but he kept it still in the flowing water as he watched the world around him. Despite the warming sun, he hadn't seen anyone. Although that was a lucky thing, it seemed odd.

He took a small sip of water, secured the skin in his bag and then headed back up to the road. Within a few minutes, while trying to determine how many more days of walking until he reached the mountains, a cart rattled up behind him. He moved across to the side of the road to allow it room to pass, and it stopped beside him.

"Where ya headed to, lad?" the older man at the reins asked. He was dressed simply and his clothes were worn.

"North," Ed said.

The man raised an eyebrow and then looked off to the distant mountains.

Ed made to keep walking, but the man put out a hand. "Climb up. North is a long way, and I could do with the company."

"I can't afford to pay you," Ed said.

The old man shrugged. "Is no matter. Talking would be payment enough, and I'm headed that way."

Ed looked over the edge of the cart, where there were some lumps beneath a rough canvas cover. He pulled his bag off and dropped it in the back, then climbed up into the seat beside the man. He was never going to make it there if he continued trying to walk.

"What is your name?" the old farmer asked.

"Ed. Ed Forest."

The man gave a nod of his head and tapped his chest. "Phillip Poales. I hail from the grasslands. And I'm taking grain to trade in the mountains, or beyond."

"Beyond?" Ed asked.

"Sheer Rock. I understand they grow their own grains, but I'm hoping they might be wanting something different."

"It is a long way to travel for a sale that might not happen."

"I have little else to occupy my time."

"Don't you have crops to grow?" Ed asked, trying to look at him without appearing to. *Who is this man?*

The man shrugged and flicked the reins, and the old horse moved into a slow walk. Ed thought he might have moved faster or done just as well on his own. Phillip flicked the reins again, and the horse surprised him by moving into a fast gait. Ed was thrown back in the seat.

"She takes a little to get going, but it would be better for you if we didn't take all day."

"Would it?" Ed asked, glancing at the man. Perhaps someone had been sent to find him after all.

Looking back over the cart, Ed couldn't tell what was beneath the canvas, but it didn't look to be enough grain to make such a journey worthwhile. Even with the horse, he must have been travelling for many days already to have come so far from the grasslands.

Ed's hand rested on the sword at his belt. This wasn't a good idea. He might just have put himself in an impossible position.

"You got any family?" he asked Phillip, trying to gauge what kind of man he was.

"I had a girl," he said, sitting forward and flicking the reins again.

Ed waited, but he didn't say any more. Perhaps she had died, he thought, worried the man might slip from the seat.

After too long in silence, the old man startled him by speaking. "She was taken."

"Who?" Ed asked.

"My daughter."

"Who took her?"

"Men thinking I owed them. They took her North."

"When?" Ed asked, glancing back again at the cart behind him.

"I could use the help," he said.

"I am no help to anyone," Ed murmured. "I might have a sword." He closed his hand around the handle. "Yet the best I can do with it is scare myself."

The old man laughed. "Any fool can use a sword," he said.

"Were you going to try to get her back on your own?"

"She is all I got," he said.

"Is that why you stopped?" Ed asked hurriedly. "You thought I could help?"

"I wanted to see if you was one of them," he said, absently flicking the reins again, and Ed wondered how hard he had driven the horse. "Fifteen men he had when he fronted on my land."

Ed felt sick, even more than he had at the idea of the watery stew. He looked down at the sword and released his strong hold on the handle. He was going to die—and not for his own actions, but because he had accepted a lift from an old man with a crazy notion that they could fight a group of men. The type of men who stole girls and had probably grown up fighting.

"Do you have a plan?" he asked, disappointed that he sounded as scared as he did.

"Only to find my girl and get her home."

"You aren't worried about what might happen to your land while you are away?"

"Ain't that much there to worry about."

"You didn't consider that they might have taken her to get you away from what they wanted."

The old man looked at him with disbelief.

"It is a possibility," Ed continued. "You would be amazed at what people will do to get what you've got."

"You sound like you got more experience than a boy your age should have," Phillip said kindly, and Ed tried not to sigh. "I will take you to where you need to go. There is no expectation that you help me get my girl back."

Ed nodded thanks, but he felt bad for not being able to help the man, and for looking out for himself first. Besides, they might come across these men before he had a chance to find the man he was searching for. And he wasn't sure what he could do to help the man if they did.

"Who are you looking for?" the old man asked.

"A family friend," Ed murmured. Or at least he hoped he was.

The memory driving him was his pale, sickly mother, holding his hand far too tightly, and that had scared him far more than the colour of her skin. She had dragged in a breath that seemed to take everything she had. Even as the small child he had been at the time, he understood what was to happen.

"If anything goes wrong, you must endeavour to go north and find my one true friend." Her grip had tightened. And he had wondered where she found the strength when it was so hard for her to breathe. "You must endeavour. Promise me."

He had nodded wildly, hoping that his promise would keep her with him longer. But he was dragged from the room, and endeavour was the last word on her lips. So here he was, endeavouring to find her one true friend, hoping with everything he had that it was the right decision.

7

Ana woke with a start, cold and uncomfortable. It took her a moment to remember where she was. At least her pillow was soft, and she was curled beneath a blanket. Then she realised she was curled against Dray's leg. His cloak was wrapped tight around her, although she was sure they had huddled together beneath it the night before.

She tried not to disturb him as she sat up. Dray still slept, his hand on his sword and his head upright. The little fire had gone out, and his hands looked blue. As he sat so very still, her heart began to beat faster. She sucked in a deep breath and reached for his hand. It was cold when she rested her fingers on it, but he twitched beneath her hold and then blinked slowly.

"I thought you had died," she blurted, a shiver covering her whole body.

"I'm much harder to kill than that."

He rubbed his hands together and looked her up and down. She slipped the cloak from her shoulders and instantly regretted the movement as the cold wind wrapped around her. "Thank you," she said.

He waved a hand at her as he climbed to his feet, then rolled his shoulders and headed into the trees. She wrapped herself back up and raced to catch him up.

"Do you know where we are going?" she asked.

"Over the mountain."

She stopped and took in the expanse of mountains above them. In fact, she found it difficult to gauge just how large they were. "We are going to die," she murmured.

"It isn't that high," he called back, increasing the gap between them.

"Yes, it is," she said, racing towards him and stumbling over the rough ground. He caught her with large hands. "Thank you," she murmured. "I am not dressed for mountain climbing. Is there a road we could travel that would be easier?"

"Of course, there is," Dray said kindly, "and the mage and his soldiers will be travelling it too."

"Oh," she said.

"We are safer in the trees. No one will see us, and we can make it over the mountains to where we need to be before anyone has any idea of where we went."

"I hope you are right."

"Of course, I am," he said with a grin, and she shook her head at his mock arrogance. This was not where she had hoped to be, but then she hadn't considered that she would have stood on the Walk the day before or remembered her father being on it. She had been so sure he had fallen from a bridge and couldn't remember exactly what had happened until the day before. Maybe someone had put the idea in her head that he had fallen from a bridge. Either way, she didn't like heights and her father was gone.

She glanced up at the back of the man she followed. He must have seen all sorts of things in his lifetime and heard more. Would she be able to learn more of her mother? Ana couldn't remember her at all, nor much of what her father had told her.

The apathetic look of the lord came to mind, and how she had barely acknowledged Ana all these years yet kept her close. The lord herself had no other family. No husband or children. Ana could have learnt so much, although she didn't really like the idea of spending time with the woman.

She looked up again to find the gap had increased between her and the soldier. Worried that someone might be following, Ana looked back over her shoulder and was sure she saw something in the trees behind her.

"Dray," she called out.

He was back by her side in a moment. "What is it?"

"I think I saw something."

"You did, or you thought you did?"

"I don't know anymore," she admitted. He took a step forward and then she pointed. "There," she whispered as something dark moved between the trees.

Dray groaned. "We are going to have to move faster," he said, turning her around and pointing her up the mountain.

"Who is it?" she asked.

"Not who, what. That appears to be a very large mountain lion."

"It is dark."

"What did you hope it would be?" he asked, pushing her along.

"I just didn't know they were black. You would think with the snow, white would be better."

"The lower down the mountain, the darker they are. If we can fool it into thinking it is only tracking us, we might reach the snow before it."

"The snow?" She stopped. "Can't you kill it?"

"It is far bigger than me, and to get close enough to drive a sword into it means getting close enough for its very sharp claws to slice through me, or you."

Ana's heart sparked into its high-paced pounding for the second time that morning. She clenched her fists to stop her hands shaking and tried desperately to focus on the path ahead so as not to fall, and to pretend it wasn't following them.

As they continued up the mountain, Ana wanted to turn back and look. She could feel it stalking behind them, and with four legs and better grip of the mountain it was moving much faster than she could. Despite her certainty that it was gaining on them, she stopped. Dray turned back at her with a questioning look.

There was something else on this mountain, and she didn't know if it was worse than the mountain lion or just an unknown. Either way, she knew it was coming. She could feel it in her bones.

Dray waved her forward, but she remained where she was. "Now," he whispered hoarsely through clenched teeth. He looked far less worried than he sounded, and she sidestepped just as the mountain lion landed where she had been standing.

It growled loudly, but although it was close enough to take Ana's head from her shoulders, it didn't move. Dray's hand was tight around his sword. It wasn't clear if he was waiting to see if he could move faster than the animal or if it would lose interest first.

The growl in its throat grew louder, and Ana felt it resonate through her. Instead of stepping forward with his sword drawn, Dray stepped backwards. Ana squeezed her eyes closed. She could feel it coming, moving faster than an avalanche down the mountainside. She looked then, in fear it was an avalanche, to see deep red scales as the large head closed around the mountain lion. She blew out a slow breath.

She held up her hand, and Dray lowered the sword he'd had ready to drive into the side of the beast. "Step back slowly," he said.

"I think if it wanted to eat me, it would have," Ana said.

"It might be saving you for a treat."

"What is it?" she asked, reaching a hand towards its warm face. It turned to look at her with the blackest eyes, and steam blew about her, warming her cold frame.

"Are you serious?" Dray snapped, and the beast turned its head towards him.

Whatever the beast was, it was huge. The head alone was the same height as Dray. More steam swirled around her, and she stepped forward to place a hand on its face. Strange images raced through her mind, the world from far above, trees as small dots and villages like toys amongst green fields. Then fighting, swords and men and blood, but she couldn't see who was fighting whom or what colours they wore.

She pulled her hand back quickly. The animal pulled back from her and folded in large leathery wings that she hadn't noticed until they rustled with the movement. It was almost as long as the bridge to Sheer Rock.

"Dragon," Dray whispered. It turned back to him again and then back to Ana.

"Do they exist?" she asked, looking at the bulk before her. It snorted again, and she smiled. Then she frowned. "Why is there a dragon here?"

"Maybe it lives in the mountains."

"Could you carry us up the mountain?" she asked, and the large black eye blinked.

"What are you doing?" Dray asked, pushing himself between her and the dragon. "Do you want to be food?"

"He seems to like us," she said.

Dray turned to face her so suddenly that she squealed, and as he put his hand to her face, the dragon nudged him away. She could tell it didn't intend to hurt him, but it was enough to knock him down.

"What are you doing?" Ana asked, unsure to whom she was asking the question.

The dragon pulled back. Dray sat amongst the rocks and glared at her. "I think you have lost your mind," he said.

"He could help," she said.

"Help?"

"I saw something," she said softly. She hadn't seen him in the vision she'd had as she touched the dragon, but she knew he was there.

"What did you see?" Dray asked, as he climbed to his feet and dusted himself off.

She shook her head. "It wasn't very clear. Fighting."

"Who was fighting?"

"I couldn't tell that either."

"We need to keep moving," he said.

She nodded. The dragon slowly turned as she started forward and followed along behind as they moved up the mountainside. Tim had once had a puppy who had followed him wherever he went, and when he grew and the puppy became a dog, it never left his side. They had both cried the day that old dog had died, but as Ana glanced back at the dragon following behind her, she had the same idea. Dray did not appear as happy about their new friend. The dragon made very little noise, other than the trees it pushed over as it walked.

"It came from nowhere," Dray said.

Ana stopped and looked at him. The dragon stopped with her, and its warm breath washed over her.

"I felt him before he arrived," Ana said, then took in the look on Dray's face. "I knew there was something else out there, something scarier than the mountain lion, but I didn't know if it was more dangerous to us."

"And?"

"He doesn't seem to be."

And then, before she could suggest again that it might help them find a way up the mountain or over it, the dragon took to the air and disappeared.

"You scared him," she snapped at Dray. He stopped and sighed as he looked at her with disappointment. She looked back at the ground and kept moving. She had no idea of this supposed skill she had, of seeing what others thought. Or was it their skill? she wondered.

"He scared me," Dray murmured, and she smiled.

She looked back the way they had come to see a clear path in the trees behind them. Then she looked back up the mountain. The trees were thick ahead of them. Although she knew that the ground rose more sharply, she had no idea how far they were from the top.

She again longed for the road, but Dray was right; the others would be travelling that way. Would they be able to stay out of their way for long? If the sharp-faced man was as strong as she suspected, he might be able to find them anywhere.

She stumbled on a rock as she thought of the man and the boy again. Dray's strong hand closed around her arm, stopping her from hitting the ground. She wanted a minute to gather herself together. She missed the dragon's warm breath already, and she was tired. But he tugged her along.

"We are going to die out here," he said. She tried to catch his eye to see if he was serious, then tried to not fall over as he released his hold and moved ahead.

"Stop," she called.

"We don't have time," he said without looking back at her.

"I can't," she whined, wishing she had been able to sound more together.

"We have only been walking a couple of hours."

She stared at him, and he sighed before walking back towards her. "I understand this is hard," he said.

"Do you?"

"There may also be more mountain lions, dragons who might actually want to eat you, or worse—my own men might have worked out the direction we took and decided that waiting for you to catch your breath is not a good way to spend their time." He watched the world behind her, as though searching the trees, as he spoke.

Ana crossed her arms. She wanted to really scowl at him, but he looked away from the trees and behind him to the mountain. They had covered enough ground that the trees knocked about by the dragon were no longer visible.

She wanted to growl at him, say something clever, but instead she found she was sucking in a sob that was trying to escape and succeeding. He took a step towards her and rested a hand on her shoulder, looking directly at her.

"We have to keep moving," he said.

She nodded, but her legs wouldn't move.

"Just a bit more, and then we may be able to find somewhere to rest. But if there is any chance they are following us, we are lost if we stay in the open."

The trees seemed to close around them. "Is this really in the open?"

He nodded and waited as she started again to move one foot in front of the other. She wrapped the cloak tighter around her and tried to watch where she was walking. She only glanced at him occasionally as they made their way through the trees. He didn't appear to feel the cold or the long hours of walking.

But the day didn't seem to be coming to an end, nor were the trees or the steady incline that continued to get steeper. If only there was a path, Ana thought. She closed her eyes and wished with everything she had that she was somewhere warm and dry. As she tried not to lean into a tree and stay there, a path appeared amongst the trees.

Ana looked along the worn ground, wondering for a moment if she had wished it into existence. She shivered and pulled the cloak tighter around her. The flashes of fighting she had seen with the dragon returned, and she wondered again just what gift she had that the mage had come so far to find. And why hadn't she known about it or seen signs of it before?

She wiped at her face, hoping that Dray hadn't noticed her tears. He must be regretting running with her even more now. Yet he had stayed with her. Nothing was as it should be. She pushed herself from the tree, determined to keep moving as he had insisted. A little way along the path, she stopped again. In the scrub she was sure she could see a crumbling stone wall.

Ana stepped closer, brushing at the plants that grew along it and following it into the trees with her eyes. She leaned into the stone wall, hoping it would support her long enough to reach the remains of the house she saw ahead.

"Where did that come from?" Dray asked as he rested his hand on her shoulder.

8

Ed watched Phillip from the corner of his eye as he intermittently flicked the reins while the horse continued pushing forward at the same quick pace. The old man grumbled something under his breath, and Ed turned to watch the world pass them by. It wasn't too different from what he had experienced on his journey so far, except he didn't have to walk and his feet appreciated the rest.

Sitting on the cart, he had the chance to see just how different the rest of the kingdom was from the capital. The world seemed to be so much larger than he imagined, although there was so little in it. He could see much further than from his previously high vantage point in the capital.

"So, when was the last time you came this way?" Phillip asked, his voice surprising Ed in the comfortable silence.

"I haven't," Ed said before he thought about it, then turned to the interested look on the old man's face.

"My mother told me of her friend, and now that she is gone, I thought it time I search him out."

"He didn't come when he learnt of her death?"

Ed shook his head and turned his attention back to the green fields they passed. The distant mountains didn't seem to be getting any closer. He didn't know who had come when his parents had died. He could only clearly remember the days leading up to his mother's death, although he remembered the acute pain when he knew she was gone. And his father's death had been too much to deal with. His chest still felt as though it was slicing open when he thought of him.

When he was a boy, the world had seemed filled with possibility. Now he felt as though he was trying to hold water in his hands while it continued to slip through his fingers. There had always been people around them, people supporting him and his family. And yet when he'd needed help, they had only acted to serve themselves.

His father's death had left him not only alone but vulnerable. His uncle had told everyone that he was doing what he could for the poor boy, yet he was like everyone else, doing what he could for himself.

If Ed had managed to find someone with magic, he might have been able to get what he needed. But those with magic were even less likely to help him. The old mage came to mind, but he shook the image away before it could take hold. He wasn't the man his father had promised him to be, either. Discovering that had hurt almost as much as losing his father.

"What is it, lad?" Phillip asked.

Ed turned to see the old man's soft face creased with concern. "Have you seen something?" he asked, looking around with more focus.

"You are huffing and sighing away over there. Is it too slow a journey for you?"

Ed shook his head and looked back over the green fields that stretched away from the dusty road. "I just hoped I would be closer to the mountains. I know the kingdom is vast, but I don't think I realised just how far away the rest of the world was when I started out."

The old man chuckled. "Most folks never want to leave their little part of the world, thinking it enough. I would imagine there is a much larger world out there beyond the shores of Ilia."

"Do you mean Sheer Rock?"

"Why anyone would want to live so high up is beyond me," Phillip muttered. "But different or no, the people of Sheer Rock are still part of the kingdom. Their lord is like that of any other province."

Ed nodded. He knew the histories of the land at least, although he didn't know who was the lord of each seat. Or region. He wasn't even sure of what he should be calling them. "Are they the Lord of the Seat, or is it the Seat of the Lord?" he asked Phillip.

"You are asking an old farmer?" he asked with a chuckle.

"But you know how the kingdom works; I'm not sure I do."

The old man nodded and flicked the reins, and the horse continued racing along the road. Ed wondered just how long it could keep it up.

"Where the lord for each region lives is called the Seat of the Lord. It is like the capital, but a much smaller version for the region. I imagine they are all a bit different. I went to the Seat of the Lord of the Grasslands when my girl was taken."

"What did the lord say?" Ed asked, giving the old man his full attention.

"Not very much—or at least he would have said not very much, if I had been given the chance to see him."

"He wouldn't see you?"

"Those who would show you in said that he wouldn't see me."

"But that is what the lords do. Isn't it?" Ed asked, not quite sure what they were meant to do. "They look after the people." At least that was what he had been told as a child.

"Well, they look after those they want to." Phillip stared ahead of him and flicked the reins once more. Despite the constant speed, Ed thought the horse danced along the road even faster.

When Phillip didn't continue, Ed asked, "Do you think you can get her back?"

"I'm sure I can."

Ed nodded. Maybe other girls had been taken as well. Why would the lord not want to help the man get her back? Or did he know the men who had taken her? "When you do get her back," Ed started, and the old man turned a crooked smile on him, "you should take her to the lord and tell him that you did what he should have."

"Might be that we go somewhere else," Phillip said. "No good ruffling feathers of those you might one day need."

"Maybe," Ed said softly, turning back to the world around him. He wondered if his father would have given him similar advice. He didn't really know how to behave in the world as he would want. "Do you know what we are going to do when we find these men?"

"Whatever we need to," Phillip said softly, and with another flick of the reins the horse moved into a pace that rattled the cart so much Ed thought he would be shaken from the seat.

9

Dray looked over the old building and tried not to sigh. He wanted to keep moving, but there was no way Ana was going to be able to. It was going to take them twice as long as he hoped to make it over the mountains, and the delay only meant an increasing chance of being found.

He had been careful to stay off any pathway, to slow any chance of them being caught. Although between her unhurried walk, a mountain lion and a giant dragon, they had very nearly lost before they had begun.

The building, although he wasn't quite sure what it had been before, was larger than he thought as they moved through the ruins. The stone looked as though it had been collected from the mountainside. All of them rough and different sizes. A thick moss covered most of them, giving it a soft green appearance that helped it blend into the trees, which he was sure were denser around the building.

There were several complete rooms, although the roof had caved in on two of them. Other rooms were large, but the walls had crumbled, the mountain claiming them back. There was no furniture and no flooring. As he moved through the crumbling stone walls, he wondered just how long ago it had been built and how long since anyone else had been there.

There were no signs of fire, nor human habitation. Not even

hunters appeared to have used it, and he wondered for a moment if there was a reason for that. The one remaining room had a single door on one side, and he worried that if he tried to open it the structure would disintegrate. On the opposite wall was a small opening that would have been a door frame, but the door had long since rotted away.

Ana stood outside the open doorway and peered into the darkness.

"I've been inside, and it is dry and safe," he said, standing behind her.

She looked again but wouldn't go in.

"Would you rather camp out here in the cold again?" he asked.

She tugged his cloak around her tighter and then looked up at him seriously. "I'm sorry," she murmured.

"Don't start that again," he said, pushing her into the room.

She sucked in a wobbly breath and pushed back against him.

"What do you see?" he asked as she turned and buried her face in his chest.

"Nothing," she said. "You must be cold."

He blew out a long, slow breath. He couldn't get frustrated with her. He had dragged her into the mountains without anything to keep her warm. An image flashed though his mind of her standing on the walkway over the empty sky. The pure fear that had gripped her whole body.

"We can light a fire," he said, patting her back. She was only a girl, he had to remind himself. "The light might show you that there is nothing in here."

She nodded but didn't move.

"Ana?" he asked carefully.

"I can't see things. I'm not what he thinks I am."

"You saw something with the dragon."

She looked back up at him and nodded, then shook her head. "I don't want to see things."

He took her shoulders and moved her back a step. "We are what we are."

She gave him a frustrated scowl that made him smile.

"You saw something with the mage, the dragon and even a scar I don't have. What can you see in here that has you so unsettled?"

"It is more a feeling," she said. "It is like I can feel the loss and pain."

"It is an old house. Whatever happened here happened a very long time ago."

"It doesn't feel like that."

"Do you want to keep moving?"

"No," she sighed. "I can't walk any further and I'm cold."

"Then sit here," he said, guiding her slowly into the room. "I'll start a fire and then see if I can find something for us to eat."

"How long will it take us to find this friend of yours?"

"I don't know."

"We aren't going to make it, are we?" she said, sitting down against the wall and tucking the cloak around her. She appeared even smaller.

"Of course, we are. You have a dragon watching over you, for a start," he said.

Dray didn't want to leave her as she stared at nothing, her lip quivering. Yet there was no sign that anyone had followed them or that anyone else was close. They might have just slipped away as he had hoped. He was vigilant as he headed back out in search of wood to start a fire. The ground was damper this far up the mountain, where the moss seemed to grow over anything that lay still long enough.

It took him far longer than he would have liked to collect enough wood, but thankfully he didn't see anyone and managed to catch a large rabbit. He just hoped the dragon wasn't coming for dinner. He shook his head as he made his way back into the last standing room. If the dragon arrived for dinner, they were most likely going to be it.

He entered the room to find Ana curled in the corner, the cloak wrapped tight around her and up over her head.

"I found a rabbit," he said, dropping the wood down, but she didn't move. "You must be tired," he said more quietly. She wasn't used to travelling in such a way for so long, he had to remind himself. No good saving her if he then finished her off in the mountains.

He worked quickly to set the fire and before long, a small blaze had warmed the room considerably. He held his hands over the flames and rolled his shoulders. He was cold too, but he had more layers beneath his armour than the girl wore even with his cloak.

He turned then to find that she hadn't moved at all. An odd feeling gnawed at his gut. He bent down slowly and peeled back his cloak, fearful of just what might be waiting on the other side. Perhaps they had been discovered while he'd been out searching for dry wood and they had left her dead for him to find on his return.

He forced himself to look at her pale face. Her eyes were closed, and she didn't move at all. As he studied her, she gave the smallest of shudders. If he hadn't been looking, he would have missed it.

"Ana," he called, pulling her around into his arms, trying to be gentle and yet trying to shake her awake at the same time.

She didn't move, and then he heard something scrape across the stones outside. He waited, and the noise repeated. It was something between a shuffle and a large claw moving over the stones, and he wondered if the dragon had returned. Although he had no idea if that would be good or bad.

Dray lay Ana back down carefully and wrapped the cloak around her, then stood slowly, took half a step forward and drew his sword. The dragon was too large to fit in the room, and if it was someone else, he only hoped there were not too many of them.

A shadow moved across the doorway. With his sword held firm, he took another small step forward. He didn't want any fighting to happen around Ana, but he didn't want to give anyone the opportunity to find a way behind him.

The hunched figure in a tattered cloak was a surprise.

"Hello friend," an old voice said. "Could I share your fire? I smelled the smoke a little ways across the mountain, and I hoped there might be the smell of meat." As the figure stepped into the small space and the light of the flames, Dray focused on his old, lined face and long dark grey beard.

The old face smiled, and as he blinked slowly, taking in the dimly lit room, Dray was sure his eyes were solid black for just a second before they returned to an old milky brown.

"I see you caught a rabbit," he said, a smile splitting his weathered face and revealing perfect white teeth. "Might I share…" He stepped forward then. "What happened to the girl?" he asked, concern thick in his voice as he stood straighter.

"I don't know," Dray said. "I think she is just cold and tired from the travelling."

The old man pushed him out of the way with surprising force and knelt down over Ana. He peeled the cloak back in much the same way as Dray had, then ran a hand over her face. She murmured something, but didn't wake.

"Have you got water?" he asked.

Dray nodded and then shook his head. He was sure he had a skin, but right at that moment he had no idea where it was or how he had let the man approach Ana.

"Maybe you could get that rabbit cooking," the man said, and Dray took the rabbit and headed outside to clean it. It took him a little while to skin and gut the animal, and it was only then that he thought about what he had done.

He headed straight back into the room, the rabbit hanging by his side. "What have you done to me?" he demanded.

"I haven't done anything," the man said, sitting beside Ana with the water skin in his hand. She appeared just as she had when Dray had left.

"What have you done to her?"

"I gave her a little water, made sure she was warm," the man added, and Dray noticed that he no longer wore his cloak. It was draped over his own, over Ana.

"Is she sick?" he asked.

"She isn't quite herself," the old man murmured, looking back over her.

"We can't stay here," Dray said.

"Cook the rabbit and we can decide what to do next."

Dray nodded, then set up a stand over the fire with makeshift sticks from the pile of wood he had collected and started the rabbit cooking. As the smell of it started to fill the room, his stomach growled, and he was sure he saw a glint in the old man's eye.

They had remained in silence, and the old man had stayed at Ana's side.

"Maybe it is the shock," Dray murmured. "She is scared of heights and she was up very high."

The old man nodded as though he knew just what Dray spoke of. He had been a fool, he realised, stepping in when he should have done just what he had always done—watched what the men in power wanted, or did, or let unfold.

But there had been something so innocent in the girl as she squeezed her eyes closed, and the woman who should have watched over her was so keen to watch her fall to her death. Well, not quite. She would have only watched her slip from view. He had looked all the way down as he lay across the walkway, holding the girl by her hand as he prayed to every god he knew of to save her. The cliff face had disappeared beneath them, yet he was surprised he could hear the distant water. A mist covered what he would have seen of the water, yet through the soft white vapour, sharp black rocks jutted towards him. They may have been a long way off, but they seemed scary enough from his vantage point.

"It was right that you were there," the old man said, and Dray looked up at him as he took Ana's hand in his and wrapped his old hands around it.

❀

Ana tried not to look down. She knew there was nothing beneath her and very little stopping her from slipping over the edge. It would only take the wind to swirl up around her and she would be gone. She wanted to squeeze her eyes closed against what she knew was coming, but the world before her was strange and she needed to understand it.

In the circular opening back into the lord's office stood the lord herself, although she avoided looking at Ana as though ashamed of what she'd done. But Ana knew she would not do anything to try and stop it. Beside her was the sharp-faced mage, darkness surrounding him like a shadow. She shivered.

The third was Drayton Sterling. A soldier, a man she didn't know, and yet she knew she could trust no one like him. He held out his hand and she reached for him. A low, deep growl started, and behind the three was a large red-black dragon. Ana wondered how it could have found its way into the room. Then Dray's hand was tight around hers.

She blinked into the firelight, taking a moment to work out where she was. She was standing on the Walk, but she wasn't; and it wasn't Dray holding her hand but an old man. Concern etched his weathered face, and warmth radiated from him.

"Ahh," he said softly. "She is back."

"Are you all right?" Dray asked, almost pushing the man out of the way.

Ana nodded, but she wasn't sure. She must have been sleeping, but she didn't feel rested in any way.

Dray sighed, then clenched and unclenched his fist.

"I'm hungry," she managed.

He smiled then and turned away, returning with a greasy rabbit leg, which he held out to her. He appeared unsure whether to help her, kneel or just stand. She smiled as she sat up and pushed at the cloaks covering her. She was still cold, even with the fire, as the ground was damp and cool.

She took the meat and bit hungrily into it, but the old man rested his hand on hers. "Slow," he said.

She nodded and tried to take her time. Then she focused on the man before her. "Are you Dray's friend?" she asked.

"He has offered his hospitality," he said, looking over his shoulder to Dray.

"He came out of the cold," Dray said.

"I'm Ana," she said, putting a greasy finger to her chest and then biting into the rabbit again.

He nodded slowly. "I know who you are," he said, as though he had known her before he'd come to find them. She felt the meat slip from her fingers.

"Don't waste it, you need your strength," he said, catching it before it hit the floor and handing it back to her.

"Who are you?" she asked.

He smiled, his perfect teeth a contrast to his old face. She reached forward and placed her hand against his cheek. It was soft and warm, and she was reminded of the older people she knew on Sheer Rock. But she felt the heat and steam of something very different. She looked into his old eyes and knew they had seen far more than any other man. She could smell blood and steel, and she withdrew her hand.

"You are very gifted," he said softly.

"Sometimes I see things," she whispered.

"Did you see your father's death before it happened?" he asked, his voice not quite as kind as it had been. Ana pulled back from him and pushed the meat into her mouth. He watched her too closely.

"I was there when he died. That was enough to see."

"You saw him fall," he said. "You did not see him die."

Ana opened and closed her mouth as he continued to watch her.

"That is enough," Dray said, the timbre in his voice scaring her.

He sat down beside her and wrapped a large arm around her, pulling her against him and somehow putting himself between her and the old man.

"I was there," the man said, climbing to his feet.

"You were there in my dream," she said, and then wondered at her own words. Had he been there? She closed her eyes for a moment, overwhelmed by the sense she'd gotten from him when she had touched his face. "The dragon," she murmured.

"We won't fit him in here," Dray said. "And he might still want to eat you."

Ana looked from Dray to the old man. "Do you?" she asked.

He laughed then, and Dray seemed to hold her tighter.

"I am Ende," he said, bowing his head towards the two of them. "I think we might be able to help each other."

"In what way?" Dray asked, sounding hesitant.

"You need to get to the capital. I think I can assist you."

"Are you going to fly us there?" Ana asked, interrupting.

He laughed again. "I am going to walk with you," he said. "But we search for the same thing."

"We are looking for our friend," Dray said. "We have no plans for the capital. We have no real plans at all. This was not what was meant to happen."

"You were to accompany a mage—a powerful mage, no matter what you think of his skill—as he sought tribute. You were to protect him with your life."

"That was the plan, but I ended up saving a girl from a fall and now we are alone, unprepared and lost somewhere in the mountains."

"Lost?" Ana asked. She had thought he had a plan. An idea of where they were and where they were going. And now he was admitting they were lost.

"Once we make it over the mountains, I'll be able to determine where we are."

"Lost," she said again.

"I will keep you safe."

"I'm not questioning that," she said.

Dray rubbed his hand over his eyes. He looked exhausted. He had led them so far from the lord and the mage, and he had provided fire and food. She felt bad for questioning him.

He sighed and looked over the old man. "If Ana is happy for you to travel with us, I will watch over you both."

"He's a dragon," she said, holding out her hand to the old man. "He could be very useful."

Dray sighed again, nodded slowly, then leaned back against the wall closing his eyes. Ana leaned back beside him, unsure if he believed her about the old man. She was exhausted, yet she feared what she might find in her dreams.

Ana must have drifted, for she woke to the sound of voices. She had slept against Dray and the cold stone wall, his cloak and Ende's both covering the two of them. She glanced up at Dray, who held a finger to his lips. Ende was curled up by the fire. But he appeared to give off more heat than the dying embers. He looked like a man who had lived in the mountains his whole life. She was wondering if he spent more of his time as a dragon or a man—and if the latter, where that might be—when she was drawn by the sound of voices again.

Ana was desperate to ask what to do; surely anyone finding the building in the area would investigate. They might be able to smell the fire and the remains of the rabbit. She was momentarily surprised there was in fact some meat left over. But then, Ende had eaten an entire mountain lion just the day before.

"Could we say we were robbed?" Ana asked in a soft whisper.

Dray shook his head and sat his hand on his sword. They waited, Ana desperate to move. She had been in the same position for far too long and needed to stretch. The voices disappeared into the distance, and despite Drayton trying to hold on to her, she was at the door looking after where they might have gone.

"They can't see us," Ende murmured from his place by the fire.

She turned back to him.

"Why?" she prompted when he didn't continue.

"No one can see this place. It is enchanted," he said. "That is why it has gone undetected for so long."

"We could see it," Ana said.

"No," Ende said, stretching like a cat and then climbing slowly to his feet. "*You* could see it. The captain only saw once you put your hand on the stonework."

She turned to Dray, but he shrugged his shoulders as though he wasn't sure if what Ende said was true.

10

When the little village came into view, Ed was hopeful for a chance to get down from the cart and stretch his legs. His feet were still blistered and sore, but the hours spent on the hard bench seat had done nothing for his back or his rear end. And the continued fast pace of the horse had been unsettling.

"Should you ask after your daughter?" he suggested, as it appeared neither Phillip nor the horse were slowing when they entered the village.

"Not here," Phillip murmured.

"How can you be so sure where she was taken to?"

"Just keep your head down and your cloak up," Phillip snapped, and the cart rattled and shook over the dusty road.

Ed looked towards the houses as they passed them by. There didn't seem to be any movement. Either the town was deserted or not welcoming to strangers. He glanced at Phillip, who focused only on the road ahead as they moved through the village.

They continued in silence as they passed through the fields beyond the cottages, Ed looking over green crops. Large trees dotted the landscape, and before long it appeared that there were more trees than fields. In the distance he was sure he could hear water.

"Are we near the coast?" he asked.

"Don't be daft, boy. That's the Deep Near."

"The river?"

"Did you get an education where you came from?" Phillip asked, his voice gruffer than Ed remembered.

He nodded, but it was yet another reminder of just how little he knew the world. The continent was wider than it appeared. "Does that mean you are headed for the Forest of Near?"

"To reach anything in the north, you must pass through the Forest of Near, and it would be the best hiding place for a girl. They may also have taken others. Every seven years, one of the regions must provide brides as tribute. I'm sure they aren't that keen in the Near Forest to offer their own girls to the men of the capital, and they stole them from elsewhere."

"Are you sure or are you guessing?" Ed asked.

"About which bit?" Phillip asked, real curiosity in his voice.

Ed sighed. The lords had to pay tribute regularly to be part of the Kingdom of Ilia, to prove their loyalty and that of their people now that they were all one. Generally, supplies were presented such as grains, meat, metals—or so Ed thought. He might not have paid proper attention to just what was asked of the people.

"If you are so sure she was taken to give to the capital, would it be better to go there and ask for her return?"

If Phillip weren't in such a hurry, Ed was certain from the look on the older man's face that he would have pulled the cart to a stop and put him off.

"Do you really think they would give her back?" he asked solemnly. "They might think I am an old man desperate for a new wife. And once the kingdom has her, she belongs to the kingdom, no matter how it came about. They wouldn't be giving her back."

"I thought the people gave willingly," Ed murmured.

"Would you give your sister to a stranger, just to keep the peace?"

Ed shook his head. Not that he had family he could offer, but if he did, he would feel just as Phillip did. "We are going to get ourselves killed," he murmured.

"Maybe," the old man admitted. "But either way, they aren't sending my girl anywhere."

"We'll all die together then," Ed quipped sarcastically.

"That's the spirit. Unless you know how to use that fancy sword."

Ed put his hand on the pommel of the sword in his belt. The trees were closing in around them again. He felt claustrophobic in the darkness beneath the canopy, and the road narrowed significantly. He only hoped there were others who could bear witness in case someone ever wondered what had become of him. They should have followed the main road that traversed the kingdom. It travelled around the forest and up into the mountains before it reached the bridge to Sheer Rock.

Ed tried to swallow the uneasiness, but it stuck in his throat. If there were as many men as Phillip had said, men brazen enough to steal young women from their homes, then an old man and a boy with a sword he had never used outside the practice halls didn't stand a chance.

As the trees became denser still, Ed cleared his throat. "How far ahead of you were they?" he asked, trying to distract himself from the darkness and determine how much longer he might live.

"Maybe a day," Phillip murmured, looking through the trees.

"Do *you* know how to use a sword?"

"Been some time for me, lad, since I needed to."

"What is your plan?" Ed asked seriously. He sat up and focused on the old man rather than the shadows between the trees.

"I'm going to start with asking."

Ed was sure his jaw hit the wooden bench he sat on as he stared at the old man. "A gang of young men who stole your daughter directly from you, and maybe other men's daughters. You are just going to ask for her back?"

"No harm in asking," the old man said, glancing at him. Ed was sure he winked.

"Do you think they will give her back?"

"She can be a troublesome girl sometimes. They might think she isn't worth holding on to."

Ed sucked in a breath.

"I'm sure they still have her," Phillip muttered, a determination in his voice.

Ed could only hope he was right. If they found these men—he shivered at the idea—and Phillip's daughter was already dead, there was no telling what the man might do. Ed was starting to think he should have continued on foot.

They were only an hour or so into the forest when Ed thought he could hear voices. He tried not to wiggle in his seat as Phillip pulled up the horse and climbed down from the cart.

"Are you sure about this?" Ed asked.

The old man didn't answer him as he tied the reins to a nearby tree. The path had almost disappeared before them. Phillip climbed into the back of the cart. He lifted some of the cloth and peered at the supplies when something scraped across the base of the cart.

"Pull that sword out, lad," he said, coming around the cart with an axe in both hands. He appeared to struggle with the weight, and Ed wondered what he would really be able to do with it.

Ed drew the sword and for a moment regretted that it was as shiny as it was. It appeared to glow in the dim light of the trees. Phillip raised his eyebrows at it, then motioned for him to follow.

They moved as quietly as they could through the trees, but it took a few minutes before Ed could hear again what they were working their way towards. He wondered at the silence when they had climbed down from the cart, and perhaps at why the men would allow such noise, for surely others would hear them as well. The chatter and murmuring of women was louder than any conversation he had overheard before. Anyone trying to find them would have had little difficulty. Maybe these men weren't as scary as he first thought.

As they stopped by a large tree, Ed came around Phillip to look into a wide clearing. The women sat in a tight group and didn't appear too concerned. As he looked over the group, Ed noticed a thick rope circling the wrists of each young woman.

"You are going to have to feed us at some point, or there won't be enough for you to hand over," a fierce female voice rang out through the clearing.

Phillip nudged him and pointed to the young woman who had spoken. She climbed to her feet. Although the woman next to her tried to tug her down, she appeared very determined. She also wore a dark bruise across one side of her face, and he wondered if she had spoken out before.

"Tribute must be willing," she said. "We hardly look willing."

"By the time the soldiers come for the tribute, you will be happy enough to go anywhere you are told."

"I don't think so," she snapped.

Ed smiled. He liked her. Despite where she was and the situation she was in, she was a fighter, and he was more than a little jealous of her courage. He glanced at Phillip, who wore a look of pride, although there was an element of concern on his face.

"Girls are never keen to leave their families, even if it is an advantageous marriage," one of the men with them said, moving closer. "Now shut up and sit down, or there will be no food for any of you."

The girl beside her tugged again and, with a sigh, she sat down amongst the group. Despite her bruised face, she was still a beautiful girl. Long blond curls were loose about her face, and freckles dotted her nose. He wished he was close enough to get an idea of the colour of her eyes. Yet as he looked through the group, he saw they were all beautiful girls, each of them different but special nonetheless. He realised they had been chosen for a reason.

"They are all…" Ed started in a hoarse whisper.

"I know, lad," Phillip returned, putting a finger to his lips. "You have to offer the best of what you have."

Ed nodded. The better the tribute, the more loyal you were. He had no idea where they were in the Near Forest. Nor what they were going to do once they managed to free these girls and how they might get away. They must be headed towards the Lord's Seat. But try as he might, he couldn't remember the map of the forest or where that might be. It hadn't been his plan to come through the forest, so he hadn't taken the time to remind himself.

All of this was well outside his plan. He needed to get to the mountains, he thought, and find his mother's friend.

Then Phillip was charging out of the trees into the small clearing, axe raised, a mad scream rushing ahead of him. Ed had no choice but to follow lest he get himself killed.

There weren't as many men in the group as he'd expected. They had only seen six from their hiding spot, and they all raced at Phillip. Ed was quick with the sword, and despite his earlier concerns, it was very much like the practice hall. He blocked a scruffy man racing at Phillip's side. With a quick twist, Ed took the short sword from the man's hold. He backed off, but Ed could see he was thinking over his options.

Then he glanced over his shoulder as Phillip grunted. His axe planted deep in a man's skull. The crunch and spray of blood nearly brought Ed undone, and he was reminded that this was not practice. He blocked another man, tall with narrowed eyes. Ed tried to fend him off, but he was strong. Although Ed had some skill, he doubted he could beat this man. Then he nicked Ed's shoulder.

Ed groaned and pushed the other man back, managing to kick the short sword towards the prisoners. One girl grabbed at it eagerly and started to cut away at the rope. The man nearly caught him again as he was momentarily distracted. Ed swung at him with a solid determination not to die. He felt his own heartbeat pause as the sword pushed easily between the man's ribs.

Letting out a long sigh, the man dropped to the ground, and then the noise in the little clearing closed in around him. The girls screamed, some in fright, others like they were fighting back. He looked up to see Phillip's daughter with a sword. She sliced at a man, but he grinned as he dodged her. Then the grin slipped, and he dropped to his knees.

Phillip stood behind him as he went down and pulled the axe out of his back. The movement around the clearing stopped. The last two men standing took to the trees, dragging the injured and leaving the dead behind.

"Hello, Pa," she said, and he dropped the axe to take her in his arms.

Thankfully, the women were not as skittish as Ed expected them to be. He almost voiced this to Phillip and his daughter, but the look she gave him indicated there was no way she would put up with such comments. In fact, in didn't appear to Ed that she would put up with very much at all, from anyone.

He stood back and allowed Phillip and his daughter to determine what they should do next. How so many would make it on their own was a concern for Ed, but he still had his own journey to complete.

They remained in the clearing where, so far, the men hadn't returned. Phillip started a fire and Ed helped to ensure all were cut free as Phillip's daughter oversaw some first aid. As they sat around the fire, the consensus was reached that they would head back towards their homelands in the morning.

Ed tried not to sigh.

"So is the skinny lad coming with us?" asked Belle. Not that he had been introduced to her, but Phillip had used her name a number of times.

"No, he isn't," Ed answered for himself. "I have business in the north." He rolled his shoulder and winced.

"Business?" she asked, half laughing, looking him over as though he wasn't old enough to have left home.

"He has a family friend to find," Phillip said. "Maybe we should give you a hand. Escort you in case you get into any more trouble."

"I didn't find any trouble until I met you," Ed said with half a smile, putting his hand to his shoulder. "You need to take your daughter home. And help out some of these other girls." The material under his fingers was wet, and he tried not to wince again as he remembered the sword catching him earlier.

"You aren't worried what might happen to them?" Belle asked with a curious look he couldn't quite read. Any hint of the laughter she had shown before was gone.

"You managed to look after yourselves fairly well so far."

"We might have had men around to ensure no one else took us."

"And they took such care," he said in jest. But when she looked away, he regretted the words. He wasn't used to talking to many people, let alone a large group of pretty girls. He just wanted to be on his way. He stood, unsure what else he could do, and brushed himself off.

"Wait till morning, lad," Phillip said. "Sit yourself back down."

"What happened to your shoulder?" Belle asked, her face still unreadable.

He shrugged, and groaned involuntarily with the movement. She gave him a look that scared him somewhat, and as she took a step towards him, he took a step back.

"Take that shirt off and I'll have a look," she said. Her words were kinder than the look on her face, but he made no move to do as she instructed. "It might not be a serious injury, but if you leave a wound out here, it will quickly turn into something serious."

He nodded slowly and pulled his jerkin off, groaning again as the material dragged across his shoulder. Before he could put it down, Belle was standing before him, her fingers against his skin as she pulled at his shirt. They were warm and gentle, and he focused on the top of her head.

"Pa, can you fetch the water?"

Ed had forgotten anyone else existed in that moment.

"Sit down," she instructed, but as he made to move away, her fingers were still on his shirt. "Can you pull it off?"

He nodded and pulled it over his head, surprised by the blood marking the shoulder and the material sliced open. He looked around for a moment, wondering where he had put his bag. "I have another," he said as he lowered himself to the ground.

At her continued silence, he looked up. She was balling the shirt in her hand, her face flushed as she stared at him. He wanted to cover himself.

She must think I'm such a boy.

As Phillip returned with water, she tore his shirt. The ripping material was loud in the space, and the general conversation amongst the girls quietened. He watched as she continued to tear the material into long strips. Phillip knelt beside him.

"It isn't too bad, lad," he said.

"Just a scratch," Ed murmured.

Then Belle was squatting in front of him, her hand on his chest as she wiped wet cloth over the wound. He grimaced, but bit his lip to prevent any further unmanly groans from escaping. She wrapped the long strips around it carefully, without saying a word. And then she stood up.

"You'll freeze like that," Phillip said.

"I have another in my pack."

"In the cart, I'll go," Phillip offered.

"It isn't far," Ed said, standing again.

"I'll bring her closer," Phillip said, and he disappeared into the trees.

Her eyes still down, Belle held out his jerkin and he slowly slipped into it. Belle turned back to the group of women, and he watched her walk silently away.

Ed didn't think he could stay in the company of the women much longer. Conversation was not something he had practiced very much with anyone, and he was sure Belle saw him as a useless boy. He walked out to the edge of the clearing. The men they had killed were piled up by the trees, and he wondered if they should be buried or burned. But this was also something he was not familiar with, nor did he want to sound like he was suggesting these young women dig graves or collect wood.

He walked between two large trees. Their smooth grey bark reflected the firelight, although once he passed them it was as though the fire had gone out. There was no sign of the clearing or sound of voices at all. Were they so well hidden from the rest of the world? And if that was so, how had he and Phillip managed to hear them as they approached?

He ran his hand over the nearest tree and looked out into the darkness beneath the branches. He wouldn't be able to find his way anywhere in this. He didn't even know which way was north. But then, he didn't know where to find his mother's friend either. Nor what he could do once he found him.

He stopped and sat down against the nearest tree. He could stay out here, lost amongst the trees for the rest of his life, and no one would miss him or worry about him. His uncle, he reminded himself, was probably already congratulating himself that he had disappeared. And yet he still wondered how he might explain that. And what might his mother's friend do when he found him? He might not want to keep him safe; he might not want to help, if that was what Ed needed from him.

Not when he met the weak-willed boy who had given away all his parents had worked for and run. He wasn't worthy of staying. He wasn't worthy of what they had hoped for him. He wiped at a lone tear. His mother would be so disappointed.

"What are you doing?" a soft voice asked, and he leapt up from the cold ground, brushing at his clothes.

"Just looking at the night sky," he murmured.

Belle looked up, the torch she carried lighting her face. Despite the shadows flickering over, her skin seemed to transform her into something else. She was one of the most beautiful creatures he had ever seen.

Her brow creased, and he looked up with her into the trees to see nothing but leaves.

"Are you hiding from us?" she asked, the hurt evident in her voice.

"I've travelled on my own for some time. I'm not so good with people."

"Pa seems to think you are."

"He doesn't know me," Ed murmured. No one did.

"You helped us. The girls would like to thank you."

He shook his head. "They aren't really safe yet, are they? Those men could return, and they need to get home to safety. I need to go north."

"You said that," she said slowly, holding out his bag. "What is in the north?"

"My mother's friend."

"And why do you seek him out?"

"You ask a lot of questions," he snapped, dragging a shirt from the bag. He didn't want to admit his weaknesses to this woman. She had stood up for herself better than he ever could have done. And he didn't know what could be done to help him.

"Pa said you helped him without question. We would like to help you."

He shook his head and quickly redressed. He made his way past her and back towards the fire. "You need to go home with your father," he murmured as he moved between the trees, where the world came alive in brilliant firelight and the sound of women talking and laughing.

He made his way to the flames and someone pressed a cup into his hand. He gulped down the contents without hesitation, then continued across the clearing for a space to sleep. He glanced back only briefly to see Belle standing between the trees, watching him walk away. She looked very determined, and he sighed. Even out on the road, his world and his life were not his own.

No matter what he insisted, he knew that somehow Belle and Phillip would find a way to come along. Would she bring these other women with them? He sat down against a tree and rested his head back.

The activity in the clearing was starting to wind down. Sleep pulled at his body, but he was wary of the unknown world around them and sure he should be doing more to help protect these women. Belle seemed to stand too long in the tree line watching those before her. Or it might have been just him, and he tried not to look like he was watching her when she finally walked through the women towards her father. Phillip sat against the cart, the horse now free to move about the clearing, although it hadn't moved very far. As Belle sat beside him, he took her hand in his, and then she leaned her head on his shoulder.

He could tell they were talking, but he couldn't hear anything over the crackle of the flames and the whispered voices of the women as they settled down for the night. They both glanced at him at the same moment, and he hoped he looked like he was watching the flames rather than them.

He closed his eyes and sighed. It might be nice to travel with others, but he wasn't sure just how many that would be.

11

Ana tried not to chew on her lip as she sat by the door and watched the sun start to light the trees around the old building. She glanced back at Dray as he picked over the last of the meat. When he looked up, she looked back to the trees.

"We are not lost," he said again.

"But you don't quite know where we are."

"Not exactly," he admitted. "As long as we are out of the way of the mage, does it matter?"

She sighed and stood up, brushing at her dirty dress. It made little difference. She pulled the threadbare cloak of Ende's tighter around her shoulders. It held a comfortable warmth close to her skin. The man himself had been similarly difficult to explain. Whenever she asked him a question, he would just smile at her, a dark twinkle in his eye. Although he appeared to be just the same as any other man his age as he sat by the fire, his hands held up to the flames.

"The end of the world," Dray murmured behind her.

"Excuse me?" Ana looked from him to the mountain, wondering what he saw.

"The mountains. They are often called the end of the world and it appears that way today."

"But they aren't," she said.

"It might depend on the point of view," Ende said.

"But Sheer Rock is on one side and the rest of the Kingdom of Ilia on the other. It is a marker, and a difficult crossing, but it is not the end of the world."

"And that is your point of view," Ende said, a cackle in the back of his throat as he moved past her and out into the morning light.

"Do you still want to keep him?" Dray asked behind her. She smiled at the idea, although he wasn't far wrong. There were moments when the dragon scared her more than she would like to admit. He knew far more than he was telling her, and he knew more of her past than she thought anyone would care to know.

"I didn't have any of these gifts until the mage arrived," she blurted. The old man stopped and turned his dark eyes on her.

"Truly?" he murmured, and she nodded vigorously. "I don't believe you," he said, striding away into the trees.

She swung around to face Dray, who put his hands up in defence and stepped back. "I believe you," he said quickly.

"I had strange feelings before," she said with a sigh. "That is all. Since I met the mage, I have strange dreams, and it is as though I can see a man's thoughts."

"Can you see mine?" Dray asked, but she turned away and headed out into the trees after the old man. She didn't want to see Dray's thoughts. They might be different from what she hoped they were, and she wasn't quite sure what she hoped for. Or why he had saved her in the first place.

"I don't want to see anyone's," she snapped as she walked away.

"We need to go *up* the mountain," he called after her.

She stopped then and looked around. Where was Ende going then, if it wasn't the same way she travelled? She took a moment to look after where he had gone, but she couldn't see any sign of him now. She turned and looked up the mountain, pulled the cloak around her again and headed into the trees.

"Wait for me," Dray called after her. "We heard men before; they might be moving through the trees looking for us."

"I no longer care if I am found," she murmured. A large hand closed around her arm, pulling her to a stop. She blinked up at him then, wondering how he had closed the distance between them so quickly. Or was she slower than she thought?

"Don't say that," he said softly. "I care if we are found, for it will mean more than your death."

"I didn't ask you to help me," she said, pulling from his hold and moving up the mountainside. The ground was getting steeper and harder to travel, and she thought they might have to start going across rather than straight up. She looked up again at the looming peaks and wondered just how they were going to find their way over and whether they would ever be able to find who Dray was looking for on the other side.

He sighed behind her. As she took a step, her foot slipped on a rock and she grabbed at a narrow, bendy tree that was luckily within reach. Dray's bulk stopped her from slipping further down the mountain.

"I can't do this," she said. The exhaustion of the day before was washing over her again, and they had barely started.

"Let's go this way," Dray suggested, his hand at her back while he pointed with the other to the left. There was an indistinct trail, which in many ways made her nervous. If there was a trail, it meant others had come this way. But it was less steep and not as gravelly as the path she was trying to take.

She glanced back at him and nodded. With his hand at her back, he directed her across and they travelled on. She glanced back occasionally, but all she could see were trees. She couldn't tell where they had been, and there was no indication that there was a building below them at all. She imagined the ruins they had stayed in had once been something grand.

Despite the easier gradient, the climb was hard. They walked in silence, Ana leading the way and Dray at her back, ensuring she didn't fall back down the mountain. It was only after she was sure the air was getting colder around them that she stopped and turned to the man behind her. "Do you think he will come with us?"

"Ende?"

She nodded, chewing on her lip again.

"He seems fond of you. I'm sure he will find you again."

"I'm worried he might want to eat me," she admitted. Remembering the gleam in his eye when he spoke to her, she shivered.

Dray smiled broadly. "I'm sure you would be very tasty, but I won't let it happen."

"You may not be able to stop him," she sighed.

"I might not want to," he said, still grinning as he pushed past her and along the path.

She blew out a long breath and started after him. She wanted to say something clever in reply, but she didn't have the energy or the words at hand. She stopped again and, leaning on a tree, looked back over where they had come.

The trees had thinned out, and she could see well beyond their tops across the Sheer Rock islands. She let out a sigh of wonder.

Dray was beside her again, looking in the same direction.

"They look so small," she murmured, "and yet so beautiful."

"Green," he said. "I can't see the bridges."

"Do you think this is why the mountains are called the end of the world? The islands might look green, but you can't tell there is anyone living out there. And you would wonder why anyone would."

"You never thought to leave?"

She shook her head. "It was scary, but home."

"And your aunt?"

"Don't call her that," she growled. The smile slipped from his face as he nodded once. "I'm sorry, I didn't know that was who she was. She was never kind, never thoughtful, and she never once talked to me as though I were anything other than a servant carrying her tea."

"I'm sorry," he murmured.

"It is not your fault," she snapped again. "It is your fault that I am lost on a mountain. But then if it weren't for you, I would be lost on the rocks."

He nodded once again and then turned back along the path.

"Drayton," she called after him. He slowed a little to allow her to catch up, but he didn't turn around or answer her. "Why did you save me?" she asked, reaching out and grabbing at his sleeve.

"You've asked me that before," he said, pulling from her grip and continuing to climb. "I don't know exactly what possessed me," he muttered. "I must have lost my mind." He stopped then and turned to take her in, his smile warm and genuine. "I didn't want to see you smashed on the rocks when you were only a serving girl."

"Thank you," she murmured. He turned back, and they continued to climb in silence.

As the snow became closer and the air colder, Ana pulled the cloak tighter around her, thankful that it carried the warmth of the dragon. But despite the cloak, she didn't know how they would survive in the snow. She trudged along, looking only at the narrow path before her, and then she walked into Drayton's back.

"Sorry," she murmured, trying not to shiver. "What are you doing?" she asked when he didn't respond.

He looked into the distance, and she wondered why anyone would think to cross these mountains, let alone cut a road through them to the sheer cliffs she had called home. Who had her people been before Ilia had found them?

"There," he said, confidence in his voice.

"What?" she asked, trying to see what he was looking at.

He raised his hand, and she looked along his arm to a dark mark in the distance. "What is that?"

"A pass through the mountains, and a way that doesn't involve snow."

"Well I'm grateful for that," she murmured. "Are you sure?"

"Not at all," he said, striding off ahead of her. A giggle started in the back of her throat. "You laugh, but you follow," he said, turning back to give her a grin.

"Where else would I go but with you, my soldier in shining armour?"

He stopped then, turning a serious face to hers. The laughter died in her throat. His black armour reflected the light, and she was sure he would be formidable in battle. Although why she could picture that, she wasn't sure. She took a step back, losing her footing, and he reached out a strong hand to save her again.

"What did you see?" he asked, almost cautiously.

She shook her head. She didn't think she had seen anything. But then as she looked up, she was sure she saw the gash across his face again, and she squeezed her eyes closed.

"You go ahead," he said. "We can take this part at your pace, but we want to reach that pass before nightfall."

Ana looked towards the dark mark on the mountainside and wondered if she would ever reach it. She nodded once. Then, without looking at his face, she headed along the path ahead of him. She found it hard to breathe, and she wasn't sure if that was because they were so high in the mountains or because she kept seeing him not as he was. She shook her head. She hadn't seen anything like it until the mage.

Ana stopped on the path and swung back to look at Dray properly.

"We need to keep moving," he said.

She studied his face. A thick stubble covered his chin, but he was not scarred. "It was you," she said, taking a step closer to him.

"What was?"

"The reason I have seen what I have."

He stood taller, his face as serious as that first moment she had seen him in the lord's study. "I don't see how."

"Neither do I," she admitted, and he relaxed a little. "But when I first saw your face, you wore a large ugly scar across it. And then it was gone."

He put a hand to his cheek as though knowing where it was.

"It was after seeing your scar and then not seeing it that I was able to see what I could for the mage, and the dragon."

"What did you see of the dragon?"

"It wasn't really clear and it didn't make sense. None of this makes sense," she cried, and he leaned back from her. Then he rested his hand on her shoulder.

"Then we will find a way for it to make sense. Someone other than the mage must know what you have and why."

"Will your friend help?"

"I don't know," he said, pointing her back along the path. "If we don't make it down from this mountain soon, we may never know."

She nodded, hurrying along the path, trying not to trip over her tired legs. They continued in silence. It took them until it was almost dark to reach what had become an opening in the mountain, the closer they got to it. It looked more like a cave than a way through the mountain, but she didn't want to question him.

"Do we camp here, or try to make it through?"

He looked back over the darkening mountain. "Let's gather some materials for a fire and see how far we get."

12

Ed sat in the back of the cart and tried not to complain. His whole body ached from the jostling he had received. They continued to travel faster than he'd thought they could; he would have expected the horse to drop from exhaustion long ago. They had only taken a day and a half to break through the trees and reach the base of the mountains, which appeared even higher than they had when he had looked at them from a distance.

They had raced along a track through the Near Forest that was clearly not the main road, yet he was still surprised they hadn't met anyone along the way. At one stage he was almost sure the forest kept them hidden, as it had the women in the clearing. Although the men of the forest must have taken them there in the first place. He shook his head. There was far more to the Kingdom of Ilia than he had thought possible, and more to its people.

Belle would glance back from her seat beside her father every now and then to ensure he was still there. Yet she didn't smile, not once. He wondered if she really wanted to continue the journey with them. With him. For he was happy to continue on his own. Although it would have taken him a lot longer to reach the mountains on foot, and he was more worried than he would like to admit to Belle, or anyone else, that there might be more men amongst the trees than he could handle on his own.

He looked down over the sword across his lap. He was amazed

at what he had managed to achieve taking on those men, killing at least one of them. He let out a slow breath. His training was aimed at such things, and yet he never imagined he would have the chance to use the sword, nor that he would manage to use it to such effect.

Life had a way of showing you that things were not what you thought they were, or that people were not what you thought. Phillip remained as silent as his daughter on the journey north, and Ed wondered again why they would want to travel with him.

He had tried asking, but the only response from either of them was that he was owed. And he was sure Belle thought he couldn't survive on his own.

Earlier that day he had looked up to the mountain and thought he saw the sun shining from something near the top, but he didn't know what that could be. How far would he have to climb to find the man he searched for, and would he be able to find him in the great expanse of the mountain ahead?

Lost in his thoughts of the mountain, Ed heard thunder. As the wagon slowed for the first time that day, he leapt over the side and walked a short distance through the trees. The sound grew louder, and he froze. It wasn't thunder—it was the sound of horses. A lot of horses, and the jingle of metal gave the indication of soldiers. Too many soldiers. He jumped as a hand rested on his arm.

"Come away," Belle whispered in his ear.

"Who are they looking for?" he asked.

"They are the King's Men. It could be anyone they think may have conspired to betray the kingdom," she murmured. He turned to the harsh look on her face, which creased her beauty into something angry.

"The King's Men?" he asked.

She nodded and waved him back towards the cart, which Phillip had guided from the path and into the trees. Ed wasn't quite sure how he had managed to fit it between the trees, but he was happy enough to stand beside it, hidden from the world as the sound moved past them.

He wondered who rode with them. He couldn't see anyone, but he could hear more soldiers than he'd realised rode under the king's banner.

"The King's Men," he said slowly.

"He is just a boy," Phillip murmured. "It would be the regent who sent them out."

"But for what reason?" Ed asked.

"He doesn't need one," Phillip said. "And if he did, we would not likely understand it. The world of kings is far beyond us."

Ed looked over his shoulder as he nodded, wondering just how far away it was. As the cart made its way onto the narrow track again, he climbed onto the back, his legs hanging over the edge and the sword across his lap.

"Why would they be this far north?" Belle asked.

"I couldn't answer that if I met the king myself," Phillip answered.

"Pa, really. As if the likes of us would meet the king," she said.

"You might have if you had been tributed to the capital," Ed said, turning slightly to find her smiling at him.

"And now you wish you hadn't saved me," she said, but there was laughter in her voice.

"I was only hoping you might meet the king," he said, turning back to look over the road. A boy who couldn't even manage his own men. He tried not to sigh as they broke free of the trees. Shivering at the cooler breeze, he turned to look over the expanse of mountain before them. "You don't have to come," he said.

"We couldn't leave you now," Belle said. "Who knows what danger you might meet."

"My point exactly," he said. "Your father came all this way just to save you—no good in you both getting killed trying to get me up a mountain."

Phillip pulled the horse to a stop and turned to look at him seriously. "Do you even know where you are going?"

Ed took the chance to jump down from the cart. The mountains were overwhelming, and he had no idea where to start. "North," he murmured.

"The Lord's Seat is along the main road, I should think. I don't know who else you might meet along the way, but that might be the best place to start. You haven't told me the name of this friend of yours."

"I'm not sure I know it."

Belle looked at him as though he were simple. "And then how do you propose to find him?"

"I thought he might find me. My mother always said if I had no other option, I had to endeavour to go north and he would help me."

"He?" Belle asked. "Is that the only thing you have to go on?" She turned to her father and shook her head. "We can't leave him out here to die."

"It is my quest," he insisted. "My journey, not yours." She looked hurt at his sharp words. He didn't want to cause her any pain, but he wasn't a child. "You were happy enough to leave those girls alone in the forest. What if those men returned and they are still sent as tribute? No one would be able to do anything to get them back, and you know that."

Phillip moved the reins in his hand but didn't allow the horse to move. It waited patiently as the serious man studied the leather in his old hands. Ed wanted to tell them to go home, but instead he turned and started walking along the narrow track ahead of him, a worn path though the grassy field that followed the steepening incline of the mountain.

"The trees will protect them," Phillip called after him.

Ed thought the man might actually be right, but he didn't want to put them in any more danger. "You need to return to your farm." The path disappeared into the sparsely growing trees. Sucking in a breath, he headed forward.

"There is no farm left," Phillip cried. Ed only just caught his words, and he stopped.

"Pa?" Belle asked.

He shook his head, his hands tightening around the reins. "We got nothing but your quest now," he said, his old eyes twinkling as he looked up at Ed.

"It isn't much of a quest," Ed admitted. "I don't even know where we are going or who I'm looking for."

Belle let out a humph in frustration.

"I'm sure it will be as you hope," Phillip said, resting a hand on Belle's arm.

Ed turned and looked back up the mountain. "I don't think the cart can follow."

"Then we leave it," Phillip said, climbing down.

Ed shook his head as he headed back to help remove it from the horse. There was an old blanket and tarp that had been in the cart, and he threw them over the horse once they were free. They put the supplies over the horse as well, but Ed looked into the back of the cart and wondered what they might do with the axe.

Phillip sighed, and Ed shook his head. "It will have to be left behind," he said.

"I know, lad. But she is an old friend."

"Perhaps if we come back this way, it will still be waiting for you."

Phillip laughed.

"Will you be able to walk?" Ed asked Belle, then instantly regretted it as she scowled at him.

"I have walked halfway across the kingdom," she growled. "I think I can walk a bit further."

He nodded. Having done nearly the same himself, he wondered when he could truly stop. But even if he could find his mother's friend, he wasn't sure it would be enough for him to stop moving.

Ed led the little group along the path. He tried to keep a reasonable pace, but the track was slippery with small rocks and the climb was steeper than he'd realised. The path at least wound through the trees rather than directly up. He only hoped his mother's words were enough to find him.

Belle followed behind, her shawl pulled in tight against the cold. He was certain she must regret insisting that they help him. Phillip guided the horse along as the last of their party, and Ed glanced back every now and then to ensure he wasn't falling behind. He was about to suggest that Belle might rather ride the horse when he glanced back and she scowled at him again.

Ed sucked in a breath and trudged on. He had walked so far before he had met Phillip, and yet here he was walking again. He stopped and shivered as a strange feeling ran down his spine.

"What was that?" Belle asked in hushed whisper.

"I don't know," he said, turning back as she pulled her shawl tighter and looked up into the sparse treetops. "Did you see something?"

"I'm not sure," she murmured.

Phillip's eyes went wide, and then the horse whinnied and pulled at the reins, rearing and twisting as the blanket slipped from her back. "Now, now, girl," Phillip tried to soothe, but the horse must have had the same odd feeling as the rest of them, and it continued to pull against Phillip.

Ed turned and continued along the path, hoping that whatever it might be would leave them alone if they just kept going. He stopped again when a dark shadow passed above them. He looked up, his heart beating fast, but there was nothing there—although the horse won her tug of war with Phillip and was racing back down the mountain.

"I suppose you think she will wait by the cart?" Belle mocked.

"You are welcome to chase her down," Ed said, turning back and continuing along the path. He had no idea if they would find somewhere to shelter for the night, or if they would continue to walk the mountain until something large and unsettling ate them.

"You are not funny," Belle snapped, too close behind him. He was sure she was holding on to the back of his cloak.

"Are you cold?" he asked, glancing back at her.

She shook her head and let go. "And I'm not scared either."

As Ed turned back to the path, a dishevelled old man suddenly appeared before him. He stopped dead, Belle squealed and Phillip swore.

The man studied Ed with intense eyes, his long grey beard moving with the wind. "Are you lost?" he asked.

"I'm looking for someone," Ed said, unsure what to do with the man before him.

"You have found me," the old man said with a smile of perfectly white teeth. "Am I the one you are looking for?"

"He doesn't know," Belle quipped, but Ed noted that she was holding the back of his cloak again. "The man he seeks is a friend of his mother's, but he doesn't even know his name."

"An interesting quest. Your mother gave you no indication of who she had sent you to find?"

Ed shook his head once, unsure just what he should tell this man.

The man took a step closer and twisted his head a little to the side. His bright eyes sparkled in the dim light, and for a moment Ed thought they were black. "Your mother..." he said slowly. "You have her eyes," he added sadly.

Ed nodded once. "So I have been told."

"You don't remember her?" the old man asked, taking another step closer.

"I do," Ed said. "I was young when she died, I remember her very clearly, although people seem to think I was too young to remember anything. They tell me stories, but they aren't always right."

"She was a truly amazing woman."

"Yes," Ed said, holding out his hand to the man, "she was."

"I could never forget her. It was so hard to leave her." The old man pulled Ed close and closed a hand around his. Despite the man's dishevelled clothing and lack of a cloak, he was warm and comforting.

"How can we be sure that this is the man you are looking for?" Belle asked.

"It is," Ed said with a smile. "Mother said that I would know you, and I do."

"As I know you, Ed Forest," the man said carefully, and Ed wondered at just who he might be. "You have come a long way. And who are your companions?" he asked, moving past Ed on the narrow track. Despite his small size, Ed felt as though he had a very large presence.

"Phillip Poales," Phillip said, holding out a hand, "and my daughter, Belle."

"A perfect name for a perfect beauty," the man said, bowing politely. Ed chewed on his lip to stop the laughter that threatened to escape, and the old man gave him a cheeky sideways glance whilst he was bent over.

"And you are?" she asked in a not so friendly manner.

"Ende," he said, standing tall and grinning. As Ed noted his bright teeth again, he found himself running his tongue over his own.

"Do you live nearby?" Ed asked.

"That would depend on your point of view," Ende said, "but I have a friend who is closer. I expect he would be able to house you for a time, and keep you warm," he added, looking back at Belle. "He doesn't mind visitors." He headed off along the path ahead of them.

"Is this a good idea?" Belle hissed in Ed's ear.

"You don't have to come," he said. "We are only half a day's walk from the forest. The horse has probably found the cart, and your part in this is over. I have found my mother's friend."

"Are you sure?" she asked. "You don't know this man."

Ed smiled. He did. He wasn't sure why, but there was something about this man that he trusted. Not that he was always a good judge of people; he had found that out the hard way. But this man he knew to be different.

"Come on, it will be dark before you realise it," Ende called from the path ahead. Ed took Belle's hand and pulled her along after him. He was surprised that she didn't pull from his hold but instead gripped very tightly.

"Not long," Ende said sometime later, as the sky darkened above them and Ed struggled to see the path. Then Ende stopped and looked up into the trees further up the mountainside. "Run!" he cried, moving along the path quickly. Ed lost sight of him.

"What is it?" Belle asked, holding tighter.

"I don't know. Phillip?"

"Right behind you, boy. Don't wait for me. Go!"

Ed ran along the path, half pulling the woman behind him and struggling to listen for what might be out in the darkening forest. Before too long, he saw light ahead and then heard movement heading in the same direction from above them. Something dark glinted in the dim light, and he slowed.

"It is a cottage," Belle said, pushing past him on the path and pulling him behind, his hand still firm in hers.

It was in fact a small cottage, almost lost in the darkness between the trees. Ende stood out from the doorway with another man behind him in the light, looking into the trees. "I'll go for them," Ende was saying.

"Hello?" he heard another man call from the mountain, deep and concerned.

Ed froze, unsure if it was a good idea to be around so many people.

"Captain?" the man in the doorway called, pushing past Ende. But Ende remained fixed to the spot, an uncertainty emanating from him that unnerved Ed.

"Thank the gods," the captain sighed and then grunted. "I can't wake her."

Ed stepped forward as a broad soldier emerged from the trees. He wore the king's armour and carried what appeared to be a sleeping girl, her hair dark loose about her face. The worried look on the soldier's face told him that this girl was important. But what was a soldier doing all the way up in the mountain?

"Bring her in," the first man said, leading the way inside the cottage. Ende brushed her hair from her face as they passed him. He followed them into the cottage, and Ed followed after him.

The cottage was larger than it looked from outside. A large square space, it had a narrow bed set along one wall, where the soldier carefully placed the sleeping girl. There was a large fire, which burned brightly, lighting the space with strange shadows. A blanket lay on the floor against the far wall. Ed wondered if someone else stayed here at times, although it didn't look very comfortable. A large square table sat in the middle of the space with bench seats around three sides and a large chair by the fire. This was the house of a man who lived alone, but he didn't appear to mind company.

Ende leaned over the girl and then took her hand. "It is happening more?"

The soldier nodded. "I haven't been able to wake her today. We stopped at the pass, camped for the night and I don't think she slept at all until just before sunrise." He shook his head.

"All day?" Ende asked.

The large man looked nervous.

"What brings you here?" asked the man who had stood at the door.

"General, I am sorry," he said, bowing towards the man. "I had nowhere else to go."

"General?" Ed asked, and they both turned and looked him over.

"Another who needs our help," Ende muttered, concentrating on the woman who still slept.

"I was a general. I am now retired, or dead to the rest of the kingdom. Same difference," he said, putting his hand on the captain's shoulder.

"Captain Drayton Sterling," the soldier said to introduce himself, snapping to attention and then bowing to Belle, who Ed noticed was blushing wildly. "Or at least I was."

"Phillip Poales and my daughter Belle," Phillip said, nodding to the man. "Thank you, General, for taking us in."

"What happened?" the general asked the captain again. But as he opened his mouth to speak, the girl moaned.

"Come along, Ana," Ende said gently.

"Dray!" she called, sitting up. He was on the edge of the bed then, his arms wrapped around her tight. A sigh of disappointment escaped Belle's lips. "The king," the girl murmured.

"What about the king?" Ende asked.

"He needs our help," she said, leaning back from the soldier and looking directly at Ed. "The king needs our help."

Everyone in the room turned to Ed, and he sighed before Belle smacked his arm. "How are *we* going to help the king?" she asked.

13

The general took a slow step forward. Ende reached out an arm to stop him, but he brushed it aside. "He has his mother's eyes," he murmured.

"Aye, that he does," Ende said. Dray rose slowly to his feet before dropping to one knee, and the boy sighed again.

He really did just look like any other boy, skinny, undernourished. Dray stood slowly again as concern washed over him. Not just for the fact that the boy king stood before him, but at the state of him. "How long have you travelled, Your Majesty?"

"Too long," he murmured. "Call me Ed."

The young girl beside him stared in horror, then dropped to her knees, and the boy sighed again.

"Get up," he snapped.

"But you are the king," she stammered. She looked over her hands and then her face blazed bright red. "I slapped the king."

"You slapped a boy who had no idea of where he was, nor what he was doing," the older man behind her said. Her father, Dray remembered. He wanted to ask more, but he was distracted by Ana moving behind him.

"You should rest," he said.

"I have done nothing but rest," she responded, pushing her loose hair from her face and rubbing at her neck. Her eyes never left the boy, and he stared at her in return. Dray wanted to put himself between them, but this was the king—even if he hadn't had the chance to be one.

"How old are you?" Dray asked before shaking his head. What was he doing asking such questions of the king?

"My name is Ed Forest," he said. His hand rested on the sword at his belt, and Dray had to laugh out loud.

"You can't claim that, carrying such a weapon around."

"I thought it was too shiny," he whispered.

"It shouts of your father," Dray said, stepping forward. "May I?" He held out his hands. The king drew the sword from the sheath and handed it to him without hesitation.

He felt the weight of it, noted the craftsmanship and the brilliant blade, although there was some dried blood still on the metal. "I could show you how to care for it, Your Majesty," Dray said, handing it back. "Did you run into much trouble?"

"Only a little," the older man said. Dray looked towards the man as he nudged his daughter and she snapped her mouth closed.

Ed looked around at her, and she looked quickly at the ground, her face still reddened by her embarrassment of not knowing her king. But then, Dray doubted anyone would have known the boy.

"The boy king," Ana said, and he turned to her as she threw her legs out of the bed. Before he could step back across to her, Ende put a hand on her shoulder. She stayed where she was. "You aren't really a boy, are you?"

He blew out another long breath and sat on the end of the bench seat at the table. "I was a boy when my father died. The title stuck."

"And your uncle treats you as a boy," she continued.

"Ana, I don't think this is a conversation—" Dray was stopped as she put up her hand.

"I have dreamt of you," she said, and it was the boy's turn to grow red. "I met a mage." Her voice was shaky, and she looked at Dray. He nodded once. "He wanted me to go to your uncle. I saw what he did."

"It doesn't matter," the king said. "Whether it was willing or by trickery, the crown is no longer mine."

"You are still king."

"Some would disagree with you. I appreciate your concern, and I thank you for your hospitality. If I may stay the night, I shall be gone by sunrise."

Belle opened her mouth to say something, but closed it quickly. Ana, despite Ende's efforts, stood slowly.

"You came here searching for…" She glanced at Ende and then back to the king. "Help. And it is help that you have found."

"An old general, a soldier who has run from his post, a farmer and his daughter, one old man and a… maid?" The king paused, and Ana nodded. "What do you think you can do to help me?"

"You will die," Ana said simply.

The young man baulked and then stood from the bench. "Are you threatening me?" he asked, his voice carrying more strength than Dray had given him credit for. "Or did you dream it?"

She shrugged then, and with the way her lip quivered, Dray was sure she would cry.

"Well?" the young man demanded, taking a step closer. Dray put himself between them as Ende moved closer to the boy. The heat in the room had increased, and Dray eyed the old man in fear he might become the dragon and crush them all.

"I don't know, I just feel it."

"You don't know me. I don't even know how you could recognise me. Where are you from?"

"Sheer Rock," she whispered.

"Have you seen an image of me? A painting perhaps?"

"No, but I know you."

"Are you a *witch*?" The word was emphasised cruelly.

"Enough," Ende whispered, but the sound flowed through the room like hot steam. The boy sat back down, the farmer and his daughter took a step back and the general smiled.

"Old friend, he came in search of you," the general said.

"He needs Ana to survive. She is right, he will die if he does not trust in her.”

“Dray,” Ana whispered. He turned as she paled and slumped back across the bed.

“Do you want to explain how you came to be separated from your men, captain? Or did you abandon them?” the general asked, looking at him through suspicious eyes.

“I couldn’t let her die,” he said. “The mage wanted her for the regent.”

“The soldiers on the road,” the king said.

Dray nodded. “We were in Sheer Rock to discuss tribute with the lord. Or at least the mage was, and then there was Ana.” He wasn’t sure why he had become so attached so quickly. “She saw something in me,” he said, putting his hand to his cheek.

“The kiss of a pretty maid and you throw away your career?”

Dray sighed and looked up from the sleeping girl. “She saw something that wasn’t there. She had no idea of what the mage wanted with her, or why the lord would so willingly give her away. She would have been yet another innocent to die at the whim of those with power for no reason other than she would not give them what they wanted.”

“And what was that?” the king asked.

“I don’t know,” he said honestly. “He thought she had a gift, but she saw more than he wanted, and she was scared because she had never seen anything like it before.”

“The Walk,” Ende murmured.

“She is scared of heights,” Dray said.

“In Sheer Rock? The whole world is high,” the general said.

“No matter the reason, we ran. And then she found Ende.”

“I think I found you,” Ende said. “I’m very good at finding those who need to be found.” He looked at the boy at the table, the strain from travel etched on his young face.

“Let us eat and rest,” the general said, breaking the growing tension in the room. “We can face tomorrow when it arrives.”

❀

Ana woke to the room in near darkness and the sound of several men snoring. She sat up slowly as she adjusted to the light. Dray slept at the foot of the bed, sitting against the wall, his legs across the bed and his hand on his sword. She smiled at his sleeping form and was tempted to curl up against him. The farmer, Phillip, also slept against the wall, yet he sat on the floor, with the general nearby and Ende curled before the fire.

She stood slowly, being careful not to wake Dray. The boy sat at the table staring at the tabletop. Without a word, she stepped over the bench and sat beside him, her shoulder rubbing against his. He winced.

"What happened?" she asked, putting her hand on his shoulder.

He shrugged and then winced again, shaking his head.

She ran her hand slowly down his arm and slipped her hand into his.

His fingers curled reflexively, locking their hands together. They sat that way in silence for some time, and Ana noticed the glare of the blonde girl sitting on the floor on the opposite side of the table. Ana smiled at her, but Belle didn't move.

"What did you see?" he asked, his voice quiet.

"I saw you hand your crown to the mage, and he in turn handed it to your uncle before you faded from view. But I understand that it was not that simple. That you didn't physically hand him anything. Other than your trust."

He nodded slowly. "I didn't know what to do, and it hurt so much."

"You should have been able to trust them. What happened when you asked for it back?"

He turned quickly, as though surprised by the question. "I didn't," he stammered.

"Why not?" she asked sharply, then took a breath to steady herself and glanced about at the same time, ensuring she hadn't woken anyone.

"What about you, little maid? How did you end up out here with a soldier?"

"Only the day before I met him, I was a maid, being chastised for stepping on my lord's papers."

"Were you dancing on her desk?" he asked, a hint of laughter in his voice.

She looked up into his shining eyes and smiled. "No, they had blown to the floor. Not only did I step on them, I slipped and spilt her tea over the remaining pages. I thought she might push me from the Walk herself in that moment."

"What was on the papers?"

Ana opened her mouth and then closed it. Closing her eyes, she tried to remember the day exactly. She shook her head. "It isn't clear. Something about the tributes, perhaps."

"Is that why the mage was there?"

"I thought so, but then he seemed to only want me." She said it slowly, realising that all of this was because the lord had already known she had a gift. One she hadn't even known herself. "How?" she mused aloud.

As he looked at her expectantly, she shook her head.

"Tell me of the soldier then. He appears to know how to follow orders."

She nodded, glancing at the sleeping man on the end of her bed. "Dray has followed orders his whole life, until that moment. I'm still not sure, no matter what he tells me, as to why he did what he did."

"What did he do that means you trust him so completely?"

"He threw himself across the Walk, miles above the rocky shores and caught me."

"You would have fallen?" he asked. Worry edged the question and she wondered at it, given that he didn't know her at all.

"I had already," she said softly, focusing on his hand. She wondered at the trust he had in her that he had taken it so readily.

"The wind had pulled me over the edge, and he only just reached me."

He squeezed her hand without saying anything further. She shivered, still feeling the cold air pull at her, threatening to tear her hand from Dray's. But he was so strong and held her so firmly, pulling her up and onto the icy-cold stone that jutted out over the gaping nothing beneath.

"We are the same, you and I," the boy said softly.

She looked up then, unsure what he meant, although she doubted he had any such gifts like her own. Not that she quite knew what that meant for her just yet.

"Orphans," he added.

"How do you know I'm an orphan?" she asked gently, not hurt by his assumption.

"Your mother would have made a fuss, and your father would not have allowed you to end up on the Walk."

She sighed. They had both stood out there before, not that she had remembered until she had been out there alone. She nodded once for the young man beside her. "You have to get it back," she whispered.

He shook his head.

"You need to sleep," she said, looking into his dark eyes set in even darker halos. She slowly pulled her hand from his. He leaned forward over the table and rested his head on his arm. She ran her fingers through his hair, wondering at this scraggy boy who was her king. She looked into the shadows and locked eyes with the angry girl. The blue shined like a light in the darkness. "You too," she whispered, and her eyes slowly closed.

The room was silent around her but for the crackle of the fire. She climbed back into the bed and watched Dray sleep for a little while before she curled up, using his strong legs as a pillow. As she closed her eyes, he sighed and a heavy hand rested on her shoulder.

14

"Something isn't right with her," the blonde girl whispered too loudly to her father, but she looked at the king as she said it. He squinted at her as through trying to remember something.

Ana sat at the table and stared into the bowl of porridge. The captain, sitting beside her, gave her a gentle nudge, but she didn't look up. Ende tried not to sigh. He had heard her whispered conversation with the king the night before and knew the power she carried, even if she didn't understand it herself just yet.

He sat opposite her at the table and smiled. "You shall stay with me," he said.

She shook her head, and the soldier rested his hand on her arm as though claiming her for himself. Ende grinned, although he felt nothing like joy at the idea. They both felt the connection too, and that meant far more than he had expected for this girl.

"You must learn what you are."

"How do you know what she is?" Drayton asked.

He breathed out slowly, allowing the room to warm around them. "I see far more than you realise, young soldier."

Drayton stared him down.

"You know this. You knew this when I found you in the mountain."

She looked at Drayton, the plea clear on her pale face. Ende wondered just what this man would do for her, and whether he understood why he would go to such lengths.

"You could come with us," the king said.

"She will join you when she is ready," Ende said, wondering where this boy thought he was going. He had run all the way to the mountains, after all. Was he that keen to return just because Ana had suggested it?

"No," Ana said, looking at him. "They need me now."

"But you are not ready."

"I saw it," she whispered faintly.

"There is little you can do," he said firmly, and the hurt flashed across her face. "It will not always be as easy as making a tired man sleep."

She stared back into her bowl, her cheeks reddening.

"Have you seen what you will become?" Ende asked, suddenly fearing she might be stronger than he anticipated. Maybe he wasn't as clear on what she was as he had thought when he'd first found her.

She shook her head without looking up.

"What have you seen?" the king asked, moving around to stand at the end of the table. The farmer's daughter made a strange noise in her throat as he left her side, but he ignored it.

Ana remained unmoving, and Ende could feel the tension in the room. The boy reached out slowly and sat his hand on her shoulder. She sighed from the weight of it, as though he carried the whole kingdom in that one hand. She would be something greater than Ende had imagined, but would she help or destroy the boy and his kingdom?

She glanced up at Ende then, her eyes wary, and he sat up straighter. Was she strong enough to read him? She'd gotten glimpses of what he had allowed her to see when she had touched him, but he hadn't allowed her in since.

"Ende?" Drayton asked, and he turned to the concerned face of the soldier. "What do you think she is?"

"Who?" he asked as though he hadn't been part of the ongoing conversation.

"You said I was dangerous," Ana murmured.

He shook his head.

"I heard you," she said.

He opened his mouth and then closed it. Had she read him?

"I did too," the boy king muttered, and the soldier nodded. He looked at the two men on either side of the little mage, one holding her arm, the other with a hand on her shoulder. He blinked at the image. Something unnatural and dark filled his heart. For a moment he thought he saw them all before a throne, and then Ana sat down and the boy handed her the crown.

"He won't do that," Ana said in a tone that scared him. "I won't let him do that."

"You must come with me," Ende said, standing from the table. He was pushing at his frame. He needed to stretch his wings.

The soldier stood and drew his sword, as though Ende was a threat to her. The boy put his hand to his sword but did not draw it.

As the two released their hold on her, Ana blinked into the light and blew out a long breath.

"You need them," he said. Pulling her away from them would not allow him to learn what she could do, but her being with them could be dangerous for more than the three of them. "Perhaps you should remain together."

"You said I had to stay with you," she said, the strength he had felt in her now dissipated.

"Why should they stay together?" the farmer's daughter asked. "If she is a danger, she should stay away from the king."

Ana looked down, the frightened child returned. The king moved around to stand at her back, shielding her from the vehemence of the girl.

"You didn't even like me until you knew I was King," he murmured.

"I did too—you helped save my life," she snapped. Then she pushed her way out of the small cottage and into the early morning light beyond. Her father took a moment to look over the group before he followed her out.

Ende could hear him calling after her.

"Others will come looking for you," the general said. "What is the plan?"

The king shook his head while Drayton remained staring at Ende.

"We restore the king," Ana whispered. "It is the only way."

Ende took a deep breath and then blew it out slowly, the room warming around him although that wasn't his intent. "How do you propose to do that?"

She shook her head without looking up.

"But you are sure?" Drayton asked.

She patted his hand on her arm. "No—I mean yes. I'm sure it is what we should do, but I'm not sure how or whether it should be us that he relies on."

"Because Ende thinks that you will take my crown?" the boy asked.

"Because I'm just a maid, scared of heights and other than helping you sleep, I don't know what use I would be."

"You were stronger before, more confident," Dray said. He looked across the table at Ende, who tried not to nod in agreement, although he wasn't sure they spoke of the same time.

"I knew what I was then," Ana murmured, finally pushing the barely touched bowl before her to the centre of the table.

"You may need to remain together to find out," Ende said, looking from her to the boy standing at her back.

"But you think I'm dangerous," she repeated. "Am I?"

"I don't know," Ende said, dragging her bowl across and pulling the spoon out of the thick, congealed substance. He tried not to screw his face up and pushed the spoon back in. He could do with chasing something down. "I thought I knew what you were, but it is as though you need them to see."

"Can you see how we might get Ed on the throne, how we

might defeat his uncle?" she asked.

Ende huffed. "A little girl, an old soldier, a farmer and his daughter." He reached across the table and took her hands, then glanced at the soldier, who removed his hand from her arm. He took a deep breath and closed his eyes. He had an idea of her standing out on the Walk, the wind blowing around her, pulling at her dark hair, her brilliant green eyes pleading for someone to save her, and then she was gone. In an instant she was there and then she wasn't.

Ende ran forward and leapt over the edge of the narrow platform, dropping towards the water and sharp rocks that pointed up to meet him. His wings held back and his body stretched, but he couldn't see the falling girl.

He opened his wings and slowed his descent, spying her on the rocks below. But as he got closer, she was standing amongst them, the waves hitting the rocks around her surrounding her with sea spray that didn't even wet her hair. She smiled at him, her confidence strong and contagious, and he landed on the narrow rocks before her. He bowed his head.

Ende pulled his hands back from hers and looked into those same green eyes, although they didn't appear as confident now. She was the scared girl standing on the end of the stone walk, out over the nothingness beneath.

"I don't know what you are," he admitted. "I have moments when I see so much, and then you are something other than what you appear."

"Can I help him?"

He nodded slowly. "You are linked to these men, and they you. I cannot fathom at where that will take you. It appears that you must travel the path together."

"Come with us," she pleaded, reaching for his hold, but he pulled his hands out of her reach. A look of disappointment washed over her features. "We could use a dragon, and you could help teach me as we go."

"I am not what I was," he whispered. "Nor is the world a place for one like me. I am living in the mountains for good reason."

"What if I hurt them?" she whispered, looking down again. The soldier's arm wrapped around her shoulders and pulled her closer.

"There would be nothing I could do to stop you. And it may not be my destiny to try."

"But you saw us coming. You came to us," she insisted, and he was sure that something sparkled in her eye. He blinked several times, unsure of what it was or what it could mean.

"I may not have seen exactly what you were. You are not what I expected."

She wrung her hands together, the skin whitening as she pulled on it. "Why did he come looking for me?"

"The mage may have seen something like I did. He may have had a glimpse of what you are."

"Could he find me again?"

Ende nodded once.

"I won't let him take you," Drayton murmured.

"Is there a plan?" the general repeated, standing back from the group. "Are you to stay or are you to go? The four or five of you can't take on the kingdom, with a dragon or without. And that is if the farmer and his daughter will follow you."

"They will," Ana whispered.

"You should seek more help then," the general offered. "Go to the Lord of Edge Mountains. Tell him who you are and what you need, and he may stand with you."

"He may not," the king murmured. "My mother sent me to find Ende. She said he would be a friend and help, but…"

"It depends on the help you need," Ende said. "I have saved you from the cold. I have provided you with those you need to regain your crown. If that is what you truly wish for."

Ana looked up at him then, pulling from the soldier's hold to stand before her king. "Do you want to be King?"

"You have asked him that before," Ende said. "I think it might be you who wants him to be King, rather than he himself.”

“I know that he needs to be King,” Ana said, the confidence returning to her voice.

“I won't make a good one,” he whispered.

“Better than your uncle,” the general said.

He shook his head then and raced from the cottage.

Ana, still standing, watched him go and then turned an angry glare on Ende that made him sit back just a little. “You think he would hand the crown to me. But he knows he won't do that.”

Ende wondered what she thought she wanted.

“He is the king,” she asserted, leaning over the table, and Ende sat back a little further. This girl was going to become something very formidable. “He needs to get his crown back.”

“Are you certain?” Ende asked.

“She looks certain,” the general muttered, and Ende noted that he too had taken several steps back.

“You might be something very different on your own,” Ende thought aloud, and she looked confused for a moment. The hard lines of her face softened.

“Then I will stay,” she said.

Drayton opened his mouth to protest, but she shook her head and he snapped it shut. The large soldier sighed and nodded once.

15

Ana tried to walk as quietly as she could behind Dray as he made his way along the narrow path behind the cottage. She looked at her hands and wondered just what Ende had seen. She closed her eyes for a moment, stopping on the path, and the image returned to her of the three of them standing before the throne. It had been Ende's image, not her own, and yet she could feel the power of the three of them and the fear it had caused in him.

At the silence around her, she opened her eyes to see Dray turned towards her a little further along the track, his face worried. She tried to give him a smile and stepped up to follow him, but he remained unmoving.

"What is it?" he asked, concerned.

She looked over his bright, black armour rather than into his face. "Ende thinks I'm dangerous," she said. "I wonder if he is right."

"You wanted to stay with him and learn what you could. Do you think he won't want to teach you?"

"What if he is right?"

He smiled broadly, then turned his back and headed along the path again. "He is an old dragon, what could he know?"

"A lot," she whispered.

"I know you. I've known you longer than he has. There is nothing remotely dangerous about you."

"I'm not sure that sentiment is comforting," she said. "I destroyed your career in a heartbeat."

"I did that," he said, turning back to her again. "I threw it away, not you." He turned back and stomped on.

"You didn't have to save me," she said.

He stopped suddenly, and she nearly walked into the back of him. He surprised her by turning, wrapping his large arms around her and pulling her tight. "I did. Ende said there is a connection and I know, little sister," he said with a smirk in his voice, "that if I had let you fall, I would have had to have followed."

Ana wrapped her arms around him and squeezed. She was thankful he had done what he had, and she was very sure that no one else would have. Although her aunt had saved her once before, she knew she wouldn't have done it again.

"How did she know?" she asked his chest.

Drayton released his strong hold and held her out, his hands comfortably on her shoulders as he looked at her seriously.

"The lord. How did she know I was gifted? I didn't know I was gifted. Not until I met you."

"Don't blame this on me." His voice was light again, although she could see the seriousness of the situation in his eyes, the weathered lines of his face creased with concern.

"Dray," she said, trying to get him to talk to her as seriously as he saw the situation.

"I don't know," he said, letting her go. "She has known you your whole life. Maybe she saw something; maybe your mother or father told her something."

"Could they have been gifted?"

"That is a question for Ende."

"It could be why they died. The reason she pushed my father from the Walk."

"She may have simply wanted to remove any chance of you taking the lordship."

"Then she would have pushed me."

"She was trying to," he insisted, then sighed as she let her hands drop to her sides. "Whatever you thought you were or might be, whatever the lord and the old mage believed, it doesn't matter now. The only thing that matters is that they tried to push you from the Walk, I managed to save you and we are here now with a dragon and the king."

"I suppose you are right," she said. "And if that is the only thing that matters now, then I suppose I should spend my time with the dragon and see if he can tell me what I am."

"I think he wants to show you what you are, or for you to learn, or for him to learn from you?"

Ana smiled despite herself and nodded. Neither of them really knew why they were where they were, but she knew they needed to stay together. Whether the king decided to return without her was another matter again, but then he wasn't as keen to get his crown back as she thought he should be.

Dray turned again, and they headed along the path. He had promised to try and catch something for the group, and she had offered to help, thinking the time outside the cottage might be nice. Belle might have said something catty, she thought, but Dray had smiled warmly at her offer and now they were searching for she wasn't sure what.

"She doesn't like me," she murmured.

"She thinks the king likes you more."

"It isn't like that," she said to his back. He stopped and held up his hand.

Ana tried not to sigh. She had never had many friends, but she had always been able to talk to people. Belle just glared at her.

"Ed probably thinks she is very beautiful," she whispered, watching as Dray crept further from the path, his hand still held in the air. Other than his slow deliberate steps through the brush, he said nothing and made no noise.

Ana pulled at her hair. The loose flyaway strands were always difficult to catch, and she was sure her dark hair was not nearly as lovely as Belle's long golden curls. It wasn't that she wanted the king to think she was beautiful. Theirs was a different connection, and whether he thought of her as anything else, she knew she would always be at his side.

It might not be as comfortable as she imagined it, if the other woman was glaring at her from his other side.

A high scream came from the woods not too far away, and she pushed through the brush after Dray. The trees were dry and sharp, pulling at her dress and cloak. She was thankful that Ende had allowed her to keep it; it might be threadbare, but it was unbelievably warm. She yelped as another branch dragged across her arm, pulling at the already torn cloak. She clutched at her arm.

Between the trees she made out the glint of Dray's armour, and then he was walking towards her with a young deer over his shoulder. Blood ran down from the opening in its neck and dripped down his dark cloak.

"Why didn't you wait on the path?" he asked.

"I worried for you," she said, her eyes on the deer.

"And now I'm worried for you. Look at your arms."

She looked down and saw little dribbles of blood running from several deep scratches. Ende's cloak was in near tatters.

"Stay behind me," he said, striding past her and through the brush. He moved slowly and she stayed right at his back. Most of the branches were held back from her as he made his way through, and soon enough they were back on the path. He lifted the deer down and laid it at his feet, then turned to her with a worried look.

"Let me look," he said, pulling at the remains of the cloak. She sighed as she held her arms out. He sucked in a breath and nodded once. "Not too bad. You should make it back to the cottage alive."

"Funny," she murmured.

He heaved the animal back up over his shoulder and they headed back. She walked directly behind him, the deer's head bouncing back and forth across his back and occasionally looking at her with unseeing eyes. Ana didn't want to focus on it too much, but it gave her mind a break from the constant worry of what she would be learning with Ende and whether he really wanted to help her or keep her from the king.

It seemed too quiet when they returned to the cottage. Dray held his hand out to her again, and she stopped as he moved slowly into the cottage first. Within seconds, his face reappeared in the doorway and he waved her in.

The world was quiet as they entered. Ende looked up from his place by the fire. "No mountain lion?" he asked, and Ana smiled at him. He had come to her first, she reminded herself, and sat by her when she needed him to.

She moved over and sat at his feet before the flames. His soft smile turned to concern. "What have you done, little one?"

She shook her head. "I'm sorry about your cloak."

"Ana?" Ed asked, standing from the table. The blonde beside him sighed heavily, and her father shook his head subtly across the table.

"I have something for that," the general said, walking to the back of the cabin.

"It is only a scratch," she said. "I followed Dray into the brush when I should have stayed where he told me."

"It is more than one scratch," Ed said, squatting down before her and taking her arm gently in his hand. The cloak fell away as he lifted it, and even the girl showed some concern.

Ana looked down at her arm, which was crisscrossed with narrow red lines.

She pulled back from his hold. "Don't fuss," she murmured. "It is only a scratch."

"I could use a hand with the deer," Dray said from the doorway. Ana tried to stand, but the king held her tight.

"I'll help," Phillip said.

Ana looked back at the king, his hand around her wrist, and raised her eyebrows.

"What can you feel?" Ende asked, and Ana realised she had

forgotten he was there.

The king shook his head as though trying to clear his thoughts. "I don't know," he murmured.

"You can let me go," Ana said, but he shook his head.

Ende leaned forward from his seat and the air around Ana grew warmer. Ed gave the old man a strange look, as though seeing him for the first time. "What are you?" he asked.

"Lots of things. Different things to different people." Ende grinned and exposed his perfect teeth to the young king. "Your mother knew what I was," he said, and there was a hint of sadness in the words.

Ana opened and then closed her mouth. She wondered whether she would have learnt his true nature if she hadn't seen him in the mountains as she had. But then as she looked at him, she wondered if that was what he meant. She knew him as both a dragon and a man, and yet she didn't really know him at all.

"How did you know what I was, what I am?" she asked, and he turned his attention to her. "On the mountain when we first met."

"I knew you were coming."

"How?"

He shrugged and sat back. "I just knew."

"Did you always know I was coming?"

"That is a very good question," he said, leaning back in the chair with a smile.

"You did," she breathed, trying again to pull from Ed's hold. She glared at him for a moment, and he shook his head.

Then the general was standing over her with a small jar in his hand. Ed reached out to take it from him.

The smile became more thoughtful on Ende's lips as she sat back down and allowed him to apply the cream. He was overly gentle, dabbing at the cuts and taking his time, although Ana did flinch and suck in her breath on occasion as the cream stung.

"Just wipe it on," she snapped after too long. "This is like a slow torture."

He nodded once, his face still serious. When he wiped the cream along the next scratch, she cried out. Ende chuckled, and she turned her glare on him. Dray moved too quickly through the door, his bulk filling the room and his bloody hand already drawing his sword. He took in the scene and then slowly put the sword away. It squealed against the sheath as he pushed it home.

"She is not an easy patient," Ed said by way of explanation.

Dray chuckled.

"They are only scratches," she snapped, trying again to pull from the king's hold and wondering why he was able to hold her so tight. "This is not necessary."

"There are a lot of them," Ed said, dabbing at the next one. She sighed, and he studied her for a moment. "Would you rather I wipe?"

"No," she said quickly. "Dabbing is just fine."

Ende laughed again.

"There is the risk of infection," the general said, shooing Dray back outside. He gave her a grin before he disappeared. "I could help. There is a whole other arm to go. Assuming you weren't scratched anywhere else?"

She shook her head. "My dress protected some of me. I just wasn't dressed for the outdoors."

Ed grabbed her chin then. She sucked in a breath as he gently touched across her neck. He sighed and then dabbed along it with the ointment from the jar.

"I think you have the best nursemaid," the general said. "I might check on this deer and see if we can eat meat this evening."

"Nursemaid?" Ed said, clearly hurt by the words although he continued to dab across her arm. Then he gently sat her arm down and reached for the other. Despite her complaints, Ana held her arm out to him, placing her hand in his and allowing him to pull the cloak back from her skin. One scratch appeared somewhat deeper than the others, and the blood had run down her arm in a narrow rivulet.

"Let me help," a quiet voice said by the door. They both looked up at Belle. She held a small bowl in her hands, and she appeared somewhat nervous as she came over to Ana's side. "I was going to take it out for the men to wash," she said. "But I think you need it first." She sat it on the floor beside Ana, dipped the cloth into the water and then gently wiped over the cut.

Ana tried not to grimace, for the girl was very gentle. Then Belle did the same by another cut further around Ana's arm, which she hadn't noticed was bleeding as much as the other. "Thank you," she said.

The girl nodded without a word and headed outside with the dish.

Ed went back to dabbing at her arm. "You know that I'm staying with you until you are ready to travel."

"I'm not unable to travel," she said, watching his hands work rather than his face. "I need to spend some time with Ende."

He nodded. "You need to learn just what you are and what you can do. And I'm not going anywhere until I know you can come too."

"You could be meeting with the Lord of Edge Mountains," Ana said.

"Or you could come with us."

She glanced up at Ende, who nodded slowly, his eyes closed and his feet too close to the fire. "I must learn what you are," he murmured.

"Should we look over your wound?" she asked Ed, and he gave her a nervous look.

"It is just a scratch," he murmured.

She leaned forward and reached for his shoulder, but he moved quickly from her reach.

She looked at Ende for help and found him watching the young king with concern. Ed sighed, stood and removed his jerkin, wincing as he did so. A yellow red mark stained his shoulder. Ana was on her feet, pulling at his shirt. "Oh Ed."

"You best sit down, boy, and let her help," Ende said slowly, leaning forward in his chair.

Ed looked down at his shoulder and then sat on the long bench seat at the table. Ana poured water from the kettle on the table into a bowl. She glanced towards the door, wondering if Belle would be better suited for this.

She took a deep breath and then carefully untied the makeshift bandage as his shirt fell away from his shoulder. He was far more than a boy, she realised as she looked over his sinewy chest. As the wound was exposed, she wanted to cry out in pain. The flesh was angry red around a deep gash that appeared greenish within.

"This is more than a scratch," she breathed.

"I'm sure others have faced much worse," he muttered, looking away.

Taking a clean part of the makeshift bandage, Ana carefully wiped warm water over the opening. He actually cried out, and although Ana heard the door open, she didn't look away from what she was doing. She wet the cloth again and, with a hand on his other shoulder, she gently wiped around the wound. Ed shook beneath her hold. She put the cloth down and indicated the cream. He remained unmoving.

"Ed," she said softly.

He looked up then and opened his hand with the small jar. She released her hold on him and took it. As she dipped her finger into the cool cream, he grabbed at her skirt, his grip strong.

"Do you want me to dab or wipe?" she asked.

He took a deep breath and closed his eyes. "Just do it," he murmured.

The sting had already gone from many of her own cuts, and she carefully dabbed around the wound, putting as much cream as she could over the angry red flesh. Then she took a deep breath. Hoping she didn't hurt him any more than he was already hurt, she deliberately wiped her finger through the wound.

He grunted in pain, his fist full of her skirt.

"Let me help," Belle said softly. Ana looked up to see her holding out some fresh bandages.

"Thank you." Ana tried to step back, but the king was not letting go. "Ed," she said, "it is all done now."

He took another deep breath and nodded, then rolled his shoulder and smiled, releasing his hold on her. "It feels much better already."

They both looked at Belle, who stood frozen to the spot. As Ed cleared his throat, Ana stepped back. When the girl didn't move, Ana held out her hand to indicate she could step in where Ana had been, but the girl shook her head.

"How did you…?" Dray asked, stepping further into the room. Ana wondered why she hadn't noticed him come in sooner.

"It was troubling him," she said, unsure why the room felt as stuffy and uncertain as it did. "He helped me; I wanted to help him."

"You have done that," Ed said. "It has troubled me for days."

Belle made a strange noise and took a step back.

"You were to dress it," Ana said, frustrated that no one else appeared to be moving. "Give it to me," she said, allowing the frustration to bubble over.

"There is no need," Ende said behind her. She couldn't read the expression on his face. He nodded back towards Ed, and she looked at the smooth calm skin beneath the cream. She reached forward and ran her thumb over the space where the wound had been moments before.

"Better," Ed said. "I can hardly feel any pain at all."

Ana looked at the fresh pink skin and then over her own arms, but the scratches were still there. She took a step back, and Ende stopped her travelling any further with a hand to her back.

"I just wanted to help," she whispered.

"You did," Ende said.

Ana felt sick. The room became hazy around her, and as Ed stood quickly from the bench, her world slipped into darkness.

❊

The following morning as the rest of the small cabin's inhabitants slept, Ana wandered out into the fresh morning air. She pulled the remains of Ende's cloak around her. Just off the path was a large boulder, which she climbed up to look out over the world beyond the mountains. There were sparse trees around them, but nothing like the sea of green in the distance. She wondered if that was the Forest of Near that Ed had travelled through.

"What are you doing?" he asked, appearing as though she had conjured him with a thought.

"Breathing, thinking." Ana looked from the expanse before her back to the young man standing on the path. He chewed on his lip as though embarrassed he had interrupted her, and as he stood there looking at her, she wondered what he wanted.

"I thought you didn't like heights," he blurted.

"It isn't really that high up here," she said, turning back to the view. "It isn't looking down as such. It is all so different from what I know. How is your shoulder?"

He rolled it and put a hand to it, nodding slowly. Ana turned back to the view. His warm hand on hers surprised her as it traced over her arm. Then the king sat gingerly on the large flat rock beside her.

"It might be magic cream, but it hasn't worked on me like it did on you."

"I don't think it was the cream," he said. Although she kept her focus on the world before her, Ana knew he was staring at her. "Why did you follow Dray?" he asked eventually.

"He saved me." She turned to him, but he looked at her arm, not her face. "I heard a cry from the trees," she said, turning back.

"What else can you do?"

Ana looked over her hands. A few days ago, she couldn't even carry a cup without making a mess. "What if Ende is right?"

"He doesn't seem sure enough of what you are to be right. One moment he thinks you can help, the next he fears you are dangerous."

"He hasn't said that I can help," Ana said, looking at Ed and wondering what he hoped she was.

"He hasn't said you can't. There is a connection between us; he said that much." Ed sounded hopeful, although for what she didn't know.

"What if I hurt you?" she asked, afraid that the old dragon might be right and that he knew far more of her than she did herself.

"What if you can help keep me safe?" he asked, real wonder in his voice.

"You want to return," she breathed.

"I don't know." He stood slowly and brushed himself down.

"Why don't you want to be king?" Ana asked, standing with him.

He sighed. "It was what my parents wished for, prepared for."

She looked at him closely then, studying every movement of his young face and wondering for the first time if she could see beyond it. "Is that why you ran away?"

He hung his head. "I don't know how to be king," he mumbled. "What if I disappoint them?"

"Who?" she asked.

"Everyone."

She nodded once, and his cheeks flared. She could see the disappointment in his eyes, as though he thought she was agreeing with the sentiment.

"I think you should go to the lord. The general is right; you need more help."

"Really?" he asked, clearly surprised she would suggest it. "What if he is aligned to my uncle?"

"It is a risk," she said. "So was searching for a man you didn't know, far from home, and only knowing he was north."

"Will he help me?"

"I think he will try, but I don't think he wants to return to the capital."

"Will you come with me?"

She smiled. "Not yet."

He opened and closed his mouth.

"Do you even know what you want to do? What you want to be?" she asked.

He jumped down from the boulder and ran his fingers through his hair as he looked up at her.

"I have things to learn, as do you. I will stay with Ende while you go to the lord." She closed her eyes and took a breath. "Take Dray and Belle. He will watch over you, and she will be what you need her to be."

"He won't leave you," Ed blurted.

"Dray will do what he knows is right. Ende and I will be fine."

"He is a strange old man, living up here alone. I wonder how he became friends with my mother."

"I'm sure he will tell you one day. But right now, you need to be a king."

"Do you want my crown?" he asked. She was surprised not only by the question but the nervousness in his voice.

"Only for you," she said.

"What are you two plotting?" Dray asked, appearing on the path.

"You need to go with Ed to the Lord of Edge Mountains."

The large man harrumphed, but when he didn't say anything, Ed turned and looked him over. "You will come?"

"If Ana thinks that is what we need to do."

"Why does everyone do as she says?" Belle asked, her tone harsh. "Your breakfast is ready."

"She thinks you should come too," Ed said, taking Ana's hand to help hold her steady as she climbed back down from the rock. Belle looked confused for a moment. "Ana thinks you can help."

Belle stood a little straighter and nodded once before disappearing back towards the cottage.

"Ende was wondering where you got to," Dray said, pulling Ana into an embrace as she stepped forward.

16

Ed stood by the large, ornate door, looking like he had travelled for weeks—which he had, but he wasn't sure he wanted this man to see him as such. Belle looked equally worn. But she held her head high as they waited to be announced. The captain standing behind them looked shiny and perfect, as he always did. Although when Ed glanced at him, he sensed a hint of nervousness that was likely due to having left Ana behind.

The general had helped them find their way, but had refused to get involved. Although Ed was fairly sure the man was involved already, taking him in would give his uncle enough reason to punish the man if this all went badly. And it had been the general's idea to visit the local lord for assistance.

The door creaked open, and Ed was surprised by the sheer size of the room before him.

"His Majesty, Edwin of Ilia and his companion, Miss Belle of the Grasslands."

Edwin stepped forward, almost pulling Belle along with him, whose confidence had disappeared the moment the door had opened. She glanced at him, and he gave a little nod. Dray followed, then stayed by the door as they continued forward.

Other than the man who had announced them, there was only one other man in the room. He sat in a large chair at the far end of the room. The wall behind him was covered in a detailed painting of the mountains, the same view of them Ed had seen from before the forest. There was a large table to the side of the room covered in papers and what appeared to be maps. The man remained seated, and Ed tried not to look as nervous as he felt as he stepped forward and bowed his head.

"I appreciate you meeting with us, Lord Welcott."

The man stood slowly then as Ed took in the size of him. He wasn't a tall man, but he was very robust. He almost teetered forward and Ed thought he might fall over. He walked around them once and then smiled, but it wasn't a smile that made Ed feel comfortable.

"It is not every day that a man gets the chance to meet the boy king."

Ed allowed his annoyance to show on his face.

"Your Majesty," the lord said slowly, but the sincerity wasn't there. Ed knew he had made a mistake in coming, for the little man would be no help. "You are welcome to stay. I might take the liberty to dress your guest and yourself. Times have not been as we would wish them to be, it seems."

Ed nodded once.

"I am sure there is much you wish to share with me. But," he said, raising a chubby hand, "it will not be now. Show them to their rooms." He directed the last part to the man by the door, who bowed. "We have other guests this evening. They have been staying with me for some days, and they are excellent company. Tomorrow we shall discuss your business, or the day after that."

Ed nodded to show his understanding. Belle opened her mouth to say something, but he squeezed her arm through his in the hope it would keep her quiet. "I thank you, Lord."

The man waved them off towards the door with a little flutter of his sausage fingers. Dray looked stern as Ed turned towards it and bowed as he passed through. This man wasn't going to take him seriously, he thought. He might have well as stayed in his room where his uncle wanted him.

The man leading the way walked quickly through long hallways and up many flights of stairs, and for a moment Ed was sure he was back in the castle in the capital, wandering alone. Then their guide stopped, bowed and indicated a door. "Madam," he said softly.

Belle looked at the door and then back to Ed, squeezing his arm. Before he could offer any assistance, the door opened and a young lady bowed her head.

"I have prepared a bath," she said.

Belle released her hold and disappeared quicker than he'd hoped through the doorway. He cleared his throat, and the manservant indicated the opposite side of the hallway and another large door. As it opened, Ed found a room that would have rivalled his father's rooms at the palace. By the fire stood a large tub filled with water, and fresh clothes were laid out over the giant-sized bed.

"A manservant will be with you shortly," their guide said.

"I can manage, thank you."

The man nodded and left the room, closing the door behind him.

"It appears you have found a home," Drayton said behind him. Ed swung around to find he looked less confident than he sounded. "It might have been worth accepting the servant, give an idea that you would behave as any other king."

"How many do you know?" Ed asked, then regretted the words as the soldier's serious face turned to his. "I am well out of my depth here," Ed admitted. "This is far grander than I have experienced. No matter what I do, I know this lord won't take me seriously."

"Maybe not initially, but I'm sure you could convince him in your way. Ana is determined this is the right course of action."

Ed sighed at the thought of her. "It was more her idea than mine that I should get the crown back."

"Then make it yours," the soldier snapped, then shook his head. "Take a bath, make yourself look like a king." He looked over the clothing laid out on the bed and ran a tentative hand over the jacket as Ed stepped up beside him.

"I wonder, if the lord can afford such luxuries for his guests, that he might be able to pay a little more tribute," Ed said.

"Now you are thinking like a king," Dray said. "Now bathe so we can eat."

The same servant led the way after they were washed and changed, and Ed was sure his stomach would give him away. They had been left far too long on their own with a little wine and some dried fruit. He only hoped the meal they were provided was of the same quality as the clothing.

Belle spent her time during the walk running her hand over the fine material of her dress. Her hair was pulled up and away from her face, making it appear softer. When she smiled at him, Ed almost lost the ability to walk. She had been pretty when he'd first seen her, and she was breathtaking now that the bruise had faded completely.

Dray coughed behind him, and Ed dragged his eyes from her neck back to the way they were walking. They arrived at another large door. This castle would have rivalled the royal residence with the expansive rooms and long corridors. And being built into the side of the mountains, it had numerous levels.

Ed paused, expecting to be announced, but when the little man opened the door they were amongst an overwhelming number of people. This was not what he needed. The more who knew who he was and what he was doing, the more likely his uncle would find out where he was—or someone would kill him before he could do as he needed.

He glanced back at Dray, but his eyes were locked on something across the large room. He looked back and there, by the round Lord Welcott, were Ana and Ende. They both looked like very different people. He marched straight towards them.

As he reached Ana, he opened his mouth to ask why she was there. But she turned and smiled, and his panic subsided. She looked even more spectacular than Belle, and the firm hold Belle had on his arm told him she knew it. Ana curtsied low while Ende bowed in a similar fashion, although his clothes weren't quite as grand as Ed would have expected.

"You know the boy king?" Lord Welcott asked.

"I imagine everyone would know their own king," Ana said, her voice not quite her own. The lord nodded and smiled.

"Have you tasted from our fine display of meats, Your Majesty?" he asked, holding out his arm with a flourish towards the side of the room. Tables longer than Ed's room in the capital were covered with food. From whole roasted pigs and pheasants to bowls of fruits and cakes.

He hoped he wasn't salivating as much as he thought he was.

"Let me guide you to the delicacies," Ana whispered, taking his arm, and he wondered for a moment what had happened to Belle. "You will be very surprised by the wonders the lord has to offer," she continued.

When they reached the table, he looked at her as though he didn't know her. She pointed to several meats and animals he had not seen in some time. "This root vegetable is a rarity of the mountains," she was saying. Ed looked around to find Belle on the arm of the lord as he strode towards the table.

"The Lady Anaise has such fine taste," the lord said. "You should follow her guidance." He pulled the leg off a pheasant and started to eat it directly.

A metal plate was thrust into his hands, and Ana was heaping food upon it.

"It is a wonder you have not met the lady in the capital."

"I didn't get out much," Ed said.

Ana smiled serenely. "You must meet my uncle," she said, steering him and his full plate away from the wonder before him.

"Your uncle?"

She pointed across the room to Ende, still standing by the wall, looking like he might explode.

"He doesn't look very comfortable," he said.

"He doesn't travel like he once did," she said, guiding him firmly towards the man by the wall. "I believe he was friends with your mother."

As they approached, Ende bowed his head again. "Your Majesty."

Ed was tempted to look around and see who else was close. As he went to open his mouth, Ana gave a very subtle shake of her head.

"You are a handsome boy," Ende said, and Ed had to take a second look at the old man. "So like your mother, although I am sure there is much of your father in your face as well." He leaned forward as though to study him. "You don't know us," he whispered faintly, and Ed leaned closer to ensure he heard him.

"No, I don't," he admitted, his eyes flitting over Ana. Her dark hair was loose about her shoulders, her dress well fitted and showing her in a very different light. He glanced around the room and realised it wasn't as full as he had thought. He was not used to being around people. All the other ladies looked like Belle, their hair up, golden and cream-coloured gowns. Ana wore a darker green. "How did you get here?"

"Before you?" she asked, glancing at Ende. "We are faster than we look."

"I thought you were training or learning?"

She shrugged without saying anything and looked across the room behind him. He glanced back and noticed that Dray was still watching her rather than Ed. He only hoped no one else noticed.

"Your companion appears to be settling in," Ana said, and although her words made him look for Belle in the crowd, they were not unkind.

Belle stood beside the lord, a plate in one hand and a glass in the other. Ed wondered why they weren't all seated around the lavish tables. It was almost as though the lord was showing off his wonders without really sharing them. Despite being unable to eat,

Belle was smiling, her eyes sparkling as she spoke to the people around them.

As he watched her, he noted the room around them had grown quiet and Belle's words echoed through the space. "He rescued me," she said. Ed was sure that if she didn't have her hands full, she would have put one to her breast. She was in her element, and Ana had been right to suggest she come.

Ed wondered if the fiery woman he had met in the forest would show herself, but then she appeared to know how to act. He was tempted to make a joke about her making it to the capital, but this was not the audience. Nor did it fit with the story they had rehearsed.

"Let me hold that for you," he offered kindly, taking the glass from her hand. She nodded and reached for the narrow fork that lay across the edge of her plate.

"You have not finished your story," the lord said as she raised the first bite to her lips. Ed realised then that he had not touched the food himself.

The other ladies who had been listening turned to him with wide eyes. "Did you really kill a man to protect her?" one asked breathlessly.

He nodded, but he couldn't smile at the idea.

"So brave to ride after her. You must care very much," a second young woman swooned.

Belle, he noticed, was looking at her plate.

As he opened his mouth to explain the situation better, he was interrupted by a third young woman with bright red hair, her dress almost glowing in the light of the room. "Did those men kidnap her to get to you? You must have been so frightened," she said to Belle, "all alone like that and so far from the capital."

Ed looked at her and then back to the young woman. "Their aim was to cheat the kingdom," he said. "In taking Belle, they wished to lure me out."

"Did they bring you all the way to the mountains?" the first girl asked.

"The Forest of Near," Belle said quickly.

"Then how did you make your way here?"

"I'm afraid we lost our horses in the struggle. I feared they would follow us back to the capital, and so we came north," Ed said, very tempted to take a sip from the glass in his hand. He wasn't very good at conversations, and he was worse at lying. He was sure this man could see right through him.

"You are safe now," Lord Welcott assured Belle. "And of course, you may stay here as long as you wish. Such a beautiful girl," he murmured, reaching up to her face. But before he could reach her, she stepped forward and pushed her plate into Ed's hands.

"Your Majesty," she said. "Forgive me, telling stories of how you saved me and yet I keep you from eating."

"I had a plate," he murmured, looking back at Ana by the wall. "Here, take your drink and let me introduce you to the Lady Anaise and her uncle." He held out his elbow, and she slipped her arm through his with a warm smile before they hurried across the room.

She downed the glass, sat it on a small table against the wall, and took her plate from Ed.

"You know, if I ever become king," he murmured, "I am seriously going to review the tributes."

"None of it is real," Ana said. When he turned from the food to her, she was smiling sweetly.

"Why are you here?" Belle asked.

"My uncle thinks I can learn," she said, and when Belle looked up from her plate, Ana's eyes flicked to the group behind her.

They were chatting and laughing, but the short man amongst his beauties was watching everything they did.

"Eat," Ana said. Then she lifted the fork and pushed more meat into her mouth.

17

Sitting by the small fire in her oversized room, Ana was surprised by the quiet knock at the door. She was more surprised when she opened it to find Dray rather than Ed standing in the dim light of the hallway. She moved back as he pushed into the room and closed the door behind him. He glanced around as though checking for danger, and then his focus settled on her. Ana was sure she looked as tired as she felt.

She still wore the same dress she had worn down to dinner despite the lord's offer of servants, which she had declined, not wanting the strange people around her again. Not that she worried about what they would do; she had been in such a position herself not so long ago. She shivered at the idea and then looked back to Dray as he scanned the room again.

"Where is Ende?" he asked.

She pointed up to the ceiling, and his eyes travelled up then back to her.

"He finds castles somewhat confining," she said with a small shrug.

Dray looked at her seriously, but then a smile broke across his face and she felt as though she could breathe again.

"Now tell me," he said, settling into a chair by the fire and indicating the one she had been sitting in not so long ago, "how and why you managed to make it here before us?"

"It took *you* longer than I expected."

"It was a long walk," he admitted, "and although the girl is strong, she wasn't as fast as I would have liked. We had talked about it, but I didn't think it was a good idea for the king to say who he was."

"That was a surprise," Ana admitted, sitting on the other chair by the fire. "I know he needs the help and I encouraged him to come, but somehow I thought he would try to keep his identity a secret."

"You haven't answered my question."

"It appears that Ende's idea of training is to drop me into the middle of a lord's castle and see what I can do."

"You appear to be doing just fine." He gave her a little smile, but there was something else in his voice she couldn't quite place.

"I nearly slipped into my serving ways—pouring wine, asking if there is anything the lord would need."

"You looked like you have lived in such a world your whole life," Dray said, raising almost sad eyes from the fire to her.

"I have," she said, disappointed at his words. "Only not quite like this."

"And the how?"

"Ende thought it best we were already here when you arrived."

He leaned forward. "He carried you here?"

She grinned and nodded.

"How did you convince him to do that?"

"Do you really think I could ask Ende to do anything he didn't want to do? This was all his idea. He is sure we need to work together, but I'm not sure if he knows as much as he says or more than he has told me."

"Do you think he still finds you dangerous? You certainly looked more than you are when you were gliding around the room."

"Really?" she asked. "More than I am?"

"Maybe closer to what you actually are," he murmured as he

stood from the chair. "I should let you rest."

Ana stood to meet him. "What do you think I am?"

"What do you mean?"

"Why do you think Ende wants to work with me? Why do you think I should travel with the king? Or am I still a maid you just couldn't let fall?"

"You are something very special," Dray said, resting his hands on her shoulders. "I don't know exactly what that is. If Ende thinks the three of us must remain together, then there is something to that. And I don't know what skills he thinks you have. You have had some dreams of us together. What else can you do?"

She shook her head. She wasn't sure what abilities she had, if any. So far, she had only managed to convince a young man who didn't want to be King that he might want to be. She looked over her fingers as she remembered the angry wound disappearing from his skin.

Perhaps the danger was that she had convinced Ed to seek assistance here and thus reveal himself to these people. She wasn't even sure he knew he was being coerced. For a moment she wondered if she could do something similar with the plump little lord.

"Do you need help?" Dray asked, looking at her dress and dragging her thoughts back to the room.

She shook her head. "The girl will help."

"What girl?" he asked, and then there was a quiet knock at the door.

As it squeaked open, he bowed.

"Thank you so much for assuring me that all is well in the capital," Ana said sweetly, with a confidence she hadn't had moments before. "I believe that our king could not be in better hands. Thank you, Captain."

Dray bowed again and left quickly.

"My lady, you should be sleeping," the young woman said as she unlaced Ana, helping her from the dress.

"Should I?" she asked, wondering just what she should be doing.

"I didn't mean to direct you," the girl stammered, stepping back, and Ana turned to her worried face. Her hands clenched before her.

Ana sighed. "I wasn't chastising; I was wondering if you were right."

"You have slept very little since you have arrived. You look…" The girl chewed her lip, and Ana wondered at her candour. She would have worn a slap if she had even suggested anything close to a conversation such as this with the Lord of Sheer Rock or any visitors to the Seat.

"Tired," Ana continued for her.

The girl nodded seriously. "And you should eat more."

"I feel far from home," Ana admitted, "and it is all very different."

"You don't like the food?" It was asked with genuine surprise.

It wasn't that she didn't like it, just that she didn't trust it. There was something about it that gave her the feeling it was something other than what it was. And although there was always so much of it, they weren't encouraged to eat as well as they should. The lord was quick to distract people. "I think I would like something a little simpler," Ana said instead. "Too much rich food."

"I could bring you crumpets and honey for breakfast."

"That sounds perfect," Ana said, allowing the girl to help her into the bed.

"Shall I extinguish the candle for you?"

Ana shook her head and snuggled further down between the stiff sheets. Despite the appearance of luxury, she didn't feel it in the room. The girl bowed her head and then blew out the other candles about the room as she left, leaving just a single one beside the bed. As soon as the girl closed the door behind her, Ana blew out a long breath. She was tired, very tired, but her dreams twisted what she thought she knew.

When she did sleep, she often woke to find Ende sitting on the edge of her bed, holding her hand. She wondered just what he could see of her as he would nod slowly. But he never discussed it. She didn't know if she was seeing something significant or just dreaming because of all the thinking she was doing during the day.

During their time at the castle, her days were too long and dull. They talked, but there was little action, little movement, and then they would be moving around whatever group was in the main room of an evening. She could play the part—she had seen others do it often enough—but so far, she had learnt little.

Ana stopped fighting her heavy lids and allowed her body to relax into the firm mattress beneath her. Dray flashed before her and disappeared. She looked around for him, worried she had lost him, and then she was standing on the Walk again.

"Help me," she pleaded. "Save me!" She felt like she was screaming. The same three stood before her again. The lord not quite looking at her, the mage with his narrowed eyes and Dray giving her a small nod as he stepped forward. In the background, the large dragon blinked slowly.

She woke with a start, her heart pounding as it had when she had stood on the Walk. The candlelight flickered across the ceiling and the soft fabric that covered the bed. Ende stood at the end of the bed, and Ana was sure the wind still moved through her hair.

"Did I call you?" she asked.

He nodded, remaining where he was. "As you did just now."

"I was dreaming and you were there. But it was when I was on the Walk, and you weren't there then. Not as a dragon. I would have noticed." She tried to sound light, but she was beginning to doubt everything around her.

"You called me then," he said. "As you called Drayton. The connection was there."

"You mean he almost fell too because I asked him to save me?" A shiver crossed her skin at the idea. She was thankful, yet the thought that he might have died because of her made it hard to breathe.

"You didn't ask him, Ana. You demanded it."

She sat up, still holding the covers tight in her hands. "I demanded it?"

"Are you going to repeat everything I tell you?"

She nodded, giving him a smile, although it didn't hold any joy. "Who am I?"

"Anaise," he said slowly. "You are possibly the only way to save the king."

"You said I was dangerous."

"Oh, you are," he said, sitting on the end of the bed. Warmth radiated from him, and in some ways she felt more comfortable. "But it might be what he needs."

"The gifts that the mage came looking for…"

"I think he saw far more in you than he wanted to. He may have seen just what you are; he may have seen what I did."

"Do you think I could hurt them?"

"Yes, I do. But that may not be your intention." She made to ask another question, but he held up his hand. "You may intend it. Yet I think there is something deep within your connection to these men that will ensure you protect them."

"I hope you are right."

"As do I," he said with a broad grin.

"I'm not able to do very much anyway. A little persuasion, dreams of a world I don't know." She couldn't put what she had done to Ed's wound into words.

"A little persuasion. You demanded that a strong knight of the kingdom risk his life to save you, and he did. You are stronger than you know, and you will become more so. Whether you have other skills, we will need to find out."

"How are you going to test that?"

"For now, I'm not. I will give you several days while we remain here to find out what you have."

"Ende," she almost whined, "how am I to find out?"

He shrugged and stood up. "For now, you can sleep." He walked over and leaned towards the low fire, and it crackled to life. He nodded and sat before it. Ana lay back down, her grip still tight on the covers as she stared at the patterns the firelight made over the ceiling. Ende had wanted to see what she could do; now he wanted her to find out for herself. She shivered again at the idea that she might be dangerous, and the image of the king handing her the crown became clear in her mind.

18

The mage looked up at the sparkling tower of the castle as it poked above the other buildings of the capital. It called to him, and yet he wished he could be anywhere else in Ilia. He had managed to convince the regent to allow him to go after the girl. But she had not been what he had hoped when he found her.

The regent would expect the girl to be with him, to have come all the way from her cliff top home to the capital ready to serve him along with the others he had found. The mage would have to explain why they would be better served by her death, and then how he had lost her. He groaned at the idea, and the soldier nearest him turned a curious glance his way.

He tried not to think about it any further as he rode into the castle, the horses'' hooves echoing from the high white walls that surrounded them. Maybe they had taken too many men, he thought as he climbed down. Although after losing the girl, perhaps he had not taken enough.

He walked away from the beast, knowing someone else would take care of it. Not that it was foremost in his mind. He would take whichever of the king's horses he pleased, should he have to leave the comfort of the castle again. Despite his concerns, he made his way directly to the regent.

The man stood with his back to the door, looking out over the kingdom from the tallest room. It wasn't very large, but it was comfortable and boasted a large balcony, which was where he now stood.

The mage took a breath, trying to ignore the hot anger radiating from him.

"Where is she?" He spoke quietly, yet his voice carried an anger that made the mage step back.

"She was not what I hoped she would be."

The regent turned slowly and looked him over. He felt as though he was being sized up for a coffin, unless the regent was strong enough to throw him from the balcony himself.

"I know that we had great hopes for the child. But I saw what she would become with the king at her side, and it would not help us."

"We could have broken her," he said.

Reluctantly, the mage shook his head. "Perhaps. Once I could see her for myself, I found she is much stronger than I anticipated."

"She *is*. You did not dispose of her?"

"I tried," the mage said through gritted teeth, wondering just what she had done to the soldier.

The regent took a step forward. "Where is she now?" he asked carefully.

"I don't know."

"How long ago did you lose her?" he asked, eyes narrowed.

"Weeks," he murmured.

"And in that time, you have not seen enough to determine where she is, or with whom?"

"Now that I am returned, I have access to my own devices."

"Find her," he said, his voice like a knife.

The mage bowed low before the regent. "Yes, sire." When he straightened, the regent was back on the balcony looking over his kingdom. The mage waited half a second before he backed out of the room. Only once on the other side of the thick wooden door did he take the opportunity to breathe. "Bring the box," he snapped at the soldier waiting by the door. Lifting his cloak, he rushed down the narrow steps towards his own rooms.

Partway across the courtyard, another soldier joined him with a small wooden box in his arms. It had travelled amongst the other items collected from the Lord of Sheer Rock, what she had been willing to give. The mage reminded himself that he was to talk to the regent about how little she had provided. She should have offered greater tribute. But then, her greatest tribute had run out the door. The girl may have appeared to have been dragged, but he knew she'd gone willingly.

He pushed through the small door and down the narrow steps before reaching another door. As he fished around in his cloak for the key, he turned around and glared at the man standing further up the steps. "That is the box I wanted?"

"Yes, sir, it is."

"Then bring it in," he snapped as the door opened and the sweet smells of home greeted him. The man followed him in and dropped the box on the table. With barely a sign that he was leaving a man of the mage's station, he disappeared through the door, which shut loudly behind him.

The mage pushed items from the table to the floor, papers, quills, and what might have been remains of his last meal. He had been keen to leave. He had been standing at this very spot when he had felt her like a rush. She was strong, young and he had thought very malleable. Only he had been very wrong. When the mage had placed his hands on her, her true power had overwhelmed him. Although he had allowed her to see something of his past, he had seen far more of her than she realised she showed.

He had been so sure he could use her. That she would work with them to defeat the king the boy would someday become. She was just what the regent needed. And the lord, even though she was family, had been eager to give her up. But then she would have allowed the kingdom to take far less in the future from the cliff top islands of the north.

Now the girl was running loose with the soldier, and he had no idea where. It was almost as though she had hidden herself from him, and yet he wasn't sure how that could happen. She was strong, but she didn't understand what she was or what she would become. He could only hope they had fallen from the islands or were lost in the mountains. He finally inserted the small key into the box and turned it one-quarter to the left, then three-quarters directly to the right. A small click announced it open, and he lifted the lid to reveal a green cloak folded neatly.

He pulled it out, careful not to shake too much of the girl from it, and took a moment to lean towards it and breath in the scent of her. Her magic emanated from it. He shivered with the excitement. Beneath the cloak were several smaller items taken from her house and things she had used or touched within the castle.

One being a broken cup from the day before he had arrived. The lord had kept it, saying it was unusual for her to be so clumsy. She thought the girl had contrived the accident to see the papers on her desk.

He held the cloak in one hand and picked up the teacup with the other. He couldn't feel the same power he held in the other hand. In fact, he couldn't feel anything. He looked over the other items, then returned his focus to the cloak. He carried it through the maze of shelves, piles of books and equipment he had invented or procured over his many years as mage, towards a small fire burning at the far end of the room. Before the fire sat a large copper bowl, reflecting the firelight.

He dropped the cape into it and then closed his eyes, moving his hand slowly over it. A small smouldering flame hummed into existence. It burned blue and then green. And as it grew, it became a brilliant red. She was much more powerful than he had imagined. He watched as the flames grew taller and then, leaning over, breathed in the smoke that swirled up in crimson curls from the material.

Snow peaks and rocky slopes came to mind. And then the short, plump Lord of Edge Mountains. Lord Welcott would send word if she was there, if he understood just what he had. The mage doubted greatly that he understood very much of anything.

A face appeared from behind a pile of books, and he tried not to sigh. There was so much potential in the world, yet it appeared difficult for it to be realised.

"What do you see?" he asked her.

"Nothing, Master," she said, glancing around the room.

He pointed to a wall covered in shelves of glass bottles. "What do you hear?" he asked another girl who sat on the floor before it. She shook her head. The world quietened around him, and he wondered at the power these women had shown him. He could only hope they would be of use when he needed them most.

19

Salima pressed her back into the wall and held her breath. No one would notice her—they never did—but her father made her promise to stay out of sight and out of the way. She usually did, and if he had listened to her sooner, he might not be in the state he was now.

She peered around the stonework at the throne room and bit into her bottom lip. The regent sat on the throne, looking at the man before him and nodding occasionally. He looked bored, as though the man he listened to was not worth his time. She wondered if the man kneeling before the throne could sense the same as he pleaded for understanding and support.

Ed would have listened to her, she thought, looking at her father standing back from the throne and waiting his turn. Although it was because of Ed that they were here. Or at least that her father was seeking audience with the regent. She was supposed to be waiting in their lodgings like a good girl.

The regent waved his hand and the man before him stopped, bowed low and wandered away. Salima wondered why they bothered. She had watched the proceedings briefly before, and no one seemed to get what they asked for. Although she didn't linger for long. Her father would scold her if he knew, and watching was rarely as interesting as she hoped.

But this day was different. Her father was waved forward, and she was surprised at how openly angry he appeared to be. The regent sat taller. Before he could ask what he needed from the crown, her father took a deep breath and Salima pulled back around the corner.

"I understand that the king must rest to ensure he has fully recovered from his illness, but I fear he has been inactive too long."

There was a long silence, and Salima risked a glance around the corner. The regent nodded slowly and then sat forward. "What are you talking about?" he asked, as though her father was talking about the price of cabbages at the market.

Her father took another deep breath and squared his shoulders. "The king has not been to his training sessions for some months. I understood him to be ill and taking the time to recover, but this is too long."

A hushed whisper moved around the people still standing in the room.

"He is usually a healthy boy," the regent said, standing and stepping forward, and her father took the smallest of steps backwards. "I should check on his health myself. His other tutors have not raised such concerns. Is he simply skipping your classes?"

"He is not the swordsman his father was," her father admitted, "but he works towards the skill."

Salima almost huffed at the words. Not that she should be watching the king at his training, but she did, and she thought he showed more skill than the average soldier in the practice halls.

"I thank you for your concerns," the regent said, bowing his head just a little as he waved her father towards the door. As he disappeared, the regent waved a manservant hovering by the throne forward. "Send for the cleric."

Salima scanned the room as she rushed away from the throne and towards the back stairs. She might be able to appear as a maid or servant and walk close enough unnoticed to see what they had to say.

By the time Salima had found an apron and made it up to the king's small living space, all was quiet. There was no guard on the door, but it was closed. She had been in it often enough, both with Ed and since he had disappeared. She stood by the door for a moment, until she was confident there was no one there. Then she opened it and slipped into the room, pushing the door closed quietly behind her. She looked down at her pale-coloured dress and apron and, with a groan, dropped to the floor and rolled under the bed.

There was a sharp knock on the door, and Salima was relieved she hadn't taken any longer to reach the room. When it opened, she could see two sets of boots, neither of which belonged to her father. One pair stayed by the door while the other moved further into the room.

"It is smaller than I remember," the regent said. "Where could he be?" he asked. He sounded more angry than worried.

Salima's father had said the very same thing only the day before, when she had finally convinced him to visit the king's room. Her father allowed Ed more freedoms than his other students, but then he was the king.

"Are there any horses missing?" the regent asked.

"No, sire," a voice belonging to the other boots answered. Salima thought a guard must be waiting. She only hoped he wouldn't wait around when the regent left.

"Where could he be?" the regent asked again.

"He doesn't visit much of the castle. Occasionally he goes up to the turrets to look out over the city. Otherwise he is busy with his tutors."

"The man who came to me, what is his name?"

"Master Forest, the sword master."

"Sword master? When might the king need to use a sword?"

"Once he is grown and in battle, perhaps," the man added,

unsure himself. "It is standard training for a king, I believe."

"I suppose it is," the regent said with a sigh, turning slowly. "Has he always stayed here?"

"I believe so. I thought he had been moved away from the royal chambers after his father…" The man's words petered to a stop.

"It was a difficult and sad time," the regent said, although Salima doubted he meant it. "We may have all lost focus on what was close to us."

"Sire," the man said.

The regent lived in the royal chambers, and Salima wondered if he had moved Ed here deliberately or had left the task to someone else. She liked Ed, and although he seemed content with the life he had, she felt something was lacking for him.

Another pair of boots approached quickly and, when they appeared, were nearly hidden by the long tunic of a cleric. "I understood the king was ill?" The statement was more of a question, and Salima could picture him looking about the room for a king who wasn't there.

"Find him," the regent growled, and the soldier ran off. "And *you* will tell me when he was last seen, by whom and where. You are to tell no one he is missing."

"Yes, Your Highness," the cleric murmured.

"I rarely hear that term," he said.

"You were always Prince Thom before you were the king's regent."

"Yes," he said, "but it feels as though it was a lifetime ago."

"I will see what I can discover."

Salima waited while the two men moved out of the room and pulled the door closed behind them. She counted to twenty, slowly, before she rolled out and stood beside the bed. She was covered in dust and was sure her copper hair looked just as bad as her skirt.

When she glanced around, the whole room appeared to be thick with dust. She wondered at the maids for not doing better at cleaning and ensuring the room was fit for a king. She was disappointed on his behalf that they didn't look after him as they should. She sat carefully on the edge of the bed. So many times she had sat back against that wall, usually with a book, while he scribbled away at his desk.

Her father had said she wasn't to disturb him, but Ed was always welcoming and happy to see her. They had both lost a mother, Salima's before she could even know her. And as much as she loved her father, Ed was her friend.

He had played ill before, but never disappeared, and part of her was angry he hadn't taken her with him. She only hoped he had gone out on his adventure willingly and hadn't been taken. She stood up and dusted again at her skirt. Why had it taken so long for someone to realise he was gone, and why had no one listened to her sooner? He could be in real danger.

20

Ana stood in the window of her room and looked out over the foggy mountains. There was often mist and fog around her islands, yet the sky always cleared. It never really seemed to clear here. They had spent too long at the Lord's Seat, and she had learnt nothing. Other than the king himself could actually act like a king when needed. But she wasn't sure if or why that would bother her; it was what she wanted for him.

Dray was a different matter. He was the soldier he had always been, and she wondered where he might be now if she hadn't called him as she had. If she hadn't made him throw himself across the Walk to catch her. She was thankful that he had, yet in some ways she wished he had just watched her fall.

She pushed the window open, the sharp breeze stinging her skin and whipping her hair around. She leaned forward just a little to see the world drop away beneath her. It didn't worry her, not like it had, perhaps because it wasn't nearly as far to the ground below as from the bridges between the islands. She closed her eyes, her hand holding tight to the latch as she leaned a little further. The wind wrapped around her, unsure if it wanted to pull her out or push her back.

She could remember the feeling of the air around her as she walked along the bridge railing when she was a child. Her father would laugh and claim he was worried, but she knew she wouldn't fall. But when she had stood beside him on the Walk, it had all changed.

"What are you doing?" Dray's concerned voice called from behind her. She opened her eyes, her feet on the narrow sill, her hand holding the edge of the window as she leaned out over the void beneath.

She should be scared. She should be terrified. She wasn't.

His strong arms closed around her and pulled her back into the room. He waited a moment too long before he let her go, and she wondered if he was scared for her. Or should he be scared of her?

"What were you doing?"

"I wanted to feel the air," she murmured, unsure now why she had opened the window in the first place. "I'm feeling a bit trapped here."

"You are free to explore; Lord Welcott has said so."

"Explore? The castle? What could I learn? I have spent my life in a castle such as this, only I was sweeping and polishing and whatever else I was told."

He took a step back. His hands were raised in defence, but he wore a soft smile.

"I'm sorry, Dray," she said, sinking to the floor. "I'm not really sure what I am."

"Don't you mean who?"

"Perhaps."

"I could escort you," he said, holding out a hand. "And I don't think those dresses are designed to be on the floor."

She ran her fingers through her hair, trying to tame some of the tangle, then took his offered hand and allowed him to pull her to her feet. She brushed at the fine, cream-coloured embroidered dress and sighed. "I'm not really used to this," she murmured.

"We shall get you used to it. If you are to stay with the king, you shall wear fine dresses all the time."

She maintained her tight hold on his hand, and he looked down at her as he took it in the other hand before moving it to his elbow.

"I'm not sure you have noticed, but the other fine ladies don't hold on to soldiers."

"You are *my* soldier, so it is a little different."

He smiled warmly and shook his head. "I am supposed to be the king's."

"Well I am friends with him too, and I'm sure he would lend you whenever I asked."

He bowed his head, and they headed out into the wide corridor.

"Where can we go?" she asked.

"Anywhere and everywhere," he said.

She nodded and allowed him to lead her through the maze of corridors. She was still amazed at how grand the castle was, much more so than the one she had worked in, grown in. Perhaps it was the golden-coloured stone, whereas she had grown up amidst grey. It had always felt as though it was pressing in on her. As she moved along the hallways, it appeared that the world was opening up before her.

She pulled from his reach a little to run her fingers over the golden stonework and was surprised it was cold. They continued on, and then she stopped and pointed to a strange doorway. "What lies beyond that?"

"What?"

"That door," she said, looking at him.

He shook his head and then looked back at her. "There is no door."

She allowed her hand to slip from his arm. She glanced around. Like so much of the castle they had walked through, there was no one around. Then she took his hand, and with the other reached out and touched the warm wood.

"How do you do that?" he asked, stepping forward to put his hand beside hers on the door.

"I don't know," she said. "Are you sure we can go anywhere? Because if no one else can see this, we might not be welcome."

"I wonder what he might be hiding."

She put her hand to the latch. With Dray's hand tight in hers, she pushed it open.

The door opened into darkness. An open, empty darkness that dropped away from them. Dray's hand closed tighter around hers. The same odd calm that washed over her as she stood on the windowsill covered her body, and she stepped forward. Despite the black around them, she could feel something solid beneath her feet. Dray tugged on her hand. When she looked at the light from the doorway, it was still strange that it didn't illuminate anything within the space.

Then Dray's hand was gone, and she was alone in the dark. She thought he stood in the doorway for a moment, but then she was surrounded by nothing. She knew she should be scared, worried for what might or might not be there, but despite her concern, she wasn't panicked.

She continued, hoping she was walking straight, and a small candle flickered ahead of her and she was home. Standing in the small cottage she had lived in with her father, and then on her own. How had she survived all that time?

It could have been her sitting at the table with her father. She hadn't remembered him looking so young. She wanted to race forward and throw her arms around him, but she hesitated. When she opened her mouth, no words formed.

"You must protect her," the woman said. Her voice sounded familiar, yet it wasn't her own. She had Ana's brilliant green eyes and raven black hair, and as Ana took a step closer, she saw that she held a sleeping baby in her arms.

"I will protect you both," her father said, reaching forward and taking her hand. "You know I will."

"I know you will try, but she won't allow it."

"You have the skill to stop her."

The woman shook her head, looking down at the child. "The risks are too great."

"I can't do it without you," he said, his voice breaking.

"You can," she reassured him, putting the child into his arms and running the back of her fingers down over his cheek. Ana noticed then that he was crying. "Allow her to do what she thinks she must, and if I can, I will find you again." He shook his head. "Don't let her know what Ana is."

"She will guess."

"Keep her safe," she said, leaning in and kissing him. She barely ran a finger over the sleeping child's cheek, and then she was gone.

He cried as he pulled the child close, and he looked up at Ana with such loss that she thought her heart would break. Then the candle went out.

"Anaise?" a voice asked in the dark. The same voice she had heard talking to her father.

"Who is there?" Ana called out, trying to sound more confident than she felt. She didn't mind the dark; she worried more for who might be hidden in it.

"How did you find this place?"

"Who are you?" Ana asked more firmly.

There was no reply, and Ana huffed out a sigh of frustration.

"Dray!" she cried.

There was nothing. No echo, no hint at the size of the space around her. "Ende?" she tried. But she knew she was alone. And she was certain that whatever lay ahead of her, it was for her to deal with alone.

The idea of the woman returned. She was unknown, yet Ana knew her. Had it been as simple as her mother had left them? The lord had hinted that something had happened to her, and that she might have been responsible. If her mother could simply leave, why hadn't she taken Ana with her?

She longed for a flame, but she wasn't sure what that might show. Another world, another time? And would it answer her questions or give her more? She thought she could smell smoke, bitter and eye watering, yet she continued towards it.

As she grew closer, or as the smell grew stronger, she thought she could see a small flame in the distance. She hurried towards it. A large bowl reflecting the firelight acted as a beacon. But as she neared it, she stopped. The world around her smelt of herbs and something she couldn't quite place. She could see nothing but the bowl, not even the fire that was reflected on its surface. She stepped forward slowly and leaned over it. Her green cloak, the one she had missed so desperately in the mountains, was neatly folded in the bottom, burning—and yet it wasn't. The acrid smoke curled upwards in long red tendrils, and she waved her hand through the smoke. Images appeared as the smoke was moved around, of the Lord's Seat and the mountains it was nestled in.

Someone was looking for her. Someone with magic was trying to find where she was. "The mage," she whispered, and he came into view, working around a messy, cluttered space. Papers and debris covered the surfaces, the walls lined with shelves filled with bottles, pots and more papers. Boxes and books were scattered amongst them, and the smell of the room took her breath away.

She put her hand to her mouth as she watched him work, pulling bottles and strange dried things from the shelves before crumbling them into another bowl. Some bottles he opened and then closed again, others he sprinkled the contents. One small bottle, filled with a blue liquid so bright it might have been a summer sky captured, he dropped in completely.

Ana stepped back. Was all of this to find her, or was it a way to kill her? He had come so far, and then all he had wanted was her death. Did he see the same danger Ende had seen? Would this man want to save the king from her, or did they want to use her to end him?

She wanted desperately to lean over the bowl to learn what he did, but she didn't understand any of it. It wouldn't matter if he were able to describe to her in detail what magic he worked. She would never be anything but a maid.

The old man scowled into the bowl. Then he blew a long slow

breath over the top of it. Another cloud of smoke moved over the bowl, very different from the one with her coat not burning away. It twirled up and around and became a woman, the shape of her clear. Ana was mesmerised at how beautiful she was. Even though there was little detail other than her shape, there was a sense of her in the pale smoke. Her long hair blew out behind her as though she stood in the wind, but her dress didn't move, and then Ana realised she was holding something in her hand. She couldn't move, desperate to know what it was. The woman raised her hand and Ana recognised the crown, which she carefully placed on her own head.

A smile broke the image, a scary smile that made Ana shiver.

"No!" she cried out, and the world was dark again.

21

"Have you seen Ana?" Ed asked, finding Drayton looking very lost in the middle of a hallway.

He nodded and then shook his head.

"Recently?" Ed tried. He had been thinking about her all morning, and although Belle was good company, he was frustrated by their time in the castle. He wanted to talk with Ana about how she thought they might be able to get the lord on their side. And what exactly they were asking him for, as the little man didn't appear to have much to offer other than words.

"She was just here," he said, turning back to the wall.

"Which way did she go?"

He pointed at the wall. Ed looked from it to him and back again. "What happened?" he asked, trying to maintain his calm in the face of the nervous soldier.

"She needed to get out, walk a bit," the man said, not looking at him.

"And?" he prompted.

"She was standing in the window."

"What window?" Ed asked louder than he should have. The soldier looked at him with a scowl, as though he was dim.

"The one in her room. She was standing up on the ledge, the window wide open, and I thought she would fall."

Ed felt his stomach drop.

"I thought she needed the distraction, and we were walking and exploring and then…" He pointed to the wall.

Ed waited. When Drayton said nothing further, he stepped forward and put his hand to the warm stone. There was something very special about the girl, but for her to just disappear was odd in itself. Although there was something very odd about this castle.

"She disappeared through the wall?"

"There was a door," he said absently.

"A door?" Ed asked slowly.

"Yes," the soldier snapped. "A door, plain and old, and I couldn't see it until she put her hand to it."

"You didn't follow her?"

"I thought I did, but it was dark and I heard a woman call for her, and then I was standing here and she was gone and so was the door." His words became more urgent, and he took Ed by the shoulders. "It was the same with the house in the mountain. I couldn't see it until she touched it. Ende understands. We need Ende."

"I haven't seen him. But he has been with Ana a lot. Perhaps he is in her room."

"Can we find this place again?" The captain looked around. Ed thought he was trying to take in other features of the hallway so he could find the wall again, but there was nothing to focus on. He studied the man before him, usually so strong and determined, now looking like a lost boy.

He still wore the dark armour of the King's Men, although given what he had done, he would never be one of them again. Unless Ed managed to regain his crown, and then he could raise this man to be whatever he wanted to be. His hand rested on his sword, and he was sure Dray carried more weapons on his person than Ed could identify.

"Do you have a dagger?"

He looked at Ed for a moment and then drew a narrow blade from somewhere.

"Mark the wall," Ed directed.

Drayton scratched the fine blade across the stonework, once and then again to make a small cross. From a distance it might almost look like a natural mark in the stone. Closer it would be clear. As Ed nodded and the soldier appeared to relax a little, the mark disappeared.

"Try here," he suggested, pointing to another part of the wall further from where Dray had indicated the door was.

He scratched the same perfect cross, and they watched as it too disappeared.

Across the hallway was a large window, the small panes of glass held together with lines of lead. "May I?" he asked, holding out his hand for the dagger. He strode across and, without hesitation, broke a single pane near the bottom corner of the window with the handle of the dagger. A light breeze blew gently through the gap. They stood and stared at it for some time, but it didn't miraculously mend itself.

He handed the dagger back to Dray and headed off towards their rooms. Ende would know what to do.

Unfortunately, Ende was nowhere to be found. At least not in Ana's room. Ed grumbled something under his breath as he pulled Ana's door shut, and they walked back into the hallway to find Belle standing in his doorway watching them.

"It is unusual that she would say anything to upset you," she said, her voice quiet and a little glint of something he hadn't seen before on her face.

"She isn't there," he said.

"Oh?"

"She's missing," Dray answered for him as Ed tried to work out just what Belle might be thinking. "Have you seen Ende?"

She shook her head. "Could she be exploring?"

"That was the plan," Dray said. "It might be what she is doing." His voice and face seemed more hopeful as he turned to Ed.

"But in a way we can't find her, in a place we can't reach?"

"It might be worth looking in the main rooms. Perhaps she is talking with the lord," Belle offered.

They walked in silence towards the main rooms, where there was no sign of any other visitor to the castle. Ed thought it strange that there appeared to be so many of an evening and yet they were unable to find anyone of a day. The room where they met to eat was empty of everything as he pushed open the doors. Even the tables were missing, and he wondered just what this place was.

Dray grumbled something under his breath. Belle looked around the room as if she too found it strange that it was so empty, yet she seemed somewhat bored with the search for Ana.

"Would you like to return to the farm?" Ed asked her, and she looked across at him with surprise.

"You want me to leave? I thought I was to be of use."

"Ana thought so," he said with a sigh.

"Then let us try the other room. I'm sure Ana knows best." Belle swung around and marched out of the room, and Dray gave Ed a frustrated look with a shake of his head.

Ed wasn't sure what the girl was for. Or what she was thinking. He had been fascinated by her earlier, but she just seemed so disappointed with life lately that he sometimes wanted her far away.

Pushing the door open, he found the plump lord sitting on his pseudo-throne. Ende stood off to the side, his features dark, as though his whole body exuded his anger. Ed paused.

"It is so disappointing," Lord Welcott said, his body lounging to the side, relaxed as though he were in the room alone. "Your ward is not what I hoped she would be." He sat forward, his elbow on the arm of the large seat, and rested his chin in his hand. "Or at least, I think she could be, but she isn't quite as willing to work with me as I thought. I imagine there are others hoping for the same thing."

Ed knew in that moment that they were not amongst friends. He opened his mouth just as Ende raised his hand, and he closed it quickly.

"You have already sent word," Ende said, his voice low and deep and dangerous.

"They would hope that I had. But as yet, I still want to see what she can do for me. The mage, I'm sure, will have worked it out. My only curiosity is how you managed to drag the young king into this, and what his uncle will say when he discovers him here."

"Very little," Ed muttered, striding forward. "What do you want with Ana?"

"The Lady Anaise," the lord said. He sat up as Ed approached, but he still didn't show the deference he should to his king. "The Lady Anaise is sure to be as wondrous as her mother. And yet she fails to show me just what she can do."

"If you were to bring her here, I am sure she would be too happy to convince you of her skill."

"I've seen it," he said, standing, "and I've felt it. Pushing at my walls and unlocking doors. But she is not sharing, you see. She must share."

"Why must she?" a quiet voice asked from the doorway, and Ed turned to Belle. "What can she do?"

"So much more than she even knows she can. You have not helped her," he said angrily, turning to Ende. "Therefore, she will stay here with me."

"She can't," Ed said for him.

"You will all stay until I have what I need."

"What do you need?" Belle asked.

"I want all of this to be real," he said, moving his arm around in a wide arc. "It is all glamour, and I'm tired of it. With her powers, she can give me so much more. She can make it all real."

"Where is everyone else?" Belle asked, taking a tentative step forward.

"There is no one else," Ende said.

"Have you told them of me?" Ed asked, unsure what his uncle

would say or do if he had even noticed that he was no longer in the capital.

"Told them? No. I don't want the King's Men turning up here, making a ruckus, upsetting the way of things. No, you shall stay here for the time being. At my hospitality," the lord said slowly. "Your company may entice the Lady Anaise to assist me."

22

The man shifted uncomfortably before the regent, his jaw opening and closing without making a sound. Salima hugged the wall in her spying spot, still unseen. It was the only way she could find out what had happened to her friend. It surprised her more and more that she appeared to be the only one who had noticed his disappearance.

"When was the king last seen?" the regent asked in a sharp tone, which made the man quiver and Salima hold her breath.

"It appears some weeks."

"Weeks!" he bellowed. "How in the name of the gods has he been gone for so long without anyone noticing?"

I noticed, Salima thought, and it had been more than weeks.

"It was thought that he was unwell."

"Why was it thought that?"

"One of the…" The man looked about. "A maid…"

"Are you telling me that a maid helped the king run away?"

"No, I'm not," he said too quickly. "He was ill. One of the maids reported to the kitchen that he hadn't eaten his meal, and that he was complaining of illness. Another servant checked when he dropped the next meal to see if he needed a cleric, but he said he wasn't ill enough for that, just not well enough to be up from his bed. It was reported to the tutors and they left him to rest. The time passed before the tutors realised they had not heard after his health."

"And yet not one of them did anything about coming to me, or checking on him."

"It appears not, Your Highness."

"Send for them, now. Leave the swords man; he at least raised the alarm. And find the maid. I want to know why no one noticed he hasn't been eating for several weeks."

"They may have assumed…" His voice trailed off.

The regent stood slowly from the throne and stepped forward. The man before him flinched. "What might they have assumed?" he asked, his voice kind and coaxing, and Salima knew he was anything but.

The man before him dropped to his knees. "That you might have been caring for him yourself," he said quickly.

The regent allowed a frustrated sigh. "In the dungeons?" he asked.

"In the royal chambers, Your Highness. He is your blood, your nephew and king. Why would people think you have locked him up?"

Half the kingdom, if they had any sense, knew just what the regent had done to maintain his place of power. Salima tried not to huff. Although Ed hadn't seemed to want to retaliate or help himself in any way, and then he had disappeared. At least she could be sure the regent was not behind the disappearance, given his behaviour over the last few days.

He sat slowly on the throne as the man ran from the room. As he smiled a little to himself, Salima wondered if she was mistaken and he was behind it. Or was he just relieved that Ed had disappeared and he could use that in his favour? Why hadn't Ed told her where he was going? She had thought they were friends.

The mage appeared from the shadows, and Salima pulled back. If anyone were to discover her, she would be in serious trouble, and the only one likely to catch her was the mage.

He whispered something over the regent's shoulder. Salima closed her eyes and focused on his voice.

"If he doesn't return, it may solve all your problems."

"Unless the little scoundrel has managed to impregnate some maid or the like," the regent returned in barely a whisper. "Would he be man enough for such a feat? Would he have had the opportunity?"

"I don't think so," the mage reassured.

"Could we spin this into treason?" The regent tapped his fingers on the arm rest and leaned back. "That might not be hard to do. The boy hardly showed any love for the kingdom. He hasn't fought for the crown. In a way, he willingly asked me to take over. And his running away only proved further that it was not what he wanted."

Would the people really turn on him in such a way? Salima wondered, missing what they said next, although she thought the mage murmured something about magic.

With the sound of approaching voices, the regent sat straighter and the look of anger returned. The mage disappeared back into the shadows, and Salima wondered if he had been there the entire time.

The tutors filed nervously into the room. Four men bowed low before the regent, and the young maid tottered along nervously behind them. She curtsied so low Salima thought she might sit down.

He waved her forward first.

"You saw him in his rooms when he told you he was unwell?" he asked kindly, and she bobbed her head. "Tell me how he looked."

"Just as he always has," she said quickly. He waved his hand to encourage more detail, and she glanced at the man who had fetched them before looking back at the regent. "Tired, as though he doesn't sleep, his fingers covered in ink and his clothes too big for him. He eats," she added quickly, "but he hasn't filled out like a man." She looked at him with wide eyes for a moment, as though this was not the thought to have of her king. "But he didn't look unwell."

"Yet you reported it to the kitchen."

She nodded quickly. "I had to explain to the cook why he didn't eat her pie."

The regent nodded and waved her to the side. "Now, gentlemen. Exactly how long did you wait before you checked on the health of your king?"

"Too long," one of them said, still looking down at the floor. "There have been times, Your Highness, when the boy—excuse me, the king—does not wish to take his lessons. We try to encourage him, but he will feign illness. We find that if we give him the space and time he requires, he is more focused when we resume."

"How often?" the regent asked, frustration clear in his voice.

"Excuse me?" one of the tutors asked.

"How often have you left him alone when he required it?"

"Two or three times a year."

"So often?"

"Almost every year since his father's death."

"And yet you didn't think I might need to know this, that I might not care for him or be able to assist him?"

They glanced nervously between themselves, and one near the middle nudged another.

"He was just a boy," he blurted.

The regent stood slowly from the throne, and the tutors all stepped back as one.

"So it would seem," he said slowly. "A boy who does not understand the requirements of a king."

The girl sucked in a breath, and the regent looked disappointed. "Send for the guard," he snapped, waving his hand towards the door. They moved quickly from the room.

Salima tried not to stare. What was he hoping to achieve?

"Tell me," he said, sitting back as the guard entered the room.

"There are no horses missing. No one else appears to have disappeared from the capital. He hardly spent time with anyone outside of his tutors and training. They haven't seen him, nor have any guesses as to where he might be hiding or where he might have gone."

"Are we sure he isn't in the castle?"

The man bowed low.

"How did he get out of the castle?"

"I am trying to find out, Your Highness."

"If he can slip though unnoticed, I wonder who might be able to just walk right in."

"I assure you…"

"Save it," the regent snapped with an impatient wave of his hand. "I'm not sure I trust any of your assurances. I want you to find him. And then I want you to find out how he walked away and who he might be with."

"No one went with him."

"Then he went to find someone else. Who might he trust enough to run to?"

The man shook his head just a little.

"Does no one know their own king?" the regent asked, his frustration overflowing. "Does no one understand this boy?"

"He hasn't allowed anyone close enough, Your Highness."

"Not even me," the regent murmured. Although Salima was confident the man didn't want to know Ed in any way. And she wondered what he might do when he found him. She squeezed her hands into tight fists, only wishing she had some way of finding him first. As hot frustration washed over her, she wondered again why he hadn't shared his plans with her in the first place.

23

Ana leaned back against the cold stone and wondered for a moment just where she was. She hadn't seen anything or anyone else in the darkness, but perhaps the mage had found her. She had curled up, closing her eyes against it and willing it away.

When she had woken, she was cold and stiff, and the beautiful golden stone of the castle had been replaced with the cold grey she knew of Sheer Rock. She rested her head back and sighed. She wasn't in Sheer Rock, as much as she had hoped she was. Shivering, Ana hugged her arms closer, longing for Ende's cloak. Above her was a high-set window, far too high to reach or see through, and the light was weak as though pushed through a thick fog.

The breeze, however, moved easily through the wide-spaced bars and around her, further chilling the already cold stone walls. The floor was partly covered in straw, loose and well worn, the ground beneath it the same cold, grey stone of the walls. The wall directly before her was the same, other than the door, which was made of rough wood faded to almost the same grey as the stone.

She hadn't yet tried it. She knew it wouldn't open and doubted she had any ability to get it open. The wide panels of wood stared back at her. A small window had been cut into the topmost part. Large enough for a face to be seen, but she hadn't tried to look out of that either.

Ana didn't seem to have the energy for anything. She allowed her legs to slide out before her; the cream dress was marked and grey from her surroundings. Her shoes were scuffed. If she had been wearing what she had arrived in, she might have looked more presentable. More like the maid she was.

For a moment, she missed the cliffs and bridges and the angry lord. She had always been angry, for as long as Ana could remember. And yet Ana had still gone to her and worked hard every day. Until that one day, when the lord had tried to push her from the Walk. Ana closed her eyes, feeling the fear and wind as though she were there again.

Could Dray hear her all the way down here? Wherever that might be. Somewhere damp. But then this castle wasn't as it appeared to be. And neither was the plump little lord.

Ana looked down at her grimy hands and thought of her mother. A woman she didn't know, who made her father's eyes mist over when he thought of her. Not that he had spoken of her often. She had been gifted, Ana realised, remembering the vision she'd had in the cottage. Had she lost her life because of those gifts? Ana stood quickly, her head spinning from the movement. Or had she hidden away somewhere?

Ana beat on the door. She had heard her voice in the darkness. Her mother might be alive and trapped here, using her gifts for this man's ego. But if that was the case, where might she be, and would Ende be able to find her?

Ana banged again. The wood was rough against the side of her fist as she repeatedly thumped on the door. She stopped and listened, and there was nothing. She tried to raise herself up onto her toes to see out of the small window, but she wasn't tall enough.

"Hello?" she cried out, then pressed her ear to the door once more. Nothing. "Help!" she screamed, putting everything she had into it. She held her ear to the wood once more—still no noise. Not the sound of a guard, or someone else similarly trapped. Nothing.

Ana put her hand on the bolts where the latch might be on the other side, and she pushed. The door continued to hold solid, but as she closed her eyes, she could feel the rust and the decay in them. It was as though the moist air of the cell pushed through the strength of the metal. She rubbed her hands together and then placed them back over the bolt. If she had a sense of it, maybe she could do something with it. Ende was sure she had some strength, enough to make her dangerous to others; maybe she could use that.

She took a deep breath and reached out her senses through the cold metal. "Let go," she whispered. The bolts released their tired hold on the world and the door. Something on the other side dropped to the flagstones with a loud clatter. As the door swung out, she found herself in the dark once more.

Ana sighed and then stepped forward. Another illusion, another dream. She wondered where she actually was and whether the castle was playing tricks on her.

She held her hand out before her, breathed in the scent of cold stone and wondered if there was any light available at all, a candle or torch. Could it be hidden in the dark, as the cottage in the mountains and the doorway had been?

"Light," she murmured, "I need light."

A small flame flickered in the distance.

Making her way to the light, Ana found a small table and chair. She paused, waiting to see if this was another dream, another insight into someone else's world. There was a pewter cup and a plate with bread and cheese. The plate and cup were fancy in their way, shiny and ornate, while the bread and cheese looked tired against the bright surface. She stepped forward slowly and picked up the cup.

It appeared to be water, although she wondered what else it might contain. She hesitated. And then she tipped it up and let the cool liquid touch her lips. She hadn't realised how dry she was. She gulped it down and reached for the chunk of bread. It was hard but edible, and she wondered how long it had waited for her. She chewed slowly, the cup still held tight in her hand. Then she put it down slowly and reached for the cheese.

Could she have touched things from her other visions in such a way? Could she have held her father? Taken items from the shelves of the mage's rooms? Could she find a way out of the darkness through other people?

She swallowed down the tough cheese and closed her eyes. Could she find Dray this way? Could she call him back to her as she had on the Walk? She tried to picture him, but she couldn't see him clearly, not like she had before. He was a distant blur. She tried calling silently to him, but he didn't grow any clearer or any closer.

She bit into the cheese again and then, in her hunger, pushed what was left into her mouth, struggling to chew it. She tried to drink, but much of it ran down her chin. She needed to slow down. She had seen so much before. Despite the dark and losing Dray, she wasn't afraid. The candle flickered and went out, and the panic rose in her chest.

The cup that had been so cold and smooth in her hand disappeared. She felt forward, but the table was no longer there, nor the bread. She slowly worked to swallow the cheese. She would have to work faster if she saw food again. She hoped it really was food.

She wiped the back of her hand over her chin and found it was still damp. Someone was playing games. Ana straightened her shoulders. She didn't like games. The lord had done the same, little things to try and get at her. She had learnt to ignore them over the years.

She had wondered at the pages on the floor of her room, that day she had slipped. As though the lord had wanted her to make a mistake. Ana let her arms drop by her sides, closed her eyes again and took a deep breath. She was stronger than this. She had endured far more than anyone should have, and she had survived.

She focused on her memory of the Lord of Sheer Rock. Her blond hair blew in the breeze that came through the entrance to the

Walk—or was it the exit? Ana didn't want to focus on that. She wanted to concentrate on the lord. And in that moment, she realised how much like her mother the woman looked.

Having no recollection of her mother, she'd had nothing to compare the lord to. Now it was as though she couldn't not see how like her she was. But when she lifted her eyes from the papers on her desk, they were hateful rather than the kind, sad eyes she had seen in the woman who'd held her as a baby. She wondered if her father saw that same similarity, felt a connection to the woman who had probably killed her mother, or at least ordered her death. And then her father's.

Ana shook her head. That wasn't what she needed. She needed to see the pages. Ed had also asked about them. Looking down, she saw the word "tribute" clearly written on the page beneath her foot. The lord opened her mouth to scream at her, but Ana held up her hand and she was silenced. She squatted down and picked up the page she had stepped on. It had a boot mark across it, and splashes of tea.

It also had her name, clearly and neatly printed in the lord's hand. In parentheses after it, "gifted" was printed. And then there was nothing else.

Was she the only tribute the lord had expected to pay to the kingdom? If she had been taken by the mage, what else might the lord have gained? But she hadn't. Dray had dragged her from the room, and the lord had nothing else to give.

That wasn't right, though. There was another list, more pages on her desk, and Ana allowed the page with her name to slip from her fingers and onto the floor. The lord stood from the desk, a broken teacup in her hand, as Ana lifted the other list. But the writing was blurred from the spilt tea, and she couldn't make out the words. What else would she give the regent if she couldn't give Ana?

The castle groaned above her, and she looked up in the dim light coming through from her cell door. The ceiling was much closer than she'd anticipated, the same hard grey stone. She reached up and brushed her fingers over the cold, damp surface. Then she closed her eyes again and sighed.

The room the Lord of Edge Mountains sat in came into sharp focus. Servants carried platters, but the food was simple; either they didn't plan to feed them as lavishly every night, or the food had run out. A servant ran her tongue over her lips. And when Ana looked again, it was the same amazing spread she had seen on previous evenings. It was all magicked. Ana had thought it odd, and that might have been why. She turned to the small group by the large chair. The lord leaned over the arm, his leg thrown over the other one. He had a large drumstick in his hand, although Ana struggled to focus on it.

He waved towards the door, and Ana took a step forward as the servants disappeared rather than step back through the door. The room seemed smaller for a moment, duller in colour.

"She is a maid," Belle said, her voice carrying in the space. Ed gave a slight shake of his head. "She is," Belle insisted. "She can't help you, and you should allow her to leave as she came."

Ende looked tired, Ana thought, his clothes more threadbare than they had been before. She focused on Dray standing at the back of the room, looking again like the soldier trying not to be seen. Yet he was looking at her. It was as though he could see her.

The walls around them creaked again, and although Ana flinched, no one else did. It was as though they didn't realise just what danger they were in. Or maybe they weren't in danger, and she was somewhere very different.

"She is to stay. The Lady Anaise will be very useful."

"It wouldn't be proper for a young woman to stay with you." Belle tried to sound forceful, but she came across as scared, and Ana wondered just what made her so. This little lord and his fake food?

"She can stay as my wife."

Ed stepped forward. As Ana took another step, she noticed that

Dray had not moved. And he was still looking at her.

She moved carefully across the room towards him. The conversation became more heated with the lord, but she couldn't focus on what they were saying. The room around her groaned again.

Dray's eyes moved forward as she stood beside him. His hands were rigid by his sides. She slipped her hand into his, surprised at how solid and warm and real he felt.

"Where is she?" he asked, his deep voice loud and echoing, and she shuddered with surprise.

The lord shrugged his shoulders as though he didn't know, and the others turned to look at Dray.

"It is cold and damp," Ana whispered. "So cold." She shivered as he squeezed her hand tight, and then she was back in the small space outside her cell.

24

Dray looked around the room. He was unsure what he was seeing, but it didn't look the same as it had moments before. Lord Welcott was going on and on about how Ana could help him, and Dray wondered why he would think that. Ana was able to do a range of things he hadn't expected when he had first seen her enter that room. It seemed so long ago now. Just a girl in a worn dress, her long dark hair loosely pulled back from her face. He hadn't noticed her green eyes until he was holding her so tightly above the sea.

He shook his head, trying to focus on where he was and what was happening around him as the walls creaked and groaned. For a moment, he thought Ana was beside him, holding his hand, seeking his protection. But she wasn't there. And the room around him wasn't quite as large as it had appeared to be. The golden shimmer of the stone looked a little duller.

The large windows didn't seem to let in as much sunlight, and he felt as though a fog had moved over the castle. Dray looked more closely at the little lord, lounging in his chair, thinking it was a throne. King of his own small world. But he would only remain the Lord of the Seat if he managed to maintain his favour with the kingdom.

So many people had appeared to move in and out of the castle, but now there was no one, and Ende had seen through that. What else had the old man seen? The mage had been searching for tribute. That had been his claim on the travels to the cliff islands. He was going to collect tribute. What might this man offer as tribute, and why would the mage not stop here?

It all came back to Ana. The Lord of Sheer Rock wanted her gone. The Lord of Edge Mountains wanted her for himself. As did the mage. Or at least he had on the way to the cliff islands. Once he had touched her, he had wanted her dead. *What had he seen?*

Dray looked at Ende, who stood a little to the side of the room. He looked hemmed in, as though the room was too small for him. Dray wondered if he might turn into a dragon to save Ana, or if she needed him to. He always knew more than he was willing to share, and he had thought Ana was dangerous. Again, Dray wondered what had the mage had seen.

The more he tried to picture the girl, the hazier the room became. The more the walls groaned and the smaller it shrank. The food piled on the table was not as sweet smelling as it had been before, the roasted meats not as glossy. For a moment, it looked like potatoes and porridge. He blinked, and the lavish dishes became brighter.

He needed to find Ana. Glancing at Ende and shifting uncomfortably, Dray caught his eye. The old man nodded his head down just enough before he looked back to the king. Dray ducked out of the room and found himself in a narrow hallway, the stonework grey and dull. He blinked back his surprise and continued on. He came across another door and, pushing it open, found the large room where they met of an evening—only the shine had gone, and the room looked barely half the size of the one he had just left.

He pulled the door closed and raced on. The hallways were not nearly as long, and with only a few turns he found himself standing in a small courtyard. Empty stables stood off to the side. On the opposite side of the courtyard, another wing of the castle, although grey and dull, jutted out towards the stables. It contained only one door, with heavy iron bands around the weathered wood and a large lock on the bolt.

He raced towards it as he heard Ana calling. She was so loud, as though she was standing beside him. He pulled at the lock, which gave way easily. Beyond was a dark set of steps. Although he couldn't see where they led, he could hear her voice, loud, clear and desperate.

The stairs spiralled down, and a little light shone from very narrow slits of windows. Dray paused and looked out, seeing snow drifting down over the sparse trees on the mountain.

At the base of the stairs was a small room with several doors leading from it. Dray closed his eyes, then took the first one on the right that led into another tunnel-like hallway. He rushed forward to find another door not too far along it.

It opened easily into a small room. Off the room were several narrow wooden doors, and as he turned slowly, he saw her standing in the middle of the room with her eyes closed. The dim light of the window showed him there was nothing else but her. The world above them groaned, and he looked up.

She hadn't moved.

"Ana," he said, and she jumped at the sound. "We need to go."

"Can you hear me?" she whispered, her voice dry.

"I can see you," he said, reaching out for her.

She turned, her hand over her mouth, her face dirty and her eyes wet as she threw herself at his chest.

"We have to go," he said.

"He knows where I am," she whispered, clinging to him. "Ed isn't safe."

"The lord?"

She shook her head. "The mage. He has seen me. They are coming."

"For the king?"

"No, they want me. But in their coming it will be Ed who is in danger."

"If we leave here, can he find you?"

"I don't know," she said, allowing him to take her hand and lead her back through the tunnel and up the steps.

Once they were standing in the courtyard, she pulled him to a stop. "Look," she breathed.

The castle was smaller than it had first appeared. The grey stone now blended into the mountainous backdrop. "It was all an illusion."

"Who for?" she asked.

"I don't know," Dray admitted, looking up at the castle from the small courtyard. A distant window had a small corner pane broken, the light not reflecting as it did the rest of the windows. Appearing as a broken tooth.

"How did you get here?" he asked.

"I think the castle put me here."

"He wants your help."

"Why? What could I help with?" she asked.

"I think the kingdom's collectors are on the way. Tribute will be expected."

"He doesn't want to give me as tribute."

"No, but he might want you to make it."

She opened her mouth and then closed it.

"Could you hide the king if required?" he asked.

"I don't know," she whispered.

"Can I hide you?"

"Not here; not in the mountains. I don't know how well he can track me."

Ed watched the world flicker around him, Ende shifted uncomfortably and Belle made a strange squeak. He looked from her to the lord and back again before he understood the look on her face was fear.

"I don't think this is a good idea," Dray said.

The lord gave a low growl.

Ed turned as Dray led Ana into the room. She looked even more concerned than Belle, and dirty, and he honestly expected something rude and catty from Belle about her.

She stepped forward and placed a hand on Ed's arm as she moved directly to Belle. He felt a moment of calm, as though all would be well now that they were together.

"What do you see?" Ana asked the girl.

"He…" she stammered.

"May I?" Ana held out her hand and Belle looked at it, clearly confused.

Then she nodded and took Ana's hand before turning slowly towards the lord. Ed was watching them more than the little man, but there was something as Ana turned that made his heart stop. She too saw something that made her nervous.

"Who are you?" he asked, stepping between them, unsure what it was that they could see and he could not.

"I am the lord of all you see," the man snapped. Anger was thick in his voice, and Ende flinched as the room appeared to grow smaller around them.

"Why did the King's Men not stop for tribute?" Ed asked.

"I am sure they would have," he said, "if they thought there was anything to give."

"I'm surprised they didn't see you shining from the forest, the great golden castle. Why would they not come?"

"Perhaps they have forgotten me," he said with a shrug, lying back in the chair, although his focus appeared to be on Belle.

"I think we should leave," she whispered.

"Oh no, my dear. That isn't going to happen. I need Ana. And Ana needs you."

"I can't help you. And the mage knows where I am," Ana replied.

Ende took a step forward, but Ana simply nodded without a

word.

"I don't fear him," the lord muttered.

"And his soldiers?" Ed asked, watching him closely and wondering why he couldn't see his face as clearly as before. "He won't come alone."

He sucked in a breath and swung his leg from the chair arm.

"Where is the Lord of Edge Mountains?" Ed asked as the room slowly began to turn grey.

"Why do you not believe that I am him?"

"There is no history of magic within the line."

"There is always some magic somewhere. Look at the girl. She is from a long line of lords, and yet she is something very different."

"What?" Belle murmured, looking at Ana. Ende huffed.

Ed was almost sure that he could feel the temperature of the room rise.

"I understand her mother had some gifts of her own."

"You did not know my mother," Ana said quietly, but there was something very dangerous in the way she spoke, and for a moment Ed understood Ende's fears.

"No one cares for the mountains, and so I can do as I like. How many people do you think are dotted amongst these slopes? How much of anything of worth could I give to the Kingdom of Ilia?"

"You appear to have much," Ed said carefully. "The stone alone could be valued by the regent."

"He has interests in other things."

"Gold," Ana murmured.

"He has some interest in that," the lord admitted.

"And you have more than enough to share."

The lord scoffed and sat back. "Gold? What gold?"

Ana closed her eyes.

"Did you see something?" Ed asked, then noticed the little man flinch.

Anger radiated from him. Ed actually stepped back, but in the heat of his anger, Ende stepped forward. He grabbed hold of the lord's arm and blew a breath into his face. The man shrieked, and the room altered.

"Gwelka," Ende said.

The plump little lord, with his thinning hair and neat trimmed beard, had been replaced with a skinny, ugly, grey creature. It squirmed in Ende's hold. "Let me go," he bellowed. His head appeared too large for his body and Ed was sure he saw small pointed teeth.

"How?" Ed asked.

"Some of them have magic," Ende said, "same as any man. You could have stayed hidden in the mountains with your gold," Ende said to him.

"I was tired of living underground."

"Where is the lord?" Ana asked. "Where are the people?"

"There hasn't been anyone here for some time."

"Someone would have noticed," Ed said.

"Who, boy, would come all the way here for some gravel?"

Ed opened his mouth and then closed it. He didn't appreciate being called boy, but then he had no real idea of how the kingdom worked.

"Everyone must pay tribute," Dray said, reminding Ed that he was still in the room.

"There is nothing to pay," the creature said.

"The mage and his men are still coming," Ana said.

The grey, wizened little man tried to shake Ende off. The castle's illusion had been broken along with his.

"He doesn't want me," he said, the grin too broad.

"But that might not stop them. And once they find a gwelka running the Seat, they might assume you have something here. They could tear this mountain apart."

His wrinkled face paled further, becoming an almost blue colour.

Ana cried out, a strangled pained plea, and then she was gone.

Vanished. Belle sucked in a scared breath, stumbling a little, so Ed reached out an arm and pulled her closer.

"She was holding my hand," she whispered.

The gwelka sighed. "It appears that my advantage is gone."

"Why would he take her when he has seen how dangerous she is?" Ende mused.

Ed's heart thumped loud in his ears. "They know I'm gone."

"You think they have only just discovered it?" Dray asked.

"I don't get out much," Ed muttered. "It doesn't take long for them to forget me."

"You are the king," Belle said.

"I am a boy in the way of my uncle." He looked down at her bright yet confused face.

"You may be off," the gwelka said, waving a skinny arm towards the door.

Ed sighed.

"I agree," Ende murmured. "As much as I think it is a bad idea."

"What idea?" Belle asked.

"We are going to need some gold," Dray said, and the gwelka scowled at him.

25

Ana was sure she would throw up. Her head spun and she ached all over, as though she had fallen a great distance. She dragged in a deep breath only to cough as the smoky, herb-infused air filled her lungs. She looked up into the dim light at the two men standing before her. She wanted desperately to pull back out of their reach, but she didn't have the strength.

One man squatted down and peered at her as though she were something he had never seen before. He tilted his head. Although she didn't know who he was, there was something familiar about him.

"Are you certain?" he asked, and the other man stepped into the light.

Ana managed to find some ability to scuttle back with the fear that rose in her chest. The mage smiled at her.

"She may be a threat still. I saw her power with the king."

"He is gone," the first man said.

Ana blinked up at him and opened her mouth to ask where Ed might be, but changed her mind. As she slammed her mouth shut and chewed on her lip, she only hoped they didn't know what she was thinking. Didn't know she had been with him.

"Where is your soldier?" the mage asked.

Ana shook her head once as she looked around the dimly lit space. She had been here before. In one of the visions in the dark.

"How?" she asked.

"I am far stronger than even you could understand."

"And yet you could only kill me by throwing me from the Walk."

"It is not the only way." She shivered despite her best efforts. "The Lord of Sheer Rock needed to prove herself."

"And did she?" Ana asked. "Has she paid her tribute?"

"She has now," the mage murmured.

"Although she need not know that," the other man added under his breath. "She was keen to give you up, despite the family connection."

"I didn't know that," Ana admitted. "I only knew her as the Lord of Sheer Rock."

He nodded and held out a hand to help her up. Then he appeared to think better of it, or at least differently, for he withdrew his hand quickly as she reached for it.

They were scared of her, she realised, and she wondered if she was really the threat Ende had thought she was. What might they hope she could do for them? "Maybe you should just send me back to the mountains, out of the way."

"Enough," the man boomed, and she pulled back from him. "I want her somewhere she cannot do harm."

"You mean where someone can't harm me?" she asked hopefully.

"No," he said, his voice determined. "I know my own mind." He turned and left the room, his dark robes swirling out around him. Although he didn't wear a crown, she felt it hover over his head.

"The king's regent," she whispered.

"And the reason you need to remember who and where you are."

"Where am I exactly?" she asked.

"Somewhere you can learn."

"I thought you wanted me dead," Ana said, sitting back against the cool wall behind her.

"It may be that you are of use to us after all."

"And if I don't want to be of use?"

"You will be, one way or another."

"How did you know where I was?"

He sighed. "So many questions. You will learn how to be useful. And until you are, you can be a maid again. You can bring me tea," he said, pointing to the fireplace on the far side of the room.

"You trust me to walk around the castle?"

"You won't be leaving this room," he said, moving back into the shadows.

Ana climbed very slowly to her feet, using the wall as support. Her head spun and she staggered a little, wishing Dray was close by to hold her steady. She chewed on her lip as she moved over to the fire. He was so very far away now, and he needed to help Ed, not worry about where she might have gone. She thought of the gwelka playing at lord. She glanced over her shoulder, but she had no idea where in the room the mage was. Could he know what it was in the mountains? Or did they not care as long as it didn't stand against them?

A small pot bubbled over the flame. Ana looked at it suspended over the heat, yet there was no metal holding it in place. A tea pot and a small pile of cups sat on a low cupboard to the side along with various jars.

She selected one and lifted the lid carefully, sniffing at the contents and then shaking her head at the spicy burn. She pushed the lid back on quickly and rubbed the back of her hand across her nose. Then she tested the next one and, using the scoop in the jar, put some into the pot.

She ran her tongue over her dried lips as she poured the water over the leaves. She lifted the pot and two cups and carried them through the maze of shelves. The room felt familiar, and without thought she moved quicker towards a desk she wasn't sure she knew existed.

"Find what you need?" the mage asked as she sat the pot and cups on the edge of the desk.

Ana nodded once as she poured tea into a cup and sat it beside the book he read. Then she poured another for herself. She turned back to the room as she sipped. He had managed to drag her all the way to the capital from the mountains. Was there any way she could protect Ed from these men?

Stifling a yawn, Ana moved back through the room. She looked over the shelves that lined the walls, and the others that sometimes filled the spaces between. There were jars, pots, books and strange ornaments tucked in amongst them. Some she wanted to touch, but she kept her hands to herself.

What did she need most? she wondered. Other than a way out of this mess—not that she had a choice of returning to the life she'd had. In any case, she was sure now it wasn't what she wanted. Her mother had wanted to protect her, but whether that was only from the lord or men like the mage, she didn't know.

In a far corner amongst the shelves and dust was a cot, narrow and covered in a thin blanket. She drained the remains of the cup, sat it on the floor and lay down, longing for the warmth of Ende's cloak. She wondered where it was now that he was so far away and the gwelka was revealed. Her fine dresses had been an illusion. How had he managed to keep it up for so long, and without her seeing it?

She had felt something strange, but she hadn't worked out what it was. She might not have the gifts Ende was so sure she had. She pulled her knees up to her chest and wrapped her arms around herself. She still wore her tatty dress, and her shoes. She was still just a maid, and she had been stupid to think she could be anything else.

26

"Is it getting smaller in here?" Dray murmured, looking over the cool grey stone and the narrow windows.

"It might be a bit tight for a dragon," the gwelka quipped.

Ende, his hand still tight around the little grey man's arm, snapped at him, and he actually flinched.

"I could do with some air," the king said. They headed as a group out into the courtyard, which didn't appear to be familiar to any of them but Dray.

"Are there horses?" Belle asked, taking a step towards the stables. Dray glanced at Ende.

"Don't look at me," he said with a scowl.

The king looked up then, and Dray wondered when they would learn what Ende was. There had been a moment of understanding when the king had first arrived, clear on his face that this was the man he had searched for. Yet he didn't know what kind of man that was.

"I ate them," the little gwelka admitted easily.

Dray looked at him closely. He had never met a gwelka in the flesh before, and the stories he had heard were varied and, frankly, unbelievable. It was half the size of a man, and it even made the king look muscular. But with the tight grip maintained by Ende, he wondered just what it might do if released.

"Are you going to call off the beast?" he asked.

Ende smiled, his perfect teeth flashing in the clouded light of the day.

"I think you should be more polite," Belle said, and Dray noticed that Ende didn't meet her eyes.

"We need horses and supplies," the king said, looking at the gwelka.

"Nothing left. Hasn't been anything left for a while."

"How did you maintain this?" Dray asked, waving his hand over the much smaller castle.

"I'm stronger than I look."

"I'm not so sure about that," Ende murmured.

"And if I ate you?" he asked the old man. "What might happen then?"

"You are not likely to survive the experience," Ende whispered.

"Were you going to eat us?" Belle asked, truly fixated on him as Dray searched her for signs of fear. She seemed unsettled, but no longer scared. He wondered what else this girl had endured on her way to the mountains.

"In time. I needed the girl first."

"We wouldn't have let you," she said, and Dray took a step forward. The gwelka laughed, the sharp sound echoing off the building around them. "We would have protected each other."

"You would have been gone before you knew what had happened. I was in your room and you never suspected me."

She narrowed her eyes, and then her pretty face turned scarlet.

"There is no one else here. Who did you think drew your bath of an evening?"

If it was possible, she turned an even deeper shade of red. The king stepped between them to shield her dignity, although somewhat too late. A girl had visited with Ana as well, Dray realised as an overwhelming urge to rip the gwelka's limbs from his little body rushed over him.

But the little man, still watching around the king to the blonde girl, licked his lips and then started to open his mouth. Dray watched, transfixed, as his mouth continued to open, the jaw unhinging. Then Ende's hand closed around his throat and it snapped shut.

"You see?" he said in a sing-song voice. "You would have been gone in a minute, and no one would have noticed until you didn't come down for breakfast. You wouldn't even have the chance to scream."

Dray gulped back his revulsion. The stories might be truer than he gave them credit for. He certainly hoped that Ende would be with them if they came across any more gwelka in the mountains.

"That explains the horses," the girl muttered, and Dray snorted. The king turned a surprised look his way.

"Ana needs to be our focus," Dray said, trying to remind himself why they were where they were. It was all because of her. The reason he had left his men, the reason they were trying to help a king who didn't want to be helped. The reason he was travelling with a dragon disguised as an old man.

"Gold," Ende said through clenched teeth, his hands closing tighter in their hold.

The gwelka made a strange squeaking noise.

"He needs to be able to tell us," the king said.

Ende nodded once and allowed the hand around the gwelka's neck to ease a little, barely enough to notice other than that his knuckles were no longer white.

"I..." the gwelka started and then stopped again. He pointed wildly in several different directions with his free arm before allowing them both to hang limp. "I'm a dead gwelka whichever way you go."

"You certainly won't be following us," Ende said.

"What if I give you what I have and you let me go home to my brothers?"

"And then you come after us in force?" It was Belle who asked the question, and Dray wondered why he hadn't noticed how quick she was before. Ana had said she would help; he wondered if she knew how much.

"Under my bed," the gwelka said.

Ende took a deep breath and, guiding the gwelka by the tight hold he had around his neck, marched him back into the castle.

Once inside, the little devil tried to escape, but Ende's grip was too tight. He hung his head as he was led through the castle. The room was no different to any other, yet it didn't feel right. The illusion of the large, open golden spaces was gone, but something tingled over Dray's skin.

Ende sniffed warily at the air as Dray held up his arm, preventing Belle and the king from coming further into the room. "What is it?" he asked.

"Not gold," Ende murmured.

Something growled from the shadows, and Dray moved the king from the room altogether. "We can't risk you," he whispered as the king made noises of protest. "Watch the girl."

"More like I would watch him," she muttered, and the boy turned disappointed eyes her way.

"That wall juts up to the mountain," Ende said, his voice low.

"You have an escape," Dray said.

"I would, but I have a dragon problem."

Dray glanced back, but the others were outside the room and out of hearing. He looked to Ende, who shook his head. They would need to tell them at some point just who it was that travelled with them.

"What is it?" the king called out.

"He is trying to get away from us."

"But we need his help to find Ana."

"No, you don't," the little man spat, wriggling again to try and get out of the grip of the dragon. "You know exactly where she is."

"How would we know that?" Belle asked.

"The mage," the king murmured.

Dray nodded. "He wanted her dead. Perhaps they think with the king gone that she isn't the threat they thought, or something has changed. But the mage is the only one who could have taken her like that. The only one who would want her like that."

"She is just a girl," Belle said.

The gwelka laughed, the hideous sound echoing from the walls even as it was strained by the hold on his neck. "She is far more than just a girl. I felt that instantly, as I'm sure the mage did."

"We don't need your opinions," Dray snapped. "We need your gold."

"It is in the mountains."

"Really?" Ende asked. "You would risk it all and travel back and forth?"

"I really don't like you," the gwelka murmured. "It is in the cellar, where all gold should be kept."

"Unguarded?" Belle asked.

"Do you see any guards? Do you think I need guards?" He flashed his pointed teeth, and she shivered.

"We don't want to take everything you have, just enough to help us reach the capital." The king stood straighter.

"Lead the way," Ende said, his voice low, and Dray was sure the room rumbled. "Or I will snap your neck and we will find it on our own."

"You will need me to allow you entry."

He sighed, and Dray indicated that the king and Belle move back from the door. They travelled again in the direction instructed by the little grey gwelka as Ende's hand remained tight around its neck. It didn't take as long as he thought it might, given that the castle was so much smaller now. The door they reached was solid but looked no different from any other door they had come across.

"Open it," Ende instructed.

"You could…"

"Open it," he said again, and this time Dray was sure the walls shook with his voice.

Closing his eyes, the gwelka held his hand out and pressed it to the wood. Something clicked, and there was another sound Dray couldn't quite place, like the unsealing of a jar.

The door squealed open, and Ende pushed the gwelka in first.

"Perhaps you should…" Dray said to the king as he made to follow Ende.

"I need to see this."

Dray took a breath and was the last to enter the room. He wasn't sure why, but he kept his hand on the door, holding it open. The room was dry and dimly lit, but there was a glow of something unnatural in the corner. Then the light increased, and Belle drew in a surprised gasp.

Leaning against a pile of what looked like rocks were the desiccated remains of a man. His hand held a rock, and his fine clothes were almost intact.

"The Lord of the Seat," the king said.

"He was," the gwelka said in a bored tone.

"Belle, do you think you could take that small token from his hand?" Ende asked, but the king reached out and took her arm to stop her stepping forward.

"I can do it," she snapped.

"It is probably best that Belle does it, rather than one of us."

The king released his hold, and she stepped forward slowly to bend over the dried body.

She chewed on her lip. Although she looked unsure, she prised his fingers from the stone and held it up. As she did, it changed to a lump of brilliant gold. "Oh," she breathed.

"You are very lucky," the gwelka said. "And you, sir," he said, turning back to Ende, "know far more than I gave you credit for. The gold is yours," he said with a wave of his hand, looking back at Belle. The gold turned into a pile of coins in her hand. "Hold it close. And as it is yours, you may give it whomever you choose. But if it is taken from you, it will appear to be a worthless rock again. One that will pull the life slowly from the man who closes his hand around it."

The king took a small step back and clenched his hands. "How does this help us?"

"As long as the girl willingly gives you the coins, it is safe," Ende said.

Belle eyed the handful of coins and then slipped them into her pockets, although the weight of them appeared to weigh her down more than physically.

"I have a pouch," the king offered.

She nodded slowly and took several coins, then handed them to the king with a smile. Dray could feel the tension in the small room, but they remained as they should. As Belle gave the king a small nod, he put them into the pouch and then secured it to his belt.

"It is time to go," Dray said.

"I'll meet you outside," Ende said.

Belle opened her mouth and then closed it. But when she reached the door, she turned back and bowed her head to the little man. "Thank you," she said and then was gone, the king not far behind.

"What do you plan?" Dray asked.

"Only to ensure he isn't a burden on our travels."

"He's coming with us?"

"No, but I need to make sure he isn't going to follow us with his brothers."

Dray shivered at the thought. A whole group of them might be too much for even Ende. They would be devoured before they even knew they were being followed.

"You can't kill me. That is not very dragon-like behaviour."

"Don't tell me what dragons can and can't do. Now out, Captain."

Dray headed out and Ende followed, then turned back and threw the gwelka back into the room. The gwelka stood and grinned in the dim light as Ende pulled the door closed. Then Ende rested his hand and forehead on the door while mumbling something. He stood this way for some time. Dray wanted to check on the king, for he knew that was where he should be, but he needed to be sure that Ende was in fact keeping the gwelka from following.

When Ende straightened, he staggered a little and looked to have aged a further ten years. Dray put a hand under his arm and held him upright. There was a solidness to the old man that gave the indication he was more than he appeared to be; Dray wondered if that was because he knew what the man really was.

"That should hold him for a bit."

"How long?" Dray asked, worried they weren't going to get very far very fast at the rate they were travelling and with whom.

"Four or five hundred years."

"Will he survive that long?"

"He might find another way out, but not for some time. Long enough that he would lose the scent of us."

"But he knows where we are going."

"Gwelka aren't that fond of crowds. Otherwise he might have kept the people around him, not just to eat. How often do you hear of a gwelka in the capital?"

"Rarely," Dray said with a smile.

"Let us find this king of ours and take him home."

"I thought we were to find Ana."

"It might be that we can do both at once."

27

Ed had assumed that with a pocket full of gold, they would head straight for the capital. But it wasn't to be. They were far from the general's cottage, and Belle wanted her father. Ende agreed that he would be of help. It took them the best part of three days to make their way back across the mountains to the cottage.

Despite his concerns that they were wasting time, it was comfortable and familiar in the cottage, and for a moment it almost felt as though he was home.

Belle and Phillip held each other for a long time, then sat by the fire as she filled him in on all the news. Ed looked between Ende and Dray, who seemed to know far more than they were saying. Ed had a connection with Ana, but she shared a similar connection with Dray, one he didn't understand.

Standing in the middle of the cottage, Ed looked over the group and then pushed his way outside. He stepped up onto a large boulder not far from the cottage and looked out over the world before him. In some ways it was like when he stood on his father's balcony, looking over the city. He had the same feeling of wonder and fear.

Sensing the two men behind him, Ed turned slowly and sat down.

"She will survive," Ende said.

"He wanted to kill her before."

"And if he still does, she will be dead and it won't make any difference as to how long it takes us to get there."

Dray stared at Ende for a moment and then let out a long breath. "He has something to tell you."

Ende stared at him.

"He is your king," Dray said, as though such a thing would influence anyone. "You were friends with his mother. Did she know?"

Ende nodded slowly, moving to sit beside Ed on the boulder.

"It is not an easy thing to explain," he started, looking down on Ed rather than at him. "I didn't have to explain it to Ana," he said, looking up at the soldier. "Or you."

"I saw it, in a way," Dray said. "Ana just knew."

"Such a clever girl."

"Ende!"

"I am," he said slowly, turning to Ed, "a dragon."

Ed laughed. Then, as he took in how serious the man was and Dray's gentle nodding, the laughter died. The words of the gwelka came back to him. "That was why you could hold on to him," Ed said, making a grabbing motion with his hand.

Ende nodded.

"A dragon? Like the beasts of the stories?"

Ende nodded again.

"How?"

"It is not an easy thing to explain. And honestly, I spend more time as a man."

"How big?"

"Huge," Dray said quickly.

Ende glared up at him.

"Could you… That is how you got to the Lord's Seat before us."

"Ana is very persuasive."

"I don't think it was all Ana," Dray said.

"But I didn't know what I was taking her into. I have lived in these mountains for a long time. How could I not know what he was up to? How could no one else know what had happened to the lord?"

"My uncle appears to keep a close eye on so much," Ed said. "Yet as long as reasonable tribute is paid, the lords of the kingdom can do as they like."

"Even if they aren't really lords," Dray said.

"So it would seem," Ed agreed, trying not to stare at the old man beside him.

"Would that change?" Ende asked.

"How could it?"

"Perhaps a king more interested in the people might change the world."

"It is easier said than done. My father changed very little. My uncle maintains the status quo."

"Does it need to be changed?" Ende asked.

"That is a good question," Ed said. "I haven't been given the chance to really think about it."

"What about the tributes offered?" Dray asked. "Would you change that?"

"I think many of the regions offer what they can rather than meet a particular request."

"Brides for the young men of the capital," Belle said, appearing beside Dray. "Is that something that should be asked for?"

He shook his head as a heat rose to his face, unsure where it came from. He didn't demand these things. But he knew it was because of this request that Belle had ended up where she was. "I would stop that," he murmured.

"You could only stop that if you were King," she snapped. Dray opened his mouth to say something and Ed held up his hand. She was right.

"I might not be the king you need," he said.

"You could try," she said, her arms crossed. "You helped before. You seemed like a man who would help."

"And then you discovered I was a king hiding from my responsibilities."

"I thought the crown was taken?"

"But he didn't try to get it back," Dray answered for him. "And you still aren't sure that you should try."

"My uncle understands the politics, how to make people happy and get them to listen."

Belle looked disappointed.

"I'm sorry," Ed said.

"If Ana were here, you would try."

"She isn't here," Ed said, pushing up from the rock. She had tried to tell him it was where he needed to be. But she might not be right either. And he wasn't sure he could get there without her. He'd had strange dreams of getting the crown back, only to hand it to her. She could convince him of anything. Maybe she had tried to convince him for her own needs rather than his.

"Don't doubt her," Ende said. "Although there are times that I have myself. She cares for you, and that might be enough to ensure the right thing is done."

Belle huffed.

"But she is far away, and the mage may be doing anything to turn her against us. And if my uncle is involved…"

"Why do you think they took her now?" Dray asked.

"They have realised I'm gone," he said. "They must have. And if he saw something similar to what Ende thought, that she was dangerous to me, they might think it is their chance to remove me before I become a threat."

"But would you?" Belle asked.

He turned to her, confused by her words.

"Be a threat," she replied to his unasked question. "You don't even want to be King. What threat do you pose to the man who not only wants to be King but currently holds all the power?"

"You don't think very much of me," Ed murmured.

"You don't think very much of yourself. I see why you needed

Ana." The disappointment was clear on Belle's face as she swung around, strands of her blond hair blowing from their hold as she marched back towards the cottage.

"Your confusion is contagious," Ende said, resting a hand on his shoulder. As he smiled, Ed stared at his perfectly white teeth. "Work out what you want and who you are, and we will follow."

Dray bowed his head. "You just need the confidence. But whether you really want to be King is not a consideration. You are the rightful heir to the throne of Ilia. You are the king."

Ed sucked in a deep breath and nodded. "My father once said the same."

"An amazing man," Ende said. "Better than his own father in many ways."

"You knew them?" he asked.

"I am an old man," Ende said, smirking a little. "I was a young man like yourself… too long ago to name," he said. "When I was younger, I spent more time in the capital than I should have. Then when your mother…"

Ed wanted to ask more, to ask if Ende knew his mother as more than the queen, but he held back as the old man gulped down what looked like regret.

"Are there many dragons out there?" he asked instead.

"Out where?"

"In the world," Ed said.

"I don't know." Ende whispered it so quietly, Ed leaned forward. "That isn't the place to focus now."

"No," Ed agreed. "It isn't. Can I do this without Ana?"

"Are you not your mother's son?" Ende asked, his words sharp. They cut deeper than Ed had thought they could.

"But I haven't had their guidance. I can barely remember my mother, and despite my father's words, since he died, I have been left alone with only the tutors and a view of the stables." He clenched his fists. He hadn't wanted to sound like a whining child, and yet he did. "And do we just walk into the capital and say,

"Here I am. Your king. Your reign is over, Uncle.""

"We might need to be little more subtle," Dray said. "But I think getting you back to the capital is the first step in getting you back to where you should be."

"Where is that?"

"On the throne," Ende said.

He blew out a long breath and nodded. It would take them long enough to try to reach the capital. It had taken him weeks to get this far. Even if they managed to find horses, it would be a slow journey. He looked again at Ende, wondering just what magic he could manage.

"You saw things," Ed said slowly.

"I get a feeling sometimes."

"Ana," he said, reaching for the old man's arm. "You saw Ana coming. You know what she is."

"She is a girl worth knowing. I only hope that she is what I hope, and not what I fear."

"Then we leave now."

"You have found your purpose then," Belle said, standing by the cottage. "The meal is ready."

"You must come with us," he blurted.

"Must I?" she asked to his utter disappointment.

He had thought she wanted to travel with him. That she liked him just a little, even if it was because he was King. "No. It is your choice," he said more calmly, trying to be the king he was supposed to be, the one his father would be proud of.

28

Ana stood by the desk and tried not to speak. The mage sat hunched over a large book, writing slowly into its pages with a fine quill. He would pause occasionally to dip into the small inkwell at the edge of the desk and then continue. Ana stood and watched him for some time, unable to determine what he was writing as it wasn't a language she knew. He would write until the ink ran dry, then dip and continue again.

She had spent days roaming the labyrinth of shelves. She could look at books, although very few of them made any sense. She had studied the bottles of creatures and specimens that lined the shelves, along with dried unknown contents. Some of them had labels, and some of those labels she could read, although it made little difference.

Despite all the hidden alcoves, piles of papers and labyrinths of shelves, she had yet to see anyone else but the mage.

"What exactly do you need from me?" she asked as he paused to dip the pen into the ink again.

"So much," he murmured.

"And how will I be able to give that to you?"

He looked up then and his brow creased. "Why have you not changed?"

"Into what? A frog?"

"The clothes that have been sent for you."

She shook her head and looked back to the little cot across the room. There was no privacy, no space of her own. She had found a privy amongst the shelves and turns between cold stone walls, and she would take a heavy volume of something with her to ensure the door wasn't opened when she was in there. Not that she lingered; it was putrid. But other than a thin blanket, she had been given nothing.

"Did I not send for clothes? I think if you were better dressed, you might consider your position more seriously."

"I haven't even bathed in weeks," she murmured.

He pointed to a wall. She turned and then looked back to him.

"In there," he said, not looking up.

She moved to the wall he had indicated and looked over the shelves that lined it. "What is here that you need?" she called back.

"Here," he said, appearing beside her. As she jumped, he waved his hand in a circular motion over the shelf and it disappeared, revealing a door. He bowed his head and went back to his desk.

She slowly pressed the latch, and the door opened into a neat room, with a fire and two narrow beds on opposite walls. There was a table with a candle in the middle of it and two simple chairs pulled up to it. In the corner was a cupboard, and against another wall was an empty shelf.

Then she noticed the other door. She moved quickly over to it and opened it easily into a cool hallway. A guard, dressed as Dray would have been, turned to look at her. And although he reminded her of her friend, he didn't look enough like him for her to think it might be him.

"Do you need the maid?" he asked.

She nodded.

He pulled the door shut, and she heard a key in the lock before his footsteps moved away. It might be a way out, but not yet. She moved back to the fire and held her hands out over the flames. The heat doing little to relieve the constant chill that seemed to follow her. She could have done with a window, but she knew that would be too much to ask for. She moved over and sat on one of the beds. It was soft, and she was tempted to lie down. But at a tap on the door, she was soon standing.

"Enter," she called, wondering who might be on the other side.

The door creaked open to reveal a young woman.

She could have been Ana not very long ago. The dress was the same, and Ana found herself looking down on her shabbiness.

"Would you like a bath, miss?"

Ana nodded, unsure what she could say that would help her feel any more comfortable in this situation. The girl moved directly to the cupboard and opened the door to reveal a number of dresses. "Do you have a preference?"

Ana shook her head, wondering where the garments had come from and just what the mage expected. They were all dark in colour. She stepped forward and ran her hand over the edge of one of them, taking in the soft, silky material.

"That is a lovely one," the girl said, pulling it out and holding it up before her so that Ana could see it.

Did it matter as long as it was clean? The girl, although similar in size and age to Ana, was freckled with small brown eyes and mouse-brown hair. On the inside of the door was a mirror that Ana hadn't noticed before, and she saw just how this girl must have seen her. Her dress in dusty tatters, her black hair mussed, her face smudged. Ana pushed the door closed.

The girl laid the dress over the bed and then left the room again. When the door creaked open a short time later, the girl looked apologetically to Ana, who was now seated on the bed. She stood.

"I need to ask you to go back to the master," the young woman said.

Ana bowed her head as though she were the maid, then disappeared through the door back into the mage's main workshop. She could hear noise behind the door and realised there must have been others who were needed, and she wasn't to be seen. But so far, she had been seen by the guard and the maid.

She waited, listening to scraping boots, water sloshing and the hushed hurried tones of a conversation she couldn't make out. Then there was a gentle knock on the door, and it opened to reveal a tub in the middle of the floor.

The tub filled the room with a sweet aroma, and Ana wondered what they had put in it. She had drawn baths for the lord at times in the castle, but it was usually someone else's task.

The girl helped Ana from her dress and into the hot water. She stood for a moment before easing herself down, allowing the water to cover as much of her as it could with her knees bent.

She leaned back and let her hair float around her, sighing at the joy of it and wondering if Ende would enjoy such luxuries. He would certainly enjoy the heat of the water, but then he might make it warmer.

Ana relaxed, allowing the warm water to soak the dirt from her skin as she moved slowly beneath the surface, closing her eyes and enjoying the luxury. The girl left her to it, sitting silently nearby in case she needed anything. She remembered such nights, sitting close in case the lord needed anything, but out of her field of vision.

"I can wash your hair," the girl offered, and Ana blinked into the dim light of the room.

She sat forward, allowing the girl access as she ran water through her hair, then rubbed soap through it. She did this several times and then added something else to her hair that smelt of fresh apples.

Ana was distracted for a moment, then realised the woman was leaning over the tub and reaching for her arm. She held it out of the water and let the girl scrub her skin. It was awkward to allow someone into her personal space, but she didn't expect such a luxury to be repeated.

Ana leaned back for a moment and then turned to the woman, who was holding out a large sheet. She sighed before lifting herself from the water, climbing carefully over the edge, shivering as the woman wrapped the sheet around her. Her wet hair ran in rivulets down her back as the woman wrapped it carefully in another sheet pulling the first one from around her body.

Ana almost squealed. The young woman rubbed vigorously over her body and then dropped the sheet on the floor before reaching for more clothing than Ana had seen before. It took almost as long to get her into the new clothes as she had taken in the tub. And when she finished, she opened the cupboard door again for Ana to look at the unknown woman in the looking glass.

No longer a maid, Ana looked like a lady of the court. Although her dress was black, it was flattering, and she looked far more like a woman than she had in the nice gowns she had been given in the mountains. Not that the man in the mountains was a lord, but he pretended.

Ana ran a hand over her hips, still unbelieving. Her face appeared pale, and her hair shone in the firelight although it hung in damp tendrils. She raised a hand to it, and the maid rushed to pull a chair from the table.

"I shall brush it for you," she said, reaching for a brush on the mantle as Ana took a seat. If she had been able to live as the family of the lord rather than as a maid, she wondered if she might have looked like this before.

The maid pulled the brush through her hair, occasionally dabbing at it with the sheet. It was dry before long, and Ana ran her fingers through it. She liked wearing it out. It had always been tied behind her head in some way so that it didn't get in the way of her tasks or fall into the food she carried. Since she had been in the mountains with Dray, she had allowed it out. But it had tangled.

"Would you like me to braid it for you?" the maid asked. And for a moment, Ana wondered how the women of the court wore their hair in the capital.

"No, thank you," she said.

⚙

The regent walked into the main reception hall and stopped. Usually there was more of a show of respect, but the murmuring and chattering continued. He sucked in a deep breath, tried not to show just how frustrated he was and continued towards the long table raised up on the platform at the end of the room.

He pulled the chair out in the middle, dragging it across the tiled floor. The squeal carried through the room as he dragged it slowly. Every face turned to him, the silence perfect, and then the chatter started again.

"Is it true?" a man asked, stepping forward as the chatter continued.

"There is much news about the capital," the regent said carefully, sitting down and placing his hands on the table. A servant appeared quickly and poured his wine. "What in particular have you heard that has caused such a commotion?"

"That the king is gone," the man said, and the murmuring continued.

The regent scowled and stood slowly. The room hushed. "How does such a rumour begin?"

"We never see him," an unknown voice called across the room.

"He is a boy, still dealing with the death of his parents."

"It has been long enough. Is he not strong enough to be King?"

Now there is an idea. "He has been laid low with illness. But," he added, raising his hands at the noise, "he is recovering well enough."

"Where is he?"

"In his rooms. Do you wish to disturb the king to ensure I'm not lying?"

Murmuring continued, but it sounded more like agreement than disbelief.

"I understand how gossip and rumour get out of hand." He sat back slowly and took his time sipping his wine. "When he is of age, you shall see him."

"We saw him when his father was alive."

"The world is a very different place," the regent snapped, and then cleared his throat. "There are those who would harm the boy. We must do what we can to ensure his place on the throne is safe."

"And why does he not sit on it now?" someone else called from the crowd. "Our history is filled with boys who were made King before they were of age."

The regent rolled his shoulders. "That may be, but he has asked for my assistance, and what can I do?"

A servant appeared and leaned over his shoulder. "She's ready," he whispered.

He waved her forward, and the room hushed again.

"We have a guest of His Majesty with us this evening. She will be staying with us now. I would hope that you make her welcome."

Ana stepped out from the alcove, a very different girl from the one who had appeared at his feet. She was a woman, a very enticing woman, and he wondered just what power she had. The mage was sure she could be of use, and of use he would make her.

As she crossed the room, her black hair reflecting the light, her pale beautiful face highlighting her glorious green eyes, the crowd watched in awed silence. He couldn't have planned it better if he had dressed her himself.

"A witch," murmured through the crowd, and she stalled in her walk. He scowled at the room.

"She is our guest. Ana," he said kindly, holding out his hand. She looked from it to the room and then back. She walked towards him. A servant pulled back her chair, and she was seated beside him.

Ana looked down at her hands. He cleared his throat, but she didn't look up. The conversation was hushed around the room, but it continued. He waved forward the servant, who poured wine into the cup before her.

She nodded once, lifted it and took a large gulp. "I am not used to such attention," she whispered.

"You will come to be more comfortable."

"Will I?" she asked, looking at him with the brilliant green eyes he was sure sparkled with something. Perhaps her magic was brighter than the mage thought.

"A guest of the king?" someone asked too loudly, and she looked across the room. "Who knew King Edwin Ilren would be able to befriend such a woman when he never leaves his rooms."

"Edwin Ilren," she said slowly, as though hearing the name for the very first time.

"Anaise," the regent said in return, and she looked back at him with bright eyes. "What is your family name?"

"Excuse me?"

"Who do you belong to? Which clan or group or family?"

"Merrin," she said, still apparently confused as to what he wanted. "But you knew who I was."

He nodded once in agreement, and he remembered the Lord of Sheer Rock had been deliberately vague with some aspects of her family. "Your parents?"

"Dead." She looked at the plate placed before her, but made no move to eat from it. "Again, sir, you know more of my history than I know myself. I had no indication of these gifts or what I could do until your mage arrived to take me away. And then he didn't want me."

"Might you use these gifts on me?"

"I may have already," she said with a small smile. She looked at the food on her plate, although she still made no move to eat.

"Would you like something else?"

"You said he was ill," she said, picking up the fork, her focus on the plate.

"Yes," he said slowly.

"Do you often lie to the people?"

"Only when it is for their own good."

"And the king being ill is good for the people?"

"Do you know where he is?" he asked in a hushed tone,

glancing about the room rather than at her to ensure they weren't overheard. When he looked back to her, she was staring at him with her bright green eyes and the smallest of smiles.

"How long have you been looking?" she asked. "Did you send your mage to search for me to find him for you?"

He shook his head. She reached for his hand and then stopped, curling her fingers in and pulling her hand back.

"Do you think I'm lying?" he asked.

"I do wonder what you think, but I may not want to see what else you are." She pushed the chair back from the table and stood. The room silenced, and all eyes were on her. She bowed her head to the room and then walked away. Although the regent watched her, he knew that every other pair of eyes in the room was focused on her as well.

29

Ana stood over the desk of the mage and watched him work. "Why am I here?" she asked as she had done so many times since she had arrived.

"I thought you would be useful."

"In finding the king?"

He looked up at her then, studying her carefully as though he didn't quite recognise her. "Why would you need to find the king?"

"Because you don't know where he is." She looked around the room for a moment, a room she knew well. "When you came to get me, you changed your mind."

He looked back at the page, as though she was no longer interesting. "What does it matter?"

"It matters," she said, her voice too loud for their proximity. He looked up again, then laid down his pen with a sigh. "You wanted me, and then you didn't, and then you did. I need to know what you saw."

"What did you see?" he asked instead, lacing together his ink-stained fingers.

"What you wanted me to. But there was more. When you first touched me, you hit me." Her hand moved automatically to her cheek.

He sighed. "You were trying to make me ill."

"I thought you might be ill because you were so thin. You used the image you allowed me to see to distract me."

"You are quicker than I thought. What do you think I saw?"

"Something that frightened you," she said, leaning over the desk.

"What could you do that would frighten a man such as myself?"

"I might have been more powerful than you imagined. I might have connected myself to those you would use me to destroy. But it might not matter now what you saw. For the king is missing, and the reason you wanted me dead is now the reason you need me alive."

He tapped his finger twice on the page before him, and a chair appeared beside her. She pulled it out slowly and sat down, folding her hands in her lap. "Where are the others?" she asked, looking around the room beyond his desk. He stared at her and, despite her frustrations, Ana filled the silence. "You were seeking others with gifts as well."

"Perhaps I did not find any?"

Ana opened her mouth and then closed it. She hadn't considered that she might be the only one, although she was sure Dray had said something. Or had it been the lord as the mage had held her face too tightly?

"Perhaps I used them for something else," he said with a shrug. "What do you think I want?" he asked.

"Power. To be more than you are now. Although you claim to work for the king's regent, to better his place in the world, I think you do far more to better your own."

"I'm an old man," he said with a laugh, leaning back from the book. "What could I get?"

"A longer life, a more comfortable life, recognition through the ages."

"Truly? I don't think any of these are important."

"But I am important enough to want dead, and now you think I can help you."

"You will, and the king is not important," he said.

"What did you see?" she asked, leaning forward.

"Would you like me to take another look?"

Ana shook her head and stood. She needed to know why she was where she was, and if what this man had seen was anything like Ende's idea of her. But she didn't want him looking, in fear he might see something else. Something of Ed and Dray. She only hoped that they weren't far away.

"Why is the king not important?" she asked, trying not to fidget with her sleeve. "He is the king."

"The boy doesn't want the title, and he doesn't care for the people. His uncle does. I need to help the people."

Ana laughed easily at how serious he sounded. "You don't care for the people. You could find the king," she said, leaning forward, "like you found me."

"I found your magic. The boy doesn't have any magic, and so I cannot trace him."

Ana wondered how right he might be. She didn't want this man knowing the whereabouts of Ed or who he was with. But she needed to know he was safe. And if she could bring him to the castle like this man had magicked her, it might be easier. Although if she could find him, she wondered if she could bring the others too.

"Tell me of the soldier," the mage asked, interrupting her thoughts.

"What soldier?"

"The one who threw himself across the Walk to save you."

"I asked and he acted." Ana tried to sound bored.

He stared at her, his sharp grey eyes trying to read her, and then his face relaxed and he leaned back. He nodded once. "Where is he now?"

"I don't know," she admitted.

"Will he try to find you?"

"We parted ways," she said.

He continued to watch her, Ana wondering if he could read her.

"Can I try to find the king?" she asked.

"We might not want him found, but you could try. You will need something personal. I shall have the maid take you to his room."

She nodded once and headed back into her room, wondering how he had come to have her coat. It had burned in the copper bowl, that must have been what he had used to find her. The idea of others with gifts niggled at her. Had he found any others? And if so, what had he used them for?

The maid knocked once and entered the room. She could learn something of etiquette herself, Ana thought. But then Ana wasn't a lady of the castle; she was a prisoner of a kind. The maid held the door open and indicated out into the hallway. Ana nodded and moved into the dimly lit passageway. The soldier, someone she hadn't seen before, bowed his head to her.

Ana had asked the maid's name previously, but she wasn't talkative, and Ana had stopped trying to bond with the girl. She might not be anyone important, but Ana was no longer a maid, no longer someone who could chatter and gossip. Ana followed the woman without a word as she led the way to Ed's room, the guard keeping pace behind them.

As they made their way up through the castle, the hallways became lighter and wider. Soon they were passing more people in their travels, some of whom stopped to stare at her. But it wasn't a lavish part of the castle. It reminded Ana of the hallways that led to the kitchens on Sheer Rock. This castle was much larger than the one she had grown up working in, and she longed for a chance to look over the city that surrounded it.

Their journey came to a stop at an ordinary door in the middle of a hallway. The maid nodded once to Ana as she stepped to the side. Ana opened the door herself, and what she saw took her breath away. He was treated as a boy—an insignificant boy—and she realised in that moment why he lacked the confidence he did.

She closed the door quickly behind her and moved into the small space.

There was a narrow bed across the wall by the door, neatly made. On the opposite wall, a large desk sat beneath a window. She leaned over the desk and looked down at the stables. Her hands rested on the desk and the papers spread over it. They didn't treat him as King. No wonder the people questioned not seeing him. He didn't have the chance to know them or himself.

She looked down at the papers beneath her hands, and her eye caught the framed images of a woman and a man at the end of the desk. His parents, she thought, wondering if he had drawn them himself. She could see a similarity between him and his father, but there were elements he shared with his mother.

She sat down on the hard chair at the desk and picked up a sheet of paper. It appeared to be notes about the general history of the kingdom. She scanned through the other pages on the desk. On one she found notes about the stables, with a series of small strokes along the side of the page. Perhaps he was counting something, or watching the men she could now see moving around. She closed her eyes. He hadn't taken a horse, instead walking most of the way to the mountains. Desperation had driven him to find Ende, although he hadn't known whom or what he was trying to find.

If someone had taken the time to look at what he was doing, they might have realised his plans. If she looked now, would she discover where he was? Would that help either of them? She ran her fingers over the ink on the page, closed her eyes and tried to picture him. The sad boy she had first met, sitting at the table in the little cottage in the mountains, came into focus. She remembered sitting beside him, his strong hand in hers, calloused from sword use, shoulder to shoulder and his strong frame.

He isn't a boy.

He hadn't been a boy for a long time, yet the kingdom still thought of him as such. The regent the night before had talked about him coming of age. Surely, he was a man now. What age must he be? Had the regent convinced the people that he was younger than he truly was?

The room was a similar size to the one she had off the side of the mage's work space. She wondered how he had felt living in such a small world. Even her cottage was larger. But he would not have been trapped here all day. He would have had classes and the like, taking him around the castle.

She stood, the chair scraping across the floor as she tried to imagine Ed living in the room. She thought she had a good sense of him, and yet she couldn't picture him here at all. Ana moved slowly to the bed and lay down, looking up at ceiling and imagining the loneliness he had grown up with. She only hoped he had more around him now to support him.

Closing her eyes, Ana tried to picture them all together. Ed and Belle and Dray. They would have made it back to the cottage by now, to Phillip and the general. She couldn't quite focus on an image of Ende, who changed between the scaly red beast and the old man. Even when he was a man, she saw the dragon when she looked at him now, as the gwelka had.

Could that be why he avoided the capital? Had he left because they knew what he was and that was a danger to him? Or had the queen tried to protect him? Ana opened her eyes and glanced across at the image of her on the desk. She had been Ende's friend, and the reason Ed had sought him out. She wondered just what he knew of the man, what he had been told.

She could hear shuffling in the hallway, so she closed her eyes and listened. The sound increased as she focused on it. She wondered what skills she could learn, whether she might have been able to listen to more if she had tried.

"Why have you brought the witch up here?" a man's voice asked. An angry man, but it wasn't a voice she knew. Not that she knew very many in the castle at all.

"The mage directed her."

"Why is that man getting involved?" There was more hatred

than she expected in the voice.

She wondered if his anger was aimed at the missing king or those who had not watched over him as they should. This man might be an ally. She sucked in a breath and waited, but he didn't open the door.

"The mage is not someone to be queried," the maid said. Anna wondered for the first time why a maid would be questioned in such a manner and what she might know.

"Does no one care where the boy is?" the man asked, desperation in his tone. "Does no one want him returned?"

Ana stood slowly and opened the door. "The whole kingdom would want him returned," she said carefully. The older man beside the maid turned a hateful look towards her, glancing at her up and down. She stood rigid, holding tight to the door. He had a weathered face, like Dray's in a way, and yet he was smaller, more sinew than muscle. "I am trying to find him," she said, looking back into the room and scanning the scant objects for something distinctly his. "He has his sword," she murmured, releasing the door, and the man was suddenly pushing her inside and closing the door behind him, leaning into it.

"How do you know that?"

"I saw it," she said carefully. These people thought she was a witch; she might be able to play on that fear to learn what she needed to find Ed.

"The idiot," he murmured, looking down.

"I do not think that an appropriate term for the king."

He glanced up at her. "Where is he?"

She shook her head. "Far," she said. She didn't know if she could trust this man, but then he might be someone who knew Ed better than others. "Does he know how to use the sword?"

"Quite well," the man said with a sigh. "But I doubt he would have the courage to use it against another man."

"He had the courage to leave."

"That surprised me too. But did he?" he asked, looking at her now. "Did he go willingly, or was he taken?"

"Who would take him?"

"The…" He stopped and looked her over again. "You are quite young yourself," he said.

She raised her eyebrows. "A boy king and a girl witch, what a kingdom we have."

He growled something under his breath that she couldn't make out, and she waited. "Why are you here?" he eventually asked.

"In the castle? I was taken from where I was, unwillingly. Here in this room? To find Ed," she said, looking around again.

At the silence, she turned slowly, cursing herself at the easy slip of the tongue. The mage would find a better use for her if he found out their connection. She reached out a hand, unsure how to plead for this man's silence when she didn't know which side he stood on or whom he reported to. Too many could make false claims as to who they were, she realised, thinking of the gwelka. She gulped down a sudden fear that they might have all been eaten.

"Where did you see him?" he asked, stepping forward.

"Who?" she asked, looking around the room.

"The king." He waited, and she turned back to his expectant face. "Edwin."

She shrugged.

"Why would you call him Ed?"

"It was how he introduced himself," she said. "I don't know where he is now. I want to find him, but I don't know how."

Now he raised his eyebrows. "I am Master Forest, Sword Master." He bowed, and she stepped back. "And you are?"

"The witch," she muttered.

"They have made it appear so. Who were you before then?"

"Ana Merrin," she whispered.

"Merrin?" he asked, his voice loud as he stepped forward again. She backed into the desk, bumping it and knocking over the image of the queen.

She nodded.

"Tevis Merrin?"

"My father," she said, straightening. "You knew him?"

"He's dead?"

She nodded, and he surprised her by taking her hands. "When?"

"Many years ago."

"Where did you meet the king?"

"In the mountains."

"Edge Mountains? What was he doing all the way up there?"

"Looking for help," she said, squaring her shoulders and pulling from his hold. "I don't know you, sir, even if you knew my father. I am just a hideous witch." She turned away from him. "You cannot trust what I say."

"You are no witch," he said. "They may have made you look like one, and I'm sure you have gifts they want for themselves. You are so like your mother."

"I cannot remember her," she said, turning back to him.

"You could be her," he said as he took her face in his hands.

"How did you know them?" she asked, pulling back and moving around the small room so he could not pin her against anything else.

"I served together with your father in the King's Men."

She shook her head. "My father was no soldier."

"Long ago, the world was different."

"It has barely changed from my perspective," she said unkindly. "And what did you do, sir, to keep the king safe?"

"I taught him all I could with a sword and his feet and his mind."

"Forest," she murmured, remembering the look on Belle's face when she pointed out the king. Had they not seen who he was because they weren't looking, or because he was better at hiding it than Ana had thought?

The man looked at her expectantly.

"He introduced himself as Ed Forest."

"He might actually survive," the man said, sitting heavily on the bed. "If he can stay away."

Ana shook her head. "He needs to claim what is his."

"His uncle will destroy him."

"Not if we protect him."

"You are a girl," he said too loudly. "What could you do to protect him?"

"Maybe you are right," she said, giving the man a shallow curtsy. "He should stay lost." She pulled the door open and then stopped. Without glancing at the sword master, she returned to the desk, picked up the fallen image of the queen and then headed back out into the hallway.

"I have all I need," she said to the maid, who glanced in at the sword master before she turned back in the direction they had come.

"Wait," he called after her, but she continued forward, the maid unwavering in her pace and the guard behind. He might think Ed better off away from the castle, but Ana would find a way to reach him.

30

Ende looked over the group before him and tried not to sigh out loud. This was a far cry from the soldiers he had travelled with previously. The captain might be worth something, and the boy could hold the sword, but he didn't know whether he could actually use it.

"We have a long way to go," he murmured.

Drayton looked at him expectantly, but he shook his head.

"We need to be sure what we are going for."

"Ana," the king said without reservation.

Belle licked her lower lip and glared at him. "I thought you wanted to reclaim your crown."

"And that," he said, but he didn't take his eyes from Ende.

"I can only do so much for you," Ende said. "In many ways, you will need the girl. But long before we reach her, we need to make it through this kingdom alive. I have my doubts as to whether we can do that to any degree of competency."

"You think we are going to die." Belle scowled, and the king reached out to put a hand on her arm. She turned her glare on him, but the anger eased. "What can we do?"

Ende closed his eyes and tried not to sigh. He had no idea. There were not enough of them to make any real difference. He didn't know if they should raise a force on their way or rely on the girl. He was certain she lived, but how well he couldn't tell. And he couldn't gauge whether her time alone with the mage, and possibly Prince Thom, might twist her as they had originally wanted. They would need to find a way to keep her on their side. But then, she didn't yet have the control of her skills to do anything. He hoped.

"Ende?" the captain asked warily.

"I don't know," he admitted.

"We are packed with provisions and have gold to buy more. Let us start this journey and find ourselves along the way," Phillip said, adjusting the pack on his back and striding out before the others. "I thank you, General, for your hospitality."

The old man bowed his head. "I'm here when you need me," he said, looking at Ende.

Ende wondered if he would survive this journey himself to return to the mountains he had come to love. People were not what he had thought they were. Some were better than he hoped, but too often they disappointed him. He had hoped Ana was one of the good ones, but as he looked over the straggly group before him, he feared he might be leading them into something very different because of her.

"Time to stop thinking about this and start moving," the captain said, and Ende nodded in agreement.

With Phillip leading, they made their way slowly down the mountain. The Near Forest grew closer, and he looked at the dense canopy, wondering what might lurk beneath it. He had rarely walked beneath it, preferring to fly above it, and it had been some time since he had done that.

"Ana is better than you think she is," the captain said, walking behind him.

"She is in your head," Ende said.

"It is more than that."

"Is it?" Ende stopped and turned back to the man. He seemed very sure of himself.

"I have seen a lot in my time," he said.

Ende laughed, a loud booming noise that echoed around them and made the others ahead on the path stop and look back. "Have you indeed, young man?" Ende asked, emphasising his last words. "You have no idea of what I have seen."

"We are helping a king regain his crown."

"It will be far more than that. These things always are. The great fight of his grandfather's time. What do you think started such a battle, that it dragged the entire kingdom to war?"

The captain opened his mouth and then closed it.

"There is a reason you are the soldier you are. A reason you chose to stand with the king."

The man nodded, and he saw then what the girl had seen in him. The strength, despite his tired ways, and the dedication he had to his post. There was more to him. There had been when he was just a soldier, then as a captain and now.

"You are not the king's man," Ende said, "and she has done that, deliberately or not."

"I'll protect him with my life."

"I don't doubt that," Ende said. "But you do it not because of who you are, but because of who she is and your connection to her."

"Are you so sure she is dangerous?"

Ende sucked in a deep breath and, with a nod, turned back down the path.

They walked in silence for a time, and then the man behind him cleared his throat. "What do you think she is?"

"I don't honestly know. I see conflicting ideas of her. I can see a kindness." He stopped and turned back to the soldier, looking even more tired than when they had started out, and not due to the walking. "I can see that she truly cares, but there is something else—whether that is the idea that she is dangerous, or that when she learns what she truly is, she will become something else."

"She didn't even know she was gifted," the captain insisted.

"But others did," Ende murmured, turning back along the path.

"Ana is the lord's niece."

Ende nodded slowly. He had known her mother briefly, and he could understand that the lord would know what Ana was even if she hadn't seen it. She would know what to look for. "She had been in the castle of the Lord's Seat all that time?"

"Yes," the soldier behind him said.

"And no one told her who she was?"

"I don't know that there was anyone to tell. Her parents are gone. There was a boy," he said slowly, and as much as Ende was tempted to turn back and read his face, he continued forward. "Tim?" the captain wondered aloud. "He worried that she didn't have her cloak."

Ende stopped so suddenly that the captain nearly walked into the back of him. "Cloak," he said.

"I had marched her out. My only thought was to get her as far away from the Walk as possible," he murmured, "to save her. We didn't stop for supplies or cloaks. I shared mine," he said, looking at Ende as though for reassurance that he had looked after her well enough in running away with her.

"Did she have a cloak at the castle?"

"I don't know, but I would assume so. Does it matter now?"

"It might," Ende said, "it just might."

"Will we camp inside the forest tonight?" Belle asked. Ende shook the image forming in his mind, but it didn't quite take shape.

"Yes," Ed said, picking up his pace a little.

Ende looked out through the stringy trees that dotted the rocky landscape. They had some way to go before they would reach the base of the mountains and then make it across the plains. "Are you sure we can make the distance?" It was still early morning, but he thought it was too far, at least for Belle and Phillip.

"We have to," Ed said, stepping around Phillip and taking the lead. "It will keep us safe."

Ende slowed as he watched the young king stride out ahead of them, only slowing when his feet slipped on the gravely path and he looked back to ensure they were following.

"What did you see?" Ende asked.

He shook his head and kept walking.

Ende moved easily past the girl and her father and stopped in front of the king with his hand on his chest.

"How did you…?" he stammered, then looked down at the hand.

"What did you see?" Ende asked again.

"I don't think I saw anything, but I had a feeling."

"A feeling could be the same," Ende encouraged.

The young man sucked in a deep breath and then blew out softly, letting his head fall back to look up at the sky.

"I'll believe you," Ende whispered.

"The forest protected the girls," he said quickly.

"Not from those men," Belle snapped.

"I think it did," he said, turning to her. "Those who ran off wouldn't have been able to find you again. When I stepped outside the clearing, I couldn't see the light or hear the chatter and laughter…"

"We weren't that loud," she said defensively.

"You were," he said, laughter in his voice, and then his brow creased. "But when I was outside the clearing it was as though you weren't there." He turned back to Ende, whose hand still rested on the young man's chest. "Will it protect us all or only some of us?"

"That is to be seen," Ende said. "It may not let me in at all," he added, allowing his hand to drop and turning to look over the distant mass of green.

"Who lives in there?"

"All sorts, including the Near Folk. It may be that they kept the girls safe, although it might be that they wanted the girls for themselves."

"If that were the case," Belle said, "they would have taken us before my father and the king arrived."

"Maybe they were waiting for an opportunity. Maybe the men

were keeping you safe from them."

Belle shivered. "Are they like the gwelka?"

Ende shook his head slowly.

"Please call me Ed," the boy said with a sad sigh.

"I don't think that I should," she said politely. "And if we want to make the trees before nightfall, I suggest we get moving."

"But do we?" the captain asked.

"The boy might be right," Ende admitted, stepping back to allow him to lead the way. He waited for the farmer and his daughter to continue down the path and then joined in at the same place he had started in the line.

"The king and his merry band," he murmured as they continued down the mountainside. "Let's hope this isn't the last the world sees of us."

"You know you have quite a negative outlook on life," Dray quipped behind him.

"Gwelka and Near Folk," Belle said ahead of him. "All we need now is a dragon to swoop from the sky and eat us, and you might actually be happy."

It was Dray who laughed first, and Ende had to laugh with him.

They travelled mostly in silence through the rest of the day. All of them focused on some different aspect of where they were going and why, or where they had come from. But Ende was surprised that the sky was only just turning orange as they made it to the edge of the forest. Ende watched the group move as one beneath the trees while he waited, unsure if this was the right path. Within moments, he lost sight of them and knew the king was right. He just wondered if the forest was saving them from him too.

"Ed?" came a desperate cry, and he raced forward to find the group standing as one not far from the edge of the forest.

The voice had sounded like Ana's, and as he joined the group, an image of a woman in black disappeared.

"Who was that?" Belle asked.

"Ana," Ed and Dray said at the same time, glancing at each other and then turning to Ende.

"I didn't see anything," he murmured, "but I heard her."

"How?" Dray asked.

He shook his head. She might be trying to find them with the same magic that dragged her away. But was she looking because she wanted to be back amongst them, or was someone else making her look?

"That was not the shape of the maid," Phillip said, his old face blushing in the dim light. "That was a woman. I think you are being tricked by a witch."

Again, the group looked to Ende. "There could be any number of explanations," he said. "And I don't know any of them with certainty. At least the boy appears to be right about the forest." He looked around and then back to the group, where the king seemed somewhat disappointed. "Sorry, Your Majesty. Slip of the tongue. But once you entered the trees, I couldn't hear you. It was only at the girl's call that I knew where you were."

"Ana," the boy said.

"Maybe," Ende conceded. "Shall we set up camp here? We can consider our way forward in the morning."

"If it was Ana…?" Ed asked.

"Then she will try and try again until she finds you," Ende said, pulling the bag from his back.

"We are meant to be saving her," he said with a shake of his head.

"Maybe you will save each other," he said, reaching for a dried branch near his feet and then another. "Now let us get a fire started so you don't freeze during the night."

31

Ana stared at the scorched edges of the ink drawing. She wasn't quite sure what she hoped she would find, or whether she would manage to reach him, but all she had seen was trees. She thought she had seen the silhouettes of Dray and Ed, but she couldn't be sure it was them. She only hoped that when she did find them, Ed wouldn't be too angry that she had damaged his mother's portrait.

She had at least taken it from the frame. Although she knew that he held it regularly, she didn't know if he had painted it himself. She turned it over now, the other side of it blank, and the burnt edges marked her fingers when she turned it back. She was almost tempted to wipe them on her apron before she remembered she no longer wore one.

It had been some weeks since she had served at the Seat of the Lord. Now it was she who was waited on in another castle, yet she couldn't quite place who she was or why her life was so different.

She had called to Dray, asked him to save her, and he had. All without really knowing what had happened. He was coming again to save her, she thought, and although she wanted to call out for him, she knew she didn't need to. She looked up from the painting towards the door.

The mage provided her space and time to explore what she thought she might be and, surprisingly, how she might be able to reach the king. She didn't think they had worked out her connection to him. Although the sword master had.

He cared about the whereabouts of the king for a different reason than these other men, and she wondered if he would help her. Although seeking him out risked angering the mage, and she was sure there was much she could learn from him.

"Any luck?" the mage asked, appearing in the doorway.

Standing in the middle of her room, looking at the image on the bed, Ana shook her head.

"Magic calls to magic," he said.

"There has to be another way."

"You could try more of his items. The more personal the better. You have his mother's image; do you have the pen he drew her with? Or…"

"Tell me," she begged.

"Try calling to him from his room. King Edwin rarely went out and was very private. Perhaps the room itself can assist you."

"What will you do when I find him?"

He laughed as he turned back for his study. "*If* you find him?" He cackled. "I doubt you could come close."

"What do you know of my gifts?" she asked, unmoving.

He shrugged then, as he had done the last time she had asked.

"You could teach me."

"I would rather you found it on your own."

"Why?" she asked, turning fully towards him as he walked away. "How would that help you? It could take me years."

"I'm in no hurry," he called over his shoulder. "And it worked for your mother."

Ana stared after him, her heartbeat pounding in her ears. Had she been trapped in this room, trying to discover what she was and what that meant? She looked towards the empty doorway. Did he really know her? Had she been on his side, or he on hers? The world was turned around, and Ana no longer knew what she had.

She opened the other door and headed along the corridor without glancing at the soldier. She walked with purpose, and he didn't question as he followed her to the king's door. She put her hand on it and closed her eyes.

She couldn't sense him here. She feared the mage might be right that magic called magic and without it, she couldn't reach him.

Trying not to sigh, she lifted her hand from the wood and headed back the way she had come. She branched off from the main corridor, wanting to see more of the castle to get more of an idea of Ed, as well as the men who both wanted him found and yet didn't. Had it always been this way? she wondered. Did anyone in power risk losing it to those who wanted more than they had?

She paused by a lead-lined window. She didn't need anything that she hadn't had before. Despite who she was and what had been taken from her, Ana had been content in her way, every day the same. Yet here she was seeking out something she'd never thought she had, magic.

The castle was lit by large torches, although the shadows outweighed the light. Where might they be now, and should they stay away?

She walked a little further into a large open courtyard. She could hear the distant noises of horses. Other than a few soldiers, she didn't see anyone. The air was warm as she breathed it in. If she'd had nights like this, she might have spent far more time out socialising. Tim came to mind, with his concern for her lack of a cloak, and she wondered if he would have stood in the evening air with her.

She turned and looked back past the soldier. The mage hadn't just used her cloak to call her; he had used something that caused the strange flames and smoke. He had used magic to call magic. Ana had only tried to use her connection to Ed, and she had very nearly made it. She wondered then what she might learn if he took the time to teach her, and what she might achieve.

A man appeared before her, and it took all she had not to jump as he materialised out of the darkness. The sword master. She bowed her head, and he narrowed his eyes. Then he glanced at the soldier, and if she hadn't been watching him, she might have missed it.

"The king has not returned," he said.

"I'm not sure what I can do to rectify it," she said honestly.

"You are a witch. Surely you can magic something up."

The soldier stepped a little closer, but she held up her hand and was surprised at how easily he stopped. "Maybe you would like to walk with me?" she asked softly of the sword master. "I am not used to such warm evening weather."

"It won't last," he said, indicating back into the dark. She glanced at the guard, willing him to stay where he was, and then followed the master into the darkness.

"In many ways, I miss the sea breeze," she said, finding him not far into the dark. "Who else walks of a night?" she asked.

"I don't know," he whispered, and she leaned a little closer to hear him.

"I might not have the skills you hope I do."

"Or you might have more. The question is whether or not you will use them to help the crown."

"Does it matter to you who wears it?"

"The king," he whispered hoarsely.

Ana sighed. She didn't know if she could trust this man. She thought—or hoped—that she could, but she didn't know him. He might very easily be a spy of the regent. "What does he want with me?" she wondered aloud.

"The king?"

"His uncle."

"Has he not told you?"

"It wasn't very long ago they wanted me dead, and now they don't."

"They don't want him returned."

"No," she admitted easily. "But they are happy for me to try and find him."

"If something were to happen to him, it might easily be your fault. Witches are unpredictable."

She knew that his words were meant as a warning, but she regretted being unable to see his face. "Is this all it is about?" she asked, and he stopped.

Without the crunch of their shoes on the gravel, and with the sudden silence of the horses, as though they too listened to who else might be hidden in the darkness, the world seemed to cool around them. She shivered.

"What have you heard?" he asked.

"Nothing," she said. "Which is why I'm now curious about it." She took a deep breath. She had to trust someone, and this man had known her father. "They want him locked away, not taking the crown or even asking for it to be returned. Although the boy king has long ago ceased to be a boy. They need me, but I'm not sure what for. And it is far more than the crown that he wants."

"It could simply be that he wants to rule the kingdom."

"Perhaps," she murmured, walking on. "But he rules now."

"He is a proxy." The older man's voice lifted through the darkness. "The guard?"

"He will stay where he was directed to, although I cannot guarantee he did not hear you."

"The regent must become the true heir to be granted all that goes with it."

"To be seen as the rightful king," she whispered.

"Exactly. Then he would be more likely to keep the kingdom together."

"Everyone still pays tribute…"

"But not as they did. The world is not what it was in the previous king's time, and there are rumours of unrest."

Ana waited. This man had heard far more than she had herself. There were no signs of unrest on Sheer Rock. Although she rarely saw anyone, rumour spread faster than illness in a castle.

"The gwelka," she said, thinking of the little grey man.

"They may be part of the problem. And the Near Folk aren't as obliging as they were."

"The Near Folk? Are they not myth?"

He laughed and tugged at his sleeve. She leaned forward as the silver scar caught the moonlight. "I never heard of them attacking people, but it may be that they think they too have a chance to grab the power. Without the rightful heir on the throne, wearing the crown of Ilia, the regent may have no chance to leave his place to an heir of his own."

"He's not married," she said slowly.

"He may have other plans."

Ana stared out into the darkness. She didn't understand what the world wanted from her, or what it was meant to be.

Ana heard the movement before she saw it, and then a girl appeared in the dim light beside the master. She hung back, but Ana felt something from her.

"My daughter," the master murmured.

The lights around the edges of the courtyard seemed to increase, and as she stepped into the light Ana saw something she didn't expect. The girl would have only been a few years younger than herself, red blond hair and strikingly beautiful.

Her eyes were dark, and in the dim light Ana wasn't sure that she was seeing exactly what was in front of her. The sword master's arm moved slowly to block her, to protect the girl from Ana, and she knew the feeling was right.

She reached out quickly, grabbing the girl by the arm and dragging her closer.

"Papa," the girl cried, clearly frightened of the dark witch before her, but Ana didn't care. She had found her way to him.

"Ed," she whispered.

32

The firelight crackled, and a strange hush covered the clearing before Ed heard his name called. Clearly this time, pulling him from his half-sleep state. Belle stirred beside him, and then he saw a shimmer and was on his feet. As were Dray and Ende.

Standing before the fire and reaching for him was Ana. She looked very different, but it was certainly her. Her dark hair was loose and reflected the firelight, giving him the impression that she had returned to them. A strange shimmer around her indicated that she wasn't there in body. One hand reached to him while the other appeared to be closed around something, but he couldn't quite tell what.

"Don't touch her," Ende hissed, his hand on his arm. Ed hadn't even realised that he was reaching for her. "You don't know who sent her."

"You are not safe," Ana said. "I'm not sure whether to tell you to stay away or return.

"Ana?" Dray asked, stepping forward, but she didn't acknowledge him or turn his way. Her eyes only focused on Ed.

"What have they done to you?" Ed asked, taking in her changed form. He had seen her as a woman at the castle of the mountain lord, but this was something very different.

"You don't like it?" she asked, disappointment in her voice as she ran her hand over her side. He gulped down the wonder at who this woman was.

"Ana, how did you reach me?" he asked, trying to distract himself.

. She held up her hand then, and another came into focus.

"Salima," he breathed. As Ana's eyes hardened, he wondered if they had done more than dress her differently.

"He said I couldn't reach you. That only magic could find magic."

"Ana?" Ende interjected, and she only glanced his way, her focus on Ed.

"I found the magic to find you. But I don't know if I can use it to bring you here."

They stood in silence as Ed wondered if she was working for the mage, learning from him and so helping him. Dray's hand was heavy on his shoulder. He felt as though he had let them all down by allowing her to be taken, and then for Ana finding Salima.

"Dray?" she said, her voice soft, and Ed thought she might cry.

"Why is it not safe?" Dray asked, giving Ed's shoulder a gentle squeeze.

"There are too many who doubt, and his uncle… It is more than the crown."

"Can you return to us?" Dray asked, his voice soft and coaxing as though talking to a child, or to a madman on a ledge. "Can you step to us?" he asked, raising his hand to her, and Ed noticed Ende's uncertainty.

She reached forward, and for a moment Ed was sure she had taken the soldier's hand, but as soon as he thought she had become solid, she disappeared.

Dray released his hold and stepped forward. Ed's legs failed, and he slumped to the ground.

Ende looked from where she had been and then to Ed. "She has magic," he said.

"We knew that," Belle said behind them, but Ed couldn't turn.

There was too much going through his mind. He could only nod.

"Who is the girl?" Ende whispered, and Ed looked up at him.

He wasn't sure what Ana had seen in her or how she had managed to connect them. "The magic," Ed whispered, thinking of Ana's hand closed so tight around the girl's arm. "She said she found the magic."

"Who is the girl?" Ende asked more firmly, his deep voice resonating through Ed and drawing his attention.

"The sword master's daughter," he said quickly.

Ende opened his mouth and then closed it.

"How is she connected to you?" Dray asked, and Ed turned to him. "Ana found it; perhaps others can as well."

"They don't know to look," he murmured, then focused on Belle in the firelight, her face crumpling with disappointment. He looked up at the group standing around him, wanting to trust them yet uncertain as to what they might do with the information. Something had shifted in Ende, something hard, and he took a small step back. Ed wondered if he would see the dragon now.

"Ana said you were in danger," Belle said, kneeling beside him and blowing out a slow breath. "We should stay away."

"The danger will not dissipate by staying away," Dray said.

"How can it be?" Ende said more to himself than anyone else, moving away from the fire.

Ed climbed slowly to his feet and looked up at the soldier, wondering if he could ever be seen as more than just a boy in his eyes. "Are you the king's man?" he asked.

The soldier looked at Ende's back before he nodded.

"He thinks that you are hers."

"What do you ask?" Captain Drayton said, standing tall.

"Do you think I should wear the crown?"

The man blinked in surprise and then smiled, resting his hand on Ed's shoulder again. "Yes," he said. Then he looked back to the fire and where Ana had stood not so long ago. "Your doubt is because of the girl."

"The sword master doesn't have a child," Ende murmured, moving back into the light, and Ed wondered at the confusion. He was sure that he had worked out who she was just as Ana had, and yet he seemed to find it harder to accept.

"Then whose child is she that she could connect Ana to the king?" Belle asked.

"My sister," Ed admitted, fear making the words sound forced and scratchy. "Salima."

"The queen only had one child. The other died with her," Dray said, repeating the story told by so many.

"It was my father's way of keeping her safe. He was the only one who knew the truth, and when he died, the loyal soldier who had hidden her returned. I knew immediately, although he never admitted the truth. I knew her."

"As Ana did, because of her connection to you," Ende finished. "The child was never mentioned after your mother died, as it was seen to be the cause of her death. Your father at times openly admitted that he was glad the child had not survived, for he would not have been able to look upon him as a true son."

"Another way to keep her safe," Ed said. "In some ways I was an only child, and there were only three of us who knew the truth."

"Three?" Belle asked.

"She doesn't know who she truly is," Ed said, turning to Belle for the first time. "Master Forest thought it best to protect her, and I couldn't tell her. She missed a different mother."

Ende nodded slowly and sucked in a deep breath that caught in his throat.

"I'm sorry," Ed said. "I know you were my mother's friend." He stopped then and looked at the old man, who raised inky eyes to meet his. "You knew she was with child," he said slowly, and the old man nodded once. "But you didn't return when she died."

"When they died, there was nothing to return for." He sounded distant.

Ed stared at the old man for too long. "Ende," he said slowly.

"Endeavour. *You* were her truest friend."

"Not true enough, it appears." Ende moved back to the tree he had been sitting against when they had settled for the night.

Ed looked back to the flames of the fire, hoping Ana would keep Salima and their secret safe.

33

Salima pulled her arm from witch's fierce grip and took a step back. She could still see Ed's hazy outline in the darkness, as though his ghost had remained after their connection was severed.

"Why did that work? Why did you need me?" she asked hurriedly, trying to swallow the odd bitter taste that lingered at the back of her throat.

"Magic," the woman murmured, "and blood."

Salima looked at the witch, whose face had softened in the dim light of the torches as she looked in the direction Ed had been. *Who is she to Ed?*

"Mistress Merrin," her father said, drawing her attention, and Salima looked from the witch to him, reminded that he was there. "Stop."

Her father had assured her that the woman was willing to help find Ed. But there was something else she had seen when she had taken her arm and dragged them across the kingdom to Ed. Although she knew she hadn't moved at all.

The look on the woman's face at her father's instruction scared her enough that she pushed her way between them. "How did you reach him?" she asked, not satisfied with the earlier response.

"You are very determined, aren't you, little princess?"

"Don't get smart," Salima quipped. "Just tell me how you reached Ed."

"We have a connection to him, you and I," she said. She smiled, but it made Salima's skin crawl.

"He's my friend."

"And mine. Yet I needed something else to help me find him."

"Magic?"

"In a way." She actually looked a little lost for a moment.

"Can you bring him home?" Salima asked.

"I'm not sure if I could, if I should. I'm worried…" She stopped, looking to Salima's father before focusing on Salima. "You don't know what you are to him."

"I'm his friend," she said again, finding that she was standing straighter although the woman was taller, older and beautiful. Her long dark hair was even a little intimidating.

"Mistress Merrin." Her father's voice carried a dangerous edge.

The witch glanced at him again and then softened, as she had when she had stared after Ed. She nodded once. "Call me Ana."

Salima tried not to sigh. "Who are you?" she asked with frustration before she could stop herself.

Ana turned away. Salima reached forward and grabbed her arm, similarly to how the woman had grabbed her earlier, but not with the same vice-like hold. Ana looked at the hand, then at Salima and then at her father.

He shook his head once.

"There is more than you know," she said to him.

"I don't need to know anything other than where the king is," he growled. Salima turned to him, letting her hand fall from the woman's warm skin, missing the heat almost instantly. Without warning, the woman turned and took her in her arms, holding her close. She blew a slow breath over the top of her head. Salima wasn't sure which one of them it was meant to comfort. And for a moment she felt the woman reaching through her, searching for something deep within her.

"Ed travels with others," she whispered. "Those who would like to know you."

"Friends?"

Salima felt Ana nod against her. "Friends who would die to protect him."

"Why did you leave him?" Salima asked, suddenly wanting to cling to this woman and her comforting warmth. Then she remembered the frightening look on the woman's face, and she wondered if she should trust or fear her. And whether she could do both.

"It was not my choice."

Salima pulled back reluctantly. "Whose choice was it?"

"The mage and regent," her father whispered.

Ana nodded. The kinder, softer woman almost called to her. Salima had never really felt a connection to anyone as she did to Ed and her father. She couldn't remember her mother, as she had died when she was born. Her father was all she knew, and he hadn't remarried. There had never been a mother figure in her life, and she wasn't sure that this woman fit her idea of a mother.

"You and Ed are drawn together," Salima said, almost voicing what she felt for herself.

Ana nodded. "We were. I dreamt of him before we met."

"It appeared as though you spoke to others as well as the king," Salima's father said.

"Dray," she said softly. "A soldier, and Ende was with him."

"Ende?" he asked slowly. "Ende is with the king?"

She nodded. "You knew him."

He glanced quickly at Salima and then nodded.

"The old man avoids the capital. It must have been some time since he was last here," Ana said.

"Old man?"

"You know what he is?" Ana asked, confusion flitting across her face.

Salima wondered who this other man was. "You are connected with them all. That is why you saw them when I couldn't," she said.

Ana focused on her; her brow knitted. "You couldn't see the old man?"

She shook her head.

"It wasn't so long ago he was young and wild," Salima's father said.

"I think he is still wild in his way," Ana said, laughter at the edge of her voice. Salima smiled at her comfortable ease. "He has helped me greatly, although he wasn't sure he should."

"Why?" Salima asked quickly.

"He thinks I might be dangerous," Ana said almost absently.

"I can see that," Salima admitted, and her father glared at her. "Well, it is true. I'm not sure whether I should run from you or throw my arms around you."

"I'm don't think that Ende is sure either." Ana smiled, and Salima felt the urge to hold her again. When Ana reached for Salima, she took a step back.

"I feel your confusion," Ana murmured. "I need to return." She bowed her head to Salima's father and then disappeared into the darkness.

He let out a slow breath as she disappeared. "If Ende fears she is dangerous, she may well be."

"Who is Ende?" Salima asked. "I have never heard you mention him before."

"He's an old friend from before you were born."

"You didn't talk about him as though he was a friend."

"He was a difficult man. Selfish and hot headed."

"Ana described him as an old man. He might have learnt as he aged."

"Do you see me as an old man?"

"Of course not, Papa," Salima said, wrapping her arms around him. She was comfortable with him, yet she didn't feel the same comfortable warmth she had with Ana.

"He was close in age to myself. Perhaps he hasn't aged as well."

"You will always be the most handsome of men to me," she said, squeezing him tight.

Lying in her narrow bed that night, Salima couldn't sleep. Her father paced in the room next door, his feet heavy on the boards and constant in their movement. The evening's events wouldn't stop running through her mind. The vision of Ed. Just Ed, she had thought, as though she had only seen him. Yet she knew she had travelled across the world. Or at least across the kingdom.

She closed her eyes and focused on the image of Ed, his relief initially at seeing Ana and then the uncertainty at her using Salima. Was it just because they were friends, or was there something else? She didn't think that he saw her as the woman he saw in Ana. But did it change the way he looked at Ana?

He hadn't been alone. There was an older soldier, similar in age or perhaps younger than her father, yet something about him told her he could be trusted, and she didn't think it was the black armour of the King's Men.

She looked beyond him to the old man at Ed's other side. He was old, older than her father by many years. In fact, it seemed he could be old enough to be her grandfather. Was this the man her father knew? But he wasn't what her father had described.

There were other people behind him in the trees. Thick, ancient trees. Another older man, and a young woman. Another beauty, although very different from the witch. Her blond hair, although dishevelled, was still golden in the firelight. Salima looked around the clearing as though she had stepped through the magic gate created by Ana. She moved easily amongst the people in the group, hearing them all and looking back at Ana's form as Ed would have seen her.

She could feel the tension in the clearing. The uncertainty of the soldier, talking to her so calmly while she felt his worry. Ed's excitement, the old man's fear. Or was it joy? She paused by him, trying to determine what he was, and what he felt about the situation and Ana.

She reached for him, but before she could lay her fingers on his sleeve, the heat pushed her back. It was as though he was hot enough to burn her. A strange mix of emotion washed over her, and then he turned jet-black eyes on her.

Salima opened her eyes, her breath short and her heart beating fast in her chest.

It was as though she had seen her end and her beginning in those eyes.

Ana stood in the shadows of the mage's workspace. It appeared different from before. It was no longer a place of wonder; it had become a place of possibilities. She could feel items calling to her from the shelves, some of which tried to coax her forward while others screamed in fear.

Her world had changed in reaching Ed, not because she had reached him but because of how she had. It was the girl, with the blood running hot through her veins. She wondered at how such a child had come into existence, and how she had managed to remain hidden in plain sight with the sword master.

The girl had no idea of who or what she was, and yet Ana had felt it the moment she had laid eyes on her. It was a wonder that no one else had. Over the sounds of the workspace, she watched the mage bent over his book. The ink scratched across the pages. He seemed to sense so much, yet this girl escaped him.

Moving around to stand over the desk, Ana focused on the strange words he etched across the pages. Then she leaned closer, almost over his shoulder when she felt him flinch.

"What are you doing?" he asked, but there was more fear than anger in his voice.

"Why are you writing that way?"

He looked back at the book, then flicked back through the pages. "You can read it?"

"My father ensured that I learnt to read."

"But this is not a language your father could have taught you." He turned in the small space between him and the book and then stood slowly. Ana took a step back, and he closed the large book with surprising ease. It had looked so heavy.

"What have you done?"

She gave him a questioning look, then shook her head as the noise in the room increased. He held up a hand, and it ceased.

"What do you think I can do for you?" she asked instead.

"I want you to learn."

"And yet you don't teach."

"Do I need to?" He took a step forward, his hand reaching out for her, but she stepped back out of his reach and he stopped. "You are already all you need to be. You just needed to find it."

"How?"

"That I cannot answer. Your mother unlocked the magic with a trigger, but I cannot tell you what that might be, or what it was." He looked at her seriously then, as though trying to read her. "Do you know what caused the change?"

She wasn't sure if it was reaching Ed, the princess she had used to reach him or the shadow of Ende she felt in the castle. He was right, something had changed within her; something had been set free.

"You have not explained why you dragged me here, or what you want from me."

"You are to be the king's witch."

"I might already be," she said, the corner of her mouth lifting and her confidence growing at the uncertainty on his face. Then he too smiled.

"There is to be a new king. You will put him on the throne and serve him."

Ana hoped with everything she had that he meant Ed. Although he already had the title, he didn't yet hold the power. She knew he meant another. "If I refuse? Do you really think you can make me do anything I do not want to?"

"Have you changed so much?" he asked, stepping forward again, and Ana felt the shelves behind her push into her back. "I can take so much from you still if you do not do as you are required."

"I don't have anything left to give," she said.

"Don't you?" he asked. He waved his hand, and the strained sounds of the room returned, the call and cries of lost souls.

"There is nothing you could do to me." She stood straighter as he turned back to the book, his hand on the heavy, worn leather.

"I could think of something," he murmured, taking a deep breath. "It wasn't so long ago you would sacrifice for the king. Does it matter who that king is?"

"The people will care."

He gave a small laugh and waved her from the room.

"Why do you need me to do this? You are a powerful mage; you are already the regent's man."

"You don't need to flatter me. But I know you are far more than I can ever be, and he needs you."

Yes, she thought, *he does*. "Shall I bring him?" she asked, wondering if the power she felt flowing through her would do as she bid and pull Ed to her.

"Sleep now. There will be much to do on the morrow."

"But I…"

"Sleep," he whispered, drawing out the word, and she tried unsuccessfully to stifle a yawn.

Ed woke to Belle screaming and the early morning light trying to push through the thick canopy above him. As he leapt from the ground, looking around him for the continued high-pitched sound, he focused on the hanging bodies before him. Evenly spaced around their campsite were at least ten men, hung by the necks high in the canopy.

Their bluish, bloated faces were unrecognisable, but they were men. Or they had been. Ende whispered something under his breath of the Near Folk.

"Is it a threat?" Ed asked, watching the men slowly swaying from their weathered ropes. "How long?" He stepped closer to one man, curious whether they had been here already. Despite the level of decay, there was no scent.

The scream ceased, and he looked at Belle as her face grew even paler. "I think I know some of them," she whispered, her voice catching as she spoke, a shaky finger pointing.

Ed looked back to the canopy to find the bodies gone. He breathed a sigh of relief, yet the whole party was on guard.

They packed up quickly and moved towards the fire, covering up the remaining embers.

"Do we want to travel this way?" Belle asked.

Ende shook his head.

"It is the fastest way. Should we find the road?" Ed asked.

Dray nodded, and as a group they headed towards where they had entered the forest. As the trees thinned and the mountains became clear in the distance, another body dropped from the canopy before them.

"We are trapped!" Belle squealed, clinging to Ende, but Ed thought it was only because he was closest to her at the time.

"No," Ende said too calmly. "We are being directed."

"By whom?" Ed asked, but he feared he already knew the answer.

34

Ana sat on the edge of her bed, dressed and waiting for the mage to send for her. Despite her best efforts the night before, she couldn't fight the urge to sleep. She knew that no matter how strong the mage admitted she was, he was far stronger. She ran her fingers through her hair and then clasped her hands in her lap. The world around her was quiet except for the distant sound of footsteps.

Ana closed her eyes and waited. The maid was still working her way through the corridors to reach her, and yet Ana could hear her coming above every other noise in the castle. She paused to talk with the soldier before opening the door. Not even a knock or waiting to enter, and Ana wondered at just what her station was. Both the maid's and her own.

"I will be better situated," she murmured, then opened her eyes to the maid stopped mid-step across the room.

"Miss?"

"I am to help the regent, am I not?"

"It is not…"

"Then I am to be closer to him," Ana said, standing.

"The mage is to teach you," she stammered.

Ana held up a finger, and a strong wind wound around the maid, pulling her hair from its tight bun and blowing her dress about her. As Ana closed her fist, the wind eased and the young woman dropped to her knees. "Move my things," Ana said.

A soldier appeared in the doorway, his concern for the maid evident as he stepped forward, a sword in his hand. Ana stood from the bed and he advanced, anger etched across his face. Then the sword glowed hot in his hand, and he looked confused for a moment before dropping it.

"Do you know what I am?" Ana asked.

He shook his head as he moved back a step, the maid scurrying across the floor after him.

"Do you?" the mage asked from the doorway to his rooms.

"There is no respect," she whispered, but the words pushed the soldier and the maid out the door, closing it behind them. She could hear him worrying over her on the other side of the door.

"And this show of power, what did you expect that to give you?"

"What you want for me. A place by the king."

"You were not as willing to assist him yesterday."

"I have had the chance to think on it. And deep sleep reveals much."

"You dreamed of him?" the mage asked, stepping forward, excitement lighting his eyes.

Ana nodded once, but it was not the king he hoped she had dreamed of. Her dream had been confused and hazy, trees with men in the branches, and something following them, shadows she couldn't focus on. The regent had also made it to her dreams, and that too had been unclear, although she was sure she held a sword against him and the crown in her hand.

"I feel I would be better placed beside him. If I am to assist him, I cannot stay so far away."

"There may be compromise," the mage said, opening the door with a click of his fingers. The maid and the soldier stood too close together on the other side. "Tell His Majesty that the witch will join him."

The maid curtsied, brushed the loose curls behind her ears and disappeared along the hallway.

"You are to return to the barracks," the mage told the soldier, who bowed. Although he glanced towards the sword, he didn't pick it up. "You will not return to this post."

The man bowed again and followed the maid's path. Ana took a step forward.

"Leave it. Go to the regent. He will be waiting for you in the dining hall."

She nodded and headed towards the door, wondering just what punishment the soldier would face and how disappointed the maid might be. At the doorway, she stopped and turned back. "You won't replace her, will you?"

"There is no need," he said, and then turned back for his own workroom. She heard the squeal of delight as he removed a bottle from the shelf. Part of her was curious how he would use it, but she was needed elsewhere. She glanced back, and with the slightest of movement pushed the sword beneath her bed. Then she turned and headed for the regent.

The moment she stepped into the dining room, Ana was overwhelmed by the emotions of those who filled it. Amongst it all was a hint of something just a little too warm. The girl was hiding, and Ana wondered why she couldn't sit with the others. The sword master sat by a group of men she assumed were Ed's tutors, but the girl was nowhere to be seen. In fact, as she looked about, there were very few women at all.

"Your Highness," she said, curtsying low once she approached the table. A servant stepped forward and pulled the chair out for her. As she sat down, he poured wine before she could ask for it. There was too much food before her on the table.

"You have decided to do as directed," the regent murmured through a mouthful of food.

"Is there a choice when the mage is involved?" Ana asked, looking over the piles of food before her and then around the room.

"Perhaps not, but then you wouldn't play the part so well."

"Who says that I'm playing?" She reached for the leg of the

smaller of the animals before her, hoping it was a rabbit, but not sure of anything other than the pig, whose crisp, slow-roasted face stared blindly ahead.

"You have seen what I will become," he breathed, turning to her, and she could feel the excitement ebbing from him. She had felt things before, but now it seemed as though she could feel everything, including the uncertainty growing in the room.

"I have seen far more than I care to." She looked over the greasy leg, taken back to a dusty crumbling room so far away, as though it were a different world. One she no longer belonged to.

"You see the future?" he asked, his excitement flowing over. The hush that filled the room made her heart stop. She looked up from the greasy meat before her and was tempted to run her fingers over her dress, but she closed her hand into a fist instead.

"I dream of things that have not happened." She said it softly, but she was sure nearly everyone in the room heard her. A girl's face and copper hair appeared around a distant edge of the room.

"But will they happen?" someone called out.

"I don't know," she admitted.

"Do you want them to happen?" another asked.

Ana looked around at the growing uncertainty in the regent. "You know that this is not where you are meant to be," she said softly.

He grinned and then glanced at the taller chair beside him, one he had left empty although she was certain he sat on the throne often enough.

"Where am I meant to be?" he asked carefully.

Ana longed for Dray in that moment. She was still only a maid. Only a girl with no idea of what they thought she was capable of. She wished Salima was closer so that she could reach Ed again, but she didn't know who else might see him and realise the connection.

"The king is lost," she said, standing slowly. Her food, moved about her plate by her greasy fingers, was still untouched.

The voices and movement around the room grew louder.

"What do you mean?"

"What have you done to him?"

"Where is the king?"

The regent held up his hand and pushed his chair back, but the murmuring continued. "What have you done?" he hissed.

"The king was already gone when I arrived in the capital. I don't know where he is, and I cannot reach him." She bowed a little and took another step back. "Despite what you think I am. The king is my main concern."

"A new king," he said through gritted teeth. Ana put a hand to her temple, the room pressed in on her further, as though everyone was screaming at her, all at once.

"What have you done to the king?" a firm voice called out through the fog forming around her mind. She searched the people in the room, yet she couldn't determine where it came from.

"I'm trying to help him," she said.

"You are not," the regent said, pushing the chair back and raising a hand as though to hit her.

She reached out automatically and grabbed his arm. Her frustrations bubbled to the surface, as she glared at the man. "You should have killed me," she whispered, as his face paled and he tried to pull from her grip. "You are not what an uncle should be. He needed you and you stole from him."

"You don't know what you are saying," he stammered, the sweat beading on his forehead, his pale face becoming almost grey in colour.

"You are the reason he is gone," she growled. "You are the reason he cannot be king."

"He ran away," the regent cried above the din. "He didn't want to be king!"

The room around them dropped to a hush. And in the sudden silence inside her mind, Ana released her hold on the man and he staggered back, falling into the chair.

"You made him run," she said, leaning forward and he cowered from her. Ana took a deep breath, and stepped forward. The fear in the room overwhelmed her and she stopped. She was aware of someone behind her, but she couldn't quite focus on them over the uncertainty filling the room. "You pushed him out by denying him what was his. By keeping the crown for yourself."

"He is a boy," he rasped.

"He is a man," she said firmly, her voice rising above the emotions in the room. "A man who should be sitting here. I will see that he is the king he is meant to be."

"Arrest the witch," the regent finally managed to get out, his arm clutched across his chest. As the confusion and noise of the people filled the room, she became aware of the soldier all too late, and as his fist met her chin, the world went dark.

Ana's hand closed around the ice-cold bars. She instantly let go and stepped back, her hands blistered and burning. She leaned against the wall behind her, the cold seeping into her bones as she slid slowly down the rough surface to sit in the prickly straw. Her head bent, her hair fell forward to hide her tears from the man on the other side, watching her with a wicked grin.

"You are not what I hoped you would be," the mage said.

"You are just as I expected," she murmured.

He laughed then, but it was cruel. "You were to help the king," he said, all traces of laughter gone.

"I am," she said.

"Not the boy," he snapped, stepping closer and she wondered if he got close enough to the bars if she could reach him.

"He is not a boy. He is a king and you have denied the Kingdom of Ilia by keeping him hidden away."

"They don't want him to be king," the regent said, although he didn't carry the same certainty as the mage had. When she looked up at him, he flinched.

"You can't stop him. And the people will help him."

"Will they?" he asked, stepping closer to the bars of the cage she found herself in, and she wondered if he might be an easier target. He must have seen something in her face for he took a small step back. "Would anyone help a boy who ran away from his responsibilities?"

"He ran away from you. He went to find help to regain his crown."

"Is that what he wanted, or what you hoped?" The regent's nasty confidence had returned. "Who would he find to help him? If you found him in the mountains then he had travelled all that way and no one recognised him, no one offered assistance. No one of any consequence lives on the Edge Mountains. Even the Lord of the Seat is a selfish man with no influence and no resources. He is lucky the gwelka haven't come out of their burrows to steal his gravel." Ana stared at the man, but he shrugged and his smug smile returned. "Do what you want with the girl, and then we will work on the boy, but he is no threat."

She shivered involuntarily as he turned from the cage and stalked from the room. He reached a hand for his arm, but stopped midway, rolled his shoulders and continued on.

"What am I to do with you?" the mage asked. "I had such high hopes. Too much like your mother," he muttered. Ana looked at him then, searching his face for anything further, desperate for him to share what he knew of her and yet knowing that he never would. She would have to find another way to learn of her mother. "There is something inside you I had hoped to unlock," he murmured, stepping away.

Ana thought of the images Ende had shown her and the darkness in her that he feared. But all she wanted was Ed to be where he needed to be, on the throne, ruling over Ilia. She had thought the power was all in the crown, but it was empty. The power ran in the blood. Whether Ed wanted it or not, the throne was his.

As the mage wandered out of the icy space, she looked around the room, too light to be a dungeon, yet as the icy cold numbed her body, she thought she was buried deep in the earth somewhere. She rubbed at her jaw where the guard had taken her by surprise.

Ana had done the right thing. She was certain of it. She shivered again, regretted the tight, thin dress and longed for Ende's old tattered cloak as she closed her eyes and curled on the floor.

ACKNOWLEDGMENTS

The team at Deranged Doctor Designs (DDD) for absolutely brilliant cover design work and all the marketing extras. Thank you for your support and clear emails around what was needed from me to make the magic happen.

TWG members and Melissa for listening and support in all things writing related, even when we can't get together just now. Special thanks to Yasmin, Kait and Shae for taking the time to read my draft and providing ideas to make the story stronger.

Allison E Wright for wonderful editing work to make my sentences smoother and my intentions clearer.

My parents, Francine and Ken Smith. Amazing, supportive people who I don't thank often enough. Thanks for keeping me grounded and being the best grandparents ever.

As always, Temwa for being my biggest supporter.

ABOUT THE AUTHOR

Georgina Makalani survives life as a servant of the public by hiding in her office at lunch time with dragons, witches, a laptop and a little bit of magic.

For more about Georgina and her books visit her website: www.theflowofink.com